T0123319

A Room with a Roux

Books by Sarah Fox

The Literary Pub Mystery Series
Wine and Punishment
An Ale of Two Cities
The Malt in Our Stars

The Pancake House Mystery Series
The Crêpes of Wrath
For Whom the Bread Rolls
Of Spice and Men
Yeast of Eden
Crêpe Expectations
Much Ado About Nutmeg
A Room with a Roux

The Music Lover's Mystery Series
Dead Ringer
Death in A Major
Deadly Overtures

A Room with a Roux

Sarah Fox

LYRICAL UNDERGROUND
Kensington Publishing Corp.
www.kensingtonbooks.com

LYRICAL UNDERGROUND BOOKS are published by

Kensington Publishing Corp.
119 West 40th Street
New York, NY 10018

All Kensington titles, imprints, and distributed lines are available at special quantity discounts for bulk purchases for sales promotion, premiums, fund-raising, educational, or institutional use.

Special book excerpts or customized printings can also be created to fit specific needs. For details, write or phone the office of the Kensington Sales Manager: Kensington Publishing Corp., 119 West 40th Street, New York, NY 10018. Attn. Sales Department. Phone: 1-800-221-2647.

Lyrical Underground and Lyrical Underground logo Reg. US Pat.& TM Off.

First Electronic Edition: January 2021
ISBN-13: 978-1-5161-1086-5 (ebook)
ISBN-10: 1-5161-1086-2 (ebook)

First Print Edition: January 2021
ISBN-13: 978-1-5161-1088-9
ISBN-10: 1-5161-1088-9

Printed in the United States of America

Chapter One

Fluffy snowflakes swirled down from the gray sky, hitting the windshield a split second before the wipers whisked them away. I gripped the edge of my seat as my husband, Brett, steered his truck around a tight turn. Driving along winding mountain roads made me nervous at the best of times. The winter weather only added to my anxiety.

Ahead of us, the road straightened out, bordered on both sides by tall, snow-covered evergreens. I relaxed into my seat, relief allowing me to finally enjoy the view. It was the day after Thanksgiving. Winter had arrived early on the Olympic Peninsula, and although there was only frost on the ground in the seaside town of Wildwood Cove, up here in the mountains more than a foot of snow had already fallen. It had covered the world in a beautiful white blanket and it made me think of the upcoming Christmas season—when I wasn't worrying about the driving conditions.

Brett glanced my way as we continued our gentle ascent along the straight section of road. "We're almost there. You okay?" He knew I wasn't keen on mountain roads and hairpin turns.

"Yes," I said, glad that it was now the truth. "All good."

A painted wooden sign caught my eye at the same time as Brett flicked on the left turn signal and said, "This is it."

Excitement pitter-pattered through my stomach. I'd been looking forward to this getaway with Brett ever since we'd booked our stay at Holly Lodge a few weeks earlier. After our wedding in August, we'd had a short honeymoon in Victoria, Canada, but ever since our return, we'd both been busy with work. I knew Brett wanted this time alone together, without any distractions, as much as I did.

Brett followed the curving driveway that led through the trees. After a few seconds, we emerged from the woods and got our first look at Holly Lodge. I'd seen photos of the place on the Internet, but the pictures didn't do the building or its setting justice. The lodge looked cozy and welcoming, and was nestled in the middle of a winter wonderland.

Although Holly Lodge was small in comparison to many other hotels, that was partly why Brett and I had chosen it. We wanted a quiet getaway without any crowds, a place where we could focus on relaxing and on each other. It certainly seemed like we'd come to the right spot. The lodge resembled a large log home rather than a hotel. It had two stories and a covered wraparound porch. Warm light lit up the windows on the ground floor, sending a welcoming glow into the gray afternoon.

White twinkle lights lined the edge of the roof and the porch. Greenery also decorated the railing, and a large wreath hung on the front door. The effect was festive and inviting.

Holly Lodge sat in the middle of a woodland clearing, but as Brett drove around the side of the building to a small parking lot, I caught a glimpse of a frozen lake through the trees.

"It's beautiful here," I said as Brett pulled into a free parking spot. "And it looks like we'll get the peace and quiet we're after."

There were five other vehicles in the parking lot aside from ours, but even if the place was fully booked, I figured it would still be relatively quiet for a vacation destination.

"Peace and quiet and alone time," Brett said, leaning over to give me a kiss.

I smiled. "That's a definite yes to the alone time."

We climbed out of the truck and I shivered as the cold air stung my cheeks and the light wind cut through my clothes. Snowflakes still swirled down from the sky. I tipped my head back so all I could see was the falling snow and the leaden clouds. I stuck out my tongue and caught a fluffy flake on it, feeling like a kid. Already I was more relaxed than I'd been for weeks.

I joined Brett on the other side of the truck as he unloaded our suitcase, and together we headed along the shoveled pathway that led to the lodge's front door. Before going inside, we wiped our boots on the welcome mat.

Brett grinned and gently brushed a hand over my curly hair. "Snowflakes," he said by way of explanation.

"You've got some too." I stood up on tiptoes so I could return the favor.

We brushed off our jackets as well and then entered the lodge. As soon as we stepped inside, my breath caught in my throat. I stood there in the foyer, with Brett by my side, gazing around us. Once again, the photos I'd seen online didn't do the lodge justice. Straight ahead of us was a reception desk with a closed door behind it, but my attention was drawn elsewhere.

To the left was a dining room and a staircase with a carved wooden banister, and to the right was a lounge. Both rooms featured gleaming wooden floorboards and exposed beams. I took a few steps to the right to get a better view of the lounge. A massive stone fireplace dominated one wall of the room, a fire crackling away behind the grate. The lounge stretched all the way to the back of the lodge, where floor-to-ceiling windows provided a stunning view of the lake. Cozy armchairs practically called out to me to settle into one and enjoy the warmth from the fire. With the snow falling outside the windows, the interior of Holly Lodge was picture-perfect and fit for a magazine.

We'd definitely chosen the right place for our getaway.

"It looks great," Brett said quietly into my ear.

I slid an arm around his waist and leaned into him. "I'm so glad Patricia told us about this place."

Patricia Murray was a friend of mine who ran a bed-and-breakfast two doors down from our beachfront Victorian. She and her family had spent a couple of weekend getaways up here at Holly Lodge in the past and she'd recommended it to us when we'd mentioned we were planning a short vacation in the mountains. I couldn't have asked for a better spot.

Although I was itching to explore the rest of the lodge, Brett and I approached the reception desk. I thought we'd have to ring the bell for assistance, but before we had a chance, a woman emerged from an office behind the desk.

"Hello, and welcome to Holly Lodge," the woman said with a smile. She was tall and striking, with high cheekbones. She wore her short hair in glossy finger coils and moved with the grace of a dancer. "I'm Rita Omondi-Manning, one of the owners. You must be Mr. and Mrs. Collins."

I still wasn't quite used to the fact that I was now a Mrs., but the reminder put a smile on my face.

"That's right," Brett replied. "Brett and Marley."

"Did you have a good trip up the mountain?" Rita asked.

"It wasn't bad, considering the weather," I said. "It's such a beautiful place you've got here."

Rita's dark eyes lit up as she smiled again. "Thank you. I do love it. And I'm glad we're able to share our little slice of mountain paradise with our guests."

I told Rita that we'd heard about Holly Lodge from Patricia Murray, who'd highly recommended it.

"You know Patricia?" she said.

"We're neighbors and good friends," I replied.

She asked how Patricia was doing, and I filled her in briefly. Then Rita turned her eyes to a computer screen and tapped a few buttons on the keyboard. "We've got you in room five, up on the second floor. It has a lovely view of the lake."

"That sounds great," Brett said, and I voiced my agreement.

She handed over two keys, each one on a wooden keychain with a number five carved on it. "The dining room is open for breakfast from six until ten, for lunch from twelve to two, and for dinner from five to eight. You'll find a credenza in the dining room, where there's always tea, coffee, hot chocolate, and a few snacks available. There's a hot tub out back, and if you'd like to try snowshoeing or cross-country skiing, just let us know. We have plenty of equipment available."

We thanked her and headed for the staircase, Brett carrying our suitcase. On our way up the stairs, we got a better view of the dining room, and I noticed a man with graying dark hair sitting alone at a table, reading a newspaper, a mug with steam rising from it set on the table in front of him. I assumed he was another guest, but he was the only one we encountered on our way up to our room.

The second floor hallway was silent and deserted, all of the guest room doors shut tight. Brett unlocked the door to room five and pushed it open before stepping back to let me go in first.

"Holy buckets!" I exclaimed as I entered the room. "This is gorgeous!"

Our room was located at the back of the lodge and, just as Rita had told us, it offered a beautiful view of Holly Lake. Beyond the lake was a higher mountain than the one we were on, barely discernible through the falling snow, its peak shrouded in clouds.

The room itself was almost as impressive as the view. I removed my boots and left them on the mat by the door so I could explore without leaving damp footprints on the hardwood floors or rugs. I ran a hand down one of the carved posts of the king-size four-poster bed that took up one half of the room, knowing I'd sleep well that night. Matching nightstands flanked the bed and a chest of drawers and a small desk made from the same type of wood sat against one wall.

The other side of the room featured a small sitting area with a loveseat, armchair, television, and gas fireplace. A rustic but tasteful credenza was home to a kettle and an empty ice bucket. When I opened the cupboards, I discovered a mini fridge, two drinking glasses, two mugs, and an assortment of tea bags. A doorway led off the sitting room to a tiled bathroom with a shower stall and a soaker tub.

"It's pretty amazing," Brett said, gazing around with appreciation as I returned to the middle of the room.

"It's perfect."

I picked up a glossy brochure that was lying on the bedside table. It was about Holly Lodge and the activities available on-site and in the surrounding area. I sat on the edge of the bed and took a closer look at the brochure while Brett unpacked a few items from our suitcase.

The last page of the brochure featured information on the history of Holly Lodge, which had been built thirty years ago on the site of an old cabin that had stood by the lake for nearly a hundred years before it had become so derelict that tearing it down had been the only real option.

"Hey," I said to Brett as I read the next paragraph. "Apparently this place has a ghost."

"Holly Lodge is haunted?" Brett asked. "Wait—I think I saw something about that on the website. It's supposed to be the ghost of a woman, right?"

"Henrietta Franklin," I confirmed. "But it's Holly Lake that's haunted, not the lodge itself."

Brett sat next to me and put his arm around my shoulders. "We've got a good view of the lake from here, but somehow I think we'll be too distracted to notice any ghosts outside the window."

He kissed me in a way that almost made me forget what we were talking about.

The brochure slipped from my hand and fell to the floor. When I retrieved it a moment later, I returned it to the bedside table.

"I think you're right," I said, picking up our conversation where we'd left off. "But I doubt we'd see the ghost even if we weren't distracted."

I didn't know for sure if ghosts existed or not, but I figured most ghost stories were just that—stories. My experience with a supposedly haunted house in Wildwood Cove had led me to believe that more firmly than ever.

"That's probably true," Brett agreed, "but it makes for a good tale to tell the guests."

I couldn't argue with that.

As I got up from the bed, my attention strayed back to the view, and I wandered over to one of the two large windows.

Brett joined me and wrapped his arms around me from behind. "What do you want to do first?"

"Walk down to the lake? I wouldn't mind stretching my legs after the ride up here."

"Sounds good."

Neither of us made a move toward the door. I leaned into Brett, still enjoying the view from the window.

"I'm glad we decided to do this," I said.

"You're not worrying yet?" There was a note of gentle teasing in his voice.

I smiled. "Not quite yet. It helps that The Flip Side will be closed while we're gone."

It wasn't easy for me to leave the pancake house in other people's hands. Not because I didn't trust them—all my employees were excellent and my mom was always willing to step in to help out when she was in Wildwood Cove—but I didn't like to burden anyone with my responsibilities on top of their own. I also wasn't keen on leaving our pets, even for a few days, but they were in good hands.

My mom and her husband, Grant, had come to Wildwood Cove for Thanksgiving and now they were staying on at our house to look after our goldendoodle, Bentley, and our orange tabby cat, Flapjack. I missed the animals already, but I knew they'd be fine with my mom and Grant, so I was determined to keep my worries at bay and focus on enjoying myself.

After another minute of soaking in the view and each other's company, we put our boots back on and headed downstairs. Rita was no longer in sight, but a man with chestnut-brown hair stood behind the reception desk. His face was tanned and weathered, as if he spent a lot of time outdoors. He had his attention fixed on the computer screen, but he raised his eyes and smiled when he heard us coming into the lobby.

"You must be our newly arrived guests," he said, coming out from behind the desk. "I'm Kevin Manning."

He offered his hand, first to me and then to Brett. As we shook, we introduced ourselves and assured him that we were settling in well so far.

While we chatted, a woman descended the stairs from the second floor. She had a pale complexion and dark hair that was tied back in a messy bun. She wore glasses with purple frames and a thick sweater with a long black skirt.

"How are you doing this afternoon, Lily?" Kevin asked the woman as she reached the bottom of the stairs.

"Very well, thank you." She held up a paperback novel that she had with her. "I'm going to get in some reading time in front of the fire."

"I'm hoping to do some of that myself this weekend," I said. I'd packed a mystery novel that I'd started reading two days ago. I was only a few chapters in, but the story already had me hooked.

"Lily," Kevin said, "Brett and Marley are our latest guests." He addressed us next. "This is Lily Spitz. She's an author as well as an avid reader."

"That's cool," I said, intrigued. "What genre do you write?"

"I've been writing romance for several years, but I've branched out into mysteries as well."

The phone on the reception desk rang, so Kevin excused himself to go answer it while Lily, Brett, and I headed into the lounge.

"I'll have to check out your books," I said to Lily. "I love mysteries."

A hint of pink showed on her cheeks. "I hope mine won't disappoint."

"I'm sure they won't."

After exchanging a few more words, Brett and I left Lily in the lounge and headed out the back door onto a large deck. In the summertime, it would be a great place for outdoor dining, if the bugs weren't too bad. The view was incredible and the air fresh, if a bit cold at the moment. A stairway led down to a shoveled path. The main part of the walkway stretched toward the lake while a branch to the left led to the hot tub, currently not in use.

The hot tub was tempting, but we bypassed it—for now—and made our way down to the frozen lake. The gray afternoon was already fading toward dusk, and lights glowed in three houses on the far side of the lake. Those dwellings were the only other buildings in sight aside from Holly Lodge. The relative isolation added to the tranquility of our location.

As we stopped to take in the view from our new vantage point, I noticed snowshoe prints along the shore, leading into the woods that surrounded most of the lake.

I pointed them out to Brett. "It's been years since I last had a chance to go snowshoeing. We should go tomorrow."

"We should," he agreed. "We might be able to trek all the way around the lake."

I liked that idea, and I could already picture us enjoying mugs of hot chocolate upon our return, either while snuggled up in our room or in front of the log fire in the lounge. We were going to have a great time at Holly Lodge.

The more the light faded from the gray sky, the more the temperature dropped, so we didn't linger by the lake. As we were about to head back up the path to the lodge, Brett put a hand on my arm to stop me and pointed into the trees to our left without saying a word.

My breath caught in my throat when I realized what Brett had seen.

Two beautiful deer stood at the edge of the forest, perfectly still, their eyes on us. With the snow falling softly and the backdrop of snowcapped evergreens, the scene looked like it belonged on a Christmas card.

Brett and I stayed as still as possible, not wanting to scare the deer. After a few seconds, however, they abruptly turned away and bounded gracefully through the snow, disappearing into the forest.

I smiled and took Brett's hand as we returned to Holly Lodge. Our vacation was off to a perfect start, and I didn't think anything could possibly ruin it.

Chapter Two

Brett and I weren't quite ready for dinner when we got back to Holly Lodge so we decided to try out the hot tub. I was glad I'd thought to pack a swimsuit and flip-flops. There were two fluffy robes hanging in the closet in our room, so we pulled them on for the trip downstairs. When we passed through the lounge again on our way out the back door, the fire was still crackling and popping away, but Lily had disappeared and there were no other guests in sight. Outside, the snow had stopped falling, and darkness had settled over the mountains.

As we made our way down the path to the hot tub, I questioned the wisdom of our decision. We could have stayed inside and enjoyed a hot drink by the fire before dinner. Instead, we were about to turn into icicles. Or, I was, anyway. Brett seemed completely unaffected by the cold. He was as relaxed as he would have been if we were out for a sunny stroll on the beach. In stark contrast, my teeth chattered and I tried to pull my robe more tightly around me, but it didn't do any good. The cold air cut right through the fabric and nipped at my bare legs.

"How can you not be shivering?" I asked Brett as we turned off the main path.

"We've barely been out here five seconds," he said.

"That's long enough to turn into a popsicle."

He laughed. "Want to turn around and go back?"

I glanced over my shoulder at the lodge, its windows glowing with warm light. We were far closer to the hot tub than the lodge now, and steam was rising from the water, visible thanks to the string of lights hanging above the small deck.

"Too far," I said through chattering teeth.

I picked up my pace and hurried up the three steps to the hot tub deck, quickly dropping my robe and climbing into the water. I let out a sigh of happiness and relief as the hot water enveloped me, instantly banishing the chill that had been working its way into my bloodstream seconds before.

Brett stepped into the water and sank down onto the bench next to me. "Better?" he asked.

I scooted closer to him and rested my head on his shoulder. "Much."

My muscles relaxed more and more with every second spent in the hot tub. Around us, the world was perfectly still and quiet. With my back to the lodge, it was easy to pretend we were in our own private world, alone in the wilderness.

"This is perfect," I said as my eyelids grew heavier.

Brett settled an arm across my shoulders. "You're not thinking of giving up beachfront living, are you?"

I smiled, hearing a note of teasing in his voice. "Never."

"Good." He kissed the top of my head. "But this is a great getaway spot."

"It really is," I said with a happy sigh. "I've never thought of having a hot tub before, but now I'm wondering if we should get one."

"Do you really think we'd use it enough to make it worthwhile?"

"Maybe not," I conceded, thinking about our busy schedules. "We'll just have to make the most of this one while we're here."

"That sounds like a good plan."

Time passed, but I barely noticed. Brett and I spoke in low voices now and then, but mostly we relaxed and enjoyed the soothing heat of the water and each other's company.

"Getting hungry?" Brett asked after a while.

"Mmmm."

"Is that a 'yes' or an 'I don't want to get out of the hot tub?'"

"Both," I said.

He leaned closer, as if about to share a secret. "I don't think they serve dinner out here."

A sleepy smile spread across my face. "You're probably right."

I decided it was time to force myself to get out of the water, though I didn't relish the thought of how cold I'd feel in the seconds before I could get my robe back on. Before I could make a move, however, the sound of approaching voices stopped me.

"Have you thought any more about my offer?" It was a man who spoke, but I didn't recognize his voice.

Brett and I twisted on the bench so we could get a look behind us. Kevin Manning was trudging along a path that came around the side of the lodge, illuminated by a floodlight mounted beneath the eaves. He was wearing jeans and a red and black plaid jacket, a hat pulled down over his ears. A broad shouldered, middle-aged man kept pace at his side. I was pretty sure it was the same man I'd seen in the dining room earlier.

"I don't need to think about it." Kevin's voice was gruff and laced with irritation.

Brett and I stayed still and quiet, not wanting to interrupt the less-than-friendly conversation. Fortunately, the men didn't notice us and continued along the path toward the lodge's back steps.

"I think my offer is more than generous," the broad-shouldered man said.

Kevin stopped abruptly at the base of the steps. "I don't need your generosity. I'm not giving up Holly Lodge, in whole or in part."

The other man continued as if he hadn't heard Kevin. "It has so much untapped potential."

"I've got my own plans for expansion," Kevin grumbled. "I'm not interested in selling."

With that, Kevin stomped up the stairs and disappeared into the lodge. The other man watched him go, only following once Kevin was out of sight.

"Real estate developer?" I guessed.

"Sounds like it could be," Brett said. He stood up, water dripping off his body while steam rose up around him. "I'm definitely hungry now."

Reluctantly, I followed him out of the hot tub, trying to brace myself against the impending unpleasantness. Getting out of the water wasn't as terrible as I expected, until a gust of icy wind blew past us. I tried not to let out a squeal of discomfort as the cold air bit at my wet skin, but I wasn't quite successful. I tugged on my robe as quickly as I could, hoping it would shield me from the wind.

Brett didn't seem as bothered, but he still wasted no time pulling on his robe. As I tied the cord of my robe tightly around my waist, I noticed someone else nearby, this time heading up to the lodge from the lake. I couldn't see the man's features, but he appeared to have a thin build, despite the bulk of his winter clothing. If he noticed us, he gave no indication.

Brett and I made our way along the pathway. I was glad for the lights that lined it. Every last hint of daylight had disappeared now, and it would have been hard to see where we were going without lights to dispel the darkness.

By the time we turned onto the main path, the man up ahead of us was already climbing the steps to the lodge. The door to the lounge opened, spilling warm light out into the dark evening.

Lily stood framed by the doorway. "Ambrose!" she called out. "Where have you been? I was getting worried!"

Whatever his response might have been, it didn't reach my ears. Lily ushered him into the lodge and shut the door behind him.

We hurried up to the deck and into the lounge, relieved to get inside. The wet ends of my hair had felt like they were starting to freeze on the walk back, and my fingers and toes had been on the verge of going numb. Lily and Ambrose had disappeared, and the room was empty as we passed through it, but I could hear quiet voices coming from the dining room.

Now that I'd left the soothing comfort of the hot tub behind, I realized that I was hungrier than I'd thought. Upstairs in our room, we dried off and changed before heading back down to the main floor of the lodge. When I was three steps from the bottom of the stairway, I drew to a halt, forcing Brett to stop behind me.

Hushed, angry voices floated toward us. I recognized Kevin's voice and I was pretty sure the other one belonged to Rita. After a second or two, I realized that they were in the office behind the reception desk. The door stood open a crack, letting their argument seep out into the lobby.

"This is my lodge just as much as yours!" Rita's anger was unmistakable. "You can't do anything without my say-so."

"You're holding us back." Kevin's words were just as heated. "We could do so much more with this place if you'd give my ideas a chance."

"People come here because it's quiet, because it's *not* busy," Rita shot back. "I won't let you destroy this place. I'm not going to let you take away what I've worked so hard to build."

"*You've* worked? What about me? I've been breaking my back here for years!"

"This is supposed to be a partnership." Rita sounded close to tears now. "You always disregard anything I have to say."

Brett stepped down next to me and put a hand to my back. By unspoken agreement, we descended the remaining stairs as quietly as possible and made a beeline for the dining room, leaving Kevin and Rita's angry voices behind us. I exhaled with relief once we could no longer hear them. I wished we hadn't overheard the argument. Kevin and Rita probably would have wished that too if they'd known their voices had carried beyond the office.

Three other guests were sitting in the dining room when we arrived. Lily was at a table with a man I figured was Ambrose. He matched the build of the man we'd seen outside. He had golden hair and wore wire-framed glasses. Ambrose and Lily both appeared to be around thirty, just a few years younger than me and Brett. At a neighboring table was the man I'd seen reading a newspaper before. I took in the sight of his broad shoulders and decided he was definitely the man who'd been outside with Kevin earlier.

"Ah," the man said when he spotted me and Brett. "New guests. Come to enjoy the winter wonderland?" He stood up as we approached, and Brett and I shook the hand he offered. "Wilson Gerrard," he said by way of introduction. "Mostly of Seattle, though I like to get around."

Brett and I introduced ourselves, both to Wilson and the other two guests.

"This is Ambrose," Lily said with a bright smile, indicating her companion. "He's a renowned poet." She practically glowed with pride.

Ambrose pushed his glasses up his nose. "I'm not sure about renowned, but I will admit to the poet."

"Are you both from Seattle too?" I asked them as Brett and I sat down at one of the free tables.

"Originally," Ambrose said, setting a cloth napkin on his lap, though he had no food in front of him yet. "I moved to the peninsula a couple of years ago. Lily lives in Seattle. That's where we met and became friends."

"We became well acquainted through various writing events around Seattle and realized that we're kindred spirits." Lily beamed at Ambrose. "Isn't that right?"

Ambrose didn't have a chance to respond before Wilson spoke up.

"Writers on vacation?" He seemed amused by the idea. "Isn't your whole life a vacation? Typing a few words and then staring out the window, waiting for inspiration to hit?"

Lily's smile faded and flinty annoyance showed in her eyes.

Ambrose didn't appear impressed either. "Actually, that's not—"

Rita swept into the dining room, her arrival cutting off the conversation. That was probably for the best, judging by Lily and Ambrose's expressions. Wilson seemed oblivious to the feathers he'd ruffled.

"Everyone's here," Rita observed with a smile. She picked up two menus from an unoccupied table and handed them to me and Brett. "Can I get you something to drink to start?"

We both requested water. I was still thinking about a mug of hot chocolate, but I decided to leave that until later so I could enjoy it by the fire.

"I'll be right back with your drinks," Rita said. Then she addressed the others. "And I'll check on your meals."

She disappeared into the kitchen. Wilson produced a cell phone from his pocket and focused his attention on the screen. Ambrose and Lily talked quietly together at their table, no longer appearing so irked by Wilson's comments.

Out the back window, I could see that snow had started falling again, thickly this time, the flakes illuminated by the lights on the back deck. That made the lodge seem even cozier, and the flickering votive candles on our table added a touch of romance.

Brett reached across the table and I gave him my hand.

"Anything catch your eye?" he asked.

I smiled at him. "Definitely."

He grinned and squeezed my hand. "I meant on the menu."

I'd forgotten all about the menus. "I knew that."

"Sure, you did."

Still smiling, I slipped my hand from Brett's and turned my attention to the list of available meals. It was fairly limited, but that wasn't surprising considering the small size of the lodge.

As I read over the options, Rita returned and placed two glasses of ice water on our table. We thanked her and she disappeared into the kitchen again, returning a moment later with two plates of food, which she delivered to Ambrose and Lily's table.

She fetched another plate from the kitchen and placed it in front of Wilson. As she headed our way, I closed the menu, having finally decided what I wanted. Brett ordered the butter chicken while I requested the quinoa-stuffed bell peppers.

Rita took our menus and headed for the kitchen once more.

"I hope Flapjack and Bentley aren't missing us too much," I said.

I was itching to send my mom a text message to ask how things were going, but I'd purposely left my phone up in our room. I didn't want anything distracting me from my time with Brett.

"I'm sure they're doing just fine," Brett said. "You know your mom will be spoiling them, and Grant loves taking Bentley for long walks."

"I know. I'm sure they're having a great time."

Brett must have sensed the residual worry lingering in my mind. "We can text them later to make sure."

I nodded and pushed my remaining worries to the back of my mind, determined to stay in the moment and enjoy every minute of our vacation.

A short while later, Rita brought out our dinner, setting the plates in front of us. Delicious smells wafted up to greet my nose and my stomach grumbled in anticipation. We thanked Rita and started in on our meals. Right from the first bite, the food didn't disappoint.

Rita had only taken a few steps away from our table when Kevin appeared from the lobby.

"Is everyone enjoying their dinner?" he asked the room at large.

We all assured him that we were.

He slid an arm around Rita's shoulders. "If there's anything you need, just let me or my wife know. We want to make sure your stay at Holly Lodge is as comfortable and enjoyable as possible."

Rita gave him a loving smile and Kevin returned it before they parted ways, Kevin heading back toward the lobby and Rita disappearing into the kitchen.

I couldn't help but wonder if they were really on such good terms as they had appeared to be a moment before. Maybe they had hot, short-lived tempers and had already put their argument behind them, but somehow I had my doubts. There had been such a bitterness underlying their angry words, and I couldn't help but think that their loving smiles hadn't quite reached their eyes. Maybe I was wrong, but I had a sneaking suspicion that the apparent affection they'd shown a moment ago was nothing more than an act.

Chapter Three

By the time Brett and I finished our dinner, we were alone in the dining room. I didn't mind at all. It was romantic to be eating by candlelight, just the two of us, with the snow falling heavily outside the windows.

We decided to pass on dessert and instead fixed ourselves mugs of hot chocolate topped with mini marshmallows. There were two flavors of cocoa to choose from—double chocolate and mint. I chose the mint while Brett went with double chocolate. We were about to carry our hot drinks through the lobby to the lounge, when the sound of voices up ahead made us hesitate.

"I'm afraid I can't agree to that," Kevin was saying to someone. It sounded like he was near the reception desk.

"But it could be such great publicity for Holly Lodge," Lily said.

"It would be negative publicity," Kevin countered. "And contrary to what some people say, there *is* such a thing as bad publicity, especially when you want people to come and stay at your lodge."

I exchanged a glance with Brett. He shrugged, and we continued on our way into the lobby. Lily was about to say something more as Brett and I drew closer, but as soon as she saw us, she snapped her mouth shut.

Kevin noticed us too, and the annoyance on his face quickly cleared away. "Got everything you need?" he asked me and Brett.

"Yes, thanks," I said, still heading across the lobby.

"We're going to enjoy the fire for a while," Brett added.

"Feel free to add more wood if it needs it," Kevin said just before we left the lobby for the lounge.

If he and Lily continued their conversation, we didn't hear any more of it. I was glad of that. Although curious by nature—sometimes to a fault—I didn't want any part of anyone else's drama while Brett and I were on vacation.

The fire was burning low, so Brett set his mug on a side table and added a log to the dwindling flames. When the log caught and the flames danced higher, Brett retrieved his mug and joined me on the couch that faced the fireplace.

I snuggled closer to him and he rested an arm across my shoulders. No one else came into the lounge while we were enjoying our hot chocolate. Silence had settled over the lodge, and I figured all the other guests had retired to their rooms. Once our mugs had been empty for a while and the fire was dying again, Brett and I decided to do the same.

Up in our room, Brett switched on the gas fireplace for some added coziness. As soon as I'd changed into my pajamas and had brushed my teeth, I climbed onto the big bed and slipped beneath the covers. I picked up the paperback mystery I'd left on the nightstand and read a few pages while Brett got ready for bed. When he switched off the fireplace and the overhead light, my eyes were drooping. I marked my place with a bookmark and returned the novel to the nightstand as Brett got into bed beside me.

"Enjoying our vacation so far?" he asked as he switched off the lamp on his side of the bed.

"Very much." I'd texted my mom when we'd returned to our room, and she'd replied soon after, assuring me that Flapjack and Bentley were happy and healthy. Knowing that had allowed me to banish my niggling concerns and relax completely.

I turned off the lamp on my nightstand, plunging the room into darkness. Brett gave me a kiss and then tucked an arm around me.

"Sleepy?" he asked.

"Mmm." I turned over to face him. "But not too sleepy."

Even in the darkness, I could see his grin.

"Glad to hear it," he said, before his lips met mine.

* * * *

I woke up to complete darkness. I didn't know where I was. Fear set my heart pumping, until I heard Brett breathing next to me. My fear dissipated in an instant, and almost at the same moment, I remembered that we were in our room at Holly Lodge. As my heart rate slowed, I rolled over, planning to go back to sleep, but then I realized I needed to make a trip to the washroom.

On my way back to bed, I moved slowly and quietly, making my way through the darkness, not wanting to wake Brett or stub a toe. I was halfway across the room when I heard a steady *crunch-crunch* coming from outside the window. I strayed off my intended path and parted the curtains. Outside, the world glowed with a faint bluish light. The snow had stopped falling and the clouds had parted to let some moonlight through.

It was a winter wonderland of a different sort than it was during the day, but it was no less magical. I thought maybe the view was even more beautiful by moonlight.

The crunching sound drew my gaze downward. A man in a winter coat and a hat with earflaps was making his way up from the direction of the lake, heading toward the lodge, snowshoes strapped to his feet. As he drew closer, he veered off to my left, around the side of the building. The crunching of his footsteps grew quieter as he disappeared from sight. I stayed by the window a moment longer, but the world outside was now completely still.

I let the curtains fall back into place and carefully made my way over to the bed. The digital clock on the nightstand told me that it was shortly after two o'clock. An odd time to be out snowshoeing. I'd caught a brief glimpse of the man's face, and hadn't recognized him. He definitely wasn't Kevin, Ambrose, or Wilson.

I pulled the covers up to my chin, but then sat up again. A door closed somewhere down the hall, not loudly, but I heard it nonetheless. Floorboards creaked as someone passed by our door out in the corridor. Apparently, the snowshoeing man wasn't the only one up and about at this hour.

Beside me, Brett stirred. "Marley?" he said sleepily. "Everything okay?"

"Yes."

I lay down again and shifted closer to Brett, grateful for the warmth of his body after my brief spell out of bed. His arm went around me and I closed my eyes, drifting off to sleep as he did the same beside me.

* * * *

I slept later than I normally did, though Brett and I were still down in the dining room by seven o'clock. I was used to getting up around five so I could be at the pancake house no later than six. Brett was a morning person too, although he didn't usually start work quite as early as I did. He had his own lawn and garden business that operated from early spring into the fall each year. He'd used to spend the winters working with his dad's company, doing home renovations for clients. But after suffering a heart attack last winter, Brett's dad had retired and his former foreman, Pedro, had taken over the business. Brett was working for Pedro this winter, but he'd cut back on his hours so he could spend some time doing renovations on our own home.

We'd been updating our beachfront Victorian bit by bit, transforming it to suit our needs better while maintaining as much of its charm as possible. The kitchen was already done and looked amazing. Now Brett was converting a spacious storage closet into a bathroom and attaching it to our master bedroom.

At the moment, however, work and renovations had been firmly pushed to the back of our minds. We'd planned to go out snowshoeing in the morning, and I was looking forward to that. Living down on the coast, we didn't often get a chance to enjoy winter sports and activities. Sometimes it snowed in Wildwood Cove, but even if the flakes managed to stick to the ground and accumulate, the snow rarely lasted for more than a day or two. Up here in the mountains, it was a completely different story, and I wanted to enjoy the winter weather as much as possible.

Before heading out into the cold, Brett and I settled in the dining room to enjoy a hearty breakfast. We both ordered eggs Benedict with smoked salmon. After the previous night's dinner, I was expecting the food to be good, and it didn't disappoint. The only time I'd had eggs Benedict that tasted better was when The Flip Side's chef, Ivan Kaminski, had made them for me. The hollandaise sauce was heavenly and perfectly complemented the eggs and fish.

We were finishing up our meals when Lily arrived in the dining room. She sent a distracted smile our way, but I didn't fail to notice how her gaze skittered over the tables before her mouth turned down in a disappointed frown. Wilson sat across the room from us, reading a newspaper while he ate pancakes and sausages, but Ambrose had yet to appear. I wondered if that was the reason for Lily's frown.

"Is Kevin around?" Lily asked when Rita appeared, carrying a coffee pot in one hand.

"Not at the moment." She stopped at Wilson's table and held up the coffee pot. When he nodded and nudged his mug her way, she refilled it.

Lily fingered the hem of her purple sweater. "Do you know when he'll be back? There's something I wanted to talk to him about."

"I'm afraid I don't know." Rita's mouth set in a firm line and annoyance made her words tense. "I'm not sure where he's gone."

Lily didn't seem too bothered by that response. She sat at a free table and ordered toast and fruit salad without looking at the menu. When Ambrose appeared a moment later, Lily's face brightened and she beckoned him over to join her.

Brett finished off his last sip of coffee and we left the dining room, making a quick stop up in our room to get ready for time spent outdoors. According to the weather app on my phone, it wasn't as cold outside as it had been the day before, but we still needed our winter gear.

When we came back downstairs, Rita was behind the reception desk, holding the phone to her ear.

"Would you pick up?" she grumbled as she drummed her fingers against the desk, her bright red nails tapping against the wood.

She slammed down the receiver. As Brett and I drew closer, her head snapped up and she quickly pasted a smile on her face.

"Heading out?" she asked when she took in the sight of us in our coats, hats, and boots.

I decided to pretend we hadn't noticed her frustration. "We thought we'd try some snowshoeing."

"You mentioned there was equipment we could use," Brett said.

"Yes, of course." Rita pointed to the front door. "If you head out that way, you'll find a path that goes off to the right. It leads to an outbuilding where we have skis and snowshoes. Help yourself to the equipment. If you need help with anything, our groundskeeper, Harvey, should be around. If you can't find him, let me know and I'll try to reach him on his cell phone."

We thanked her and left the lodge through the front door. The path Rita had mentioned had been shoveled since last night's snowfall, making the trip to the outbuilding an easy one. Brett opened the door and I stepped into the dim interior. Some daylight seeped in through the two windows, but it was still much darker than outside, where the sun shone brightly down, reflecting off the fresh snow.

"Maybe there's a light switch somewhere," Brett said, feeling along the wall next to the door.

A second later he flicked a switch and a bank of overhead lights blinked on. I barely had a chance to take in the sight of numerous pairs of skis and snowshoes leaning against the walls before a voice startled me.

"Looking for skis?"

I spun around to find a man standing in the doorway, nearly filling the frame. He stood over six feet tall and had a muscular build that even his thick coat couldn't hide. I recognized the hat with earflaps, and realized he was the man I'd seen out and about in the middle of the night.

"Snowshoes," Brett said while I was still recovering from my surprise.

The man came into the building. "I can help you out." He offered his hand to Brett, who was closest to him. "I'm Harvey, the groundskeeper."

Brett shook his hand and introduced us both.

Harvey took a look at my feet and grabbed a pair of snowshoes, passing them to me. Then he did the same for Brett.

"Those should work for you," he said. "Do you want poles? Some people need them to help keep their balance."

"We should be okay without, thanks," I said.

Brett nodded his agreement with my decision.

"Where are you heading?" Harvey asked as we emerged from the building.

I set my snowshoes on the ground. "We were thinking of going around the lake."

"You shouldn't have any problems with that." Harvey removed his hat to reveal brown hair sticking up at odd angles. He gave his head a scratch and then pulled his hat on again. "The lakeshore trail goes through the trees in some places, but it's always within view of the lake. Some of the guests like to stray deeper into the woods, which I'd advise against. It's easy to get lost. If you want to go on a forest trek, let me know and we can arrange a time when I can go with you. I know these woods like the back of my hand."

"Thanks. We'll keep that in mind," Brett said.

Harvey nodded at us and then set off around the lodge. I picked up my gear and Brett and I followed the shoveled pathway down to the lake. We stopped there to put on our snowshoes. It didn't take long to get them strapped to our feet. When we were ready, we set off along the shore. The snowshoe tracks I'd noticed the day before had been covered by the fresh snow, so we made a new trail.

Along the way, we stopped a few times to snap pictures with our phones. We didn't see any wildlife other than a few birds, but the scenery was stunning, the snow glistening in the sunlight. By the time we got about a third of the way around the lake, we had to unzip our jackets part way. We ended up removing our hats and stuffing them in our jacket pockets not long after. The bright sunshine was pushing the temperature up and up.

An hour or so after we'd left the lodge, we brushed snow off a fallen tree and sat down to rest, facing the frozen, snow-covered lake. Brett and I were both in fairly good shape—Brett more so than me—but cutting a path through the fresh snow took a lot of effort and we were both ready for a short break.

"Next time we should bring a bottle of water with us," I said. "Snowshoeing is thirsty work."

Brett pulled off his gloves and ran a hand through his blond hair. "I was just thinking the same thing."

To what I thought was the south, straight across the lake from us, stood Holly Lodge. It probably wouldn't have taken as long to get back there if we could have cut across the lake. I didn't know if the ice was strong enough to withstand our weight, though, and I wasn't about to risk it. Besides, I knew I'd enjoy the rest of the journey around the lake once I'd had a bit more time to rest.

"Looks like someone else is out on the lakeshore trail," Brett said a moment later.

I followed his gaze with my own, squinting in the bright sunlight. I caught a brief glimpse of a woman with long red hair on the path we'd taken from the lodge to where we now sat. A second later, she darted into the woods and out of sight.

"Was she wearing a dress?" I could have sworn the woman was in a green gown.

"Looked like it," Brett said.

"Strange thing to wear out in the snow." I stared at the trees lining the shore, but the woman didn't reappear.

"Maybe she's on her way to a party," Brett suggested.

I looked around us. The three homes on this side of the lake were all quiet, with no signs of life. The only other building in sight was Holly Lodge.

Brett laughed when he saw me looking around. "Okay, not likely. She's probably just eccentric."

"Could be," I agreed.

I wasn't even positive that we were right about how she was dressed. She'd been too far away to see clearly.

Brett got up and offered me a hand, pulling me to my feet. Well rested now, we continued on our way, taking our time. The lake was larger than I'd realized. It wasn't all visible from the lodge. After a couple of hours, we spotted what looked like our starting point off in the distance. As much as I'd enjoyed the journey, I was thirsty and ready to get out of my jacket. The fresh snow was starting to melt from the trees, water dripping from the ends of icicles. A few minutes later, we met up with the beginning of our trail and unfastened our snowshoes.

Brett wiped a gloved hand across his forehead. "I'm ready for a cold drink after that. And lunch."

"Me too," I said, even though it was probably still a bit early for lunch. My stomach grumbled, not caring about the time.

We carried our snowshoes up the path. Before we reached the outbuilding, Harvey approached.

"Did you have a good time?" he asked.

"It was great," Brett said.

"This is such a beautiful place." I zipped up my jacket again. Now that we'd stopped moving, I wasn't quite so warm.

"I'm glad you enjoyed it. I can take those for you." Harvey relieved us of our snowshoes. "Did you happen to see Kevin while you were out there?"

"No," Brett replied. "The only person we saw was a red-haired woman."

Harvey scratched his jaw. "I don't know of any redheads around here. Except…" He shook his head. "No sign of Kevin then. I'll have to tell Rita."

"Why? Is something wrong?" I asked, noting the grim expression on Harvey's face.

"We're not entirely sure yet," he said. "But it seems Kevin's gone missing."

Chapter Four

"When's the last time someone saw Kevin?" I asked as I followed Harvey into the equipment building.

"Last night around eleven." Harvey set the snowshoes we'd used against the wall. "That's when Rita went to bed. Kevin was still up at that point, and when Rita got up in the morning, he was nowhere to be found."

"Is it unusual for him to disappear like this?" Brett asked.

Harvey rubbed the back of his neck. "It's unusual, all right. He usually tells me or Rita if he's heading out somewhere, and he's pretty good about answering texts and returning phone calls, but he's not doing either today."

A nugget of uneasiness settled heavily in my stomach. "Maybe he forgot to charge his phone."

I was about to say more when a dog barked nearby. I stepped outside and smiled as a golden retriever bounded through the snow toward us. A woman on snowshoes followed behind the dog.

A smile broke out across Harvey's face as he crouched down. "Hey there, Scout."

The golden retriever ran right up to him and accepted a thorough rubdown of his fur, his brown eyes bright and happy. It was only once Scout had greeted Harvey that he turned his attention to me and Brett, sniffing our boots and wagging his tail.

"Hi, buddy." I gave him a pat on his head, and Brett did the same. I tried to ignore the sharp pang in my chest. Seeing Scout made me miss Bentley and Flapjack.

I glanced up to see Harvey's smile growing wider. This time his gaze was on the woman approaching us.

"Morning, Evie," he said as the woman unfastened her snowshoes and stood them upright in a snowbank.

Leaving her snowshoes behind, she walked along the shoveled pathway to join us. "Morning." She directed the greeting at all of us.

She appeared to be about my age, or maybe a little bit older. Wisps of fair hair had come loose from her braid and her cheeks were pink. She wore a cable-knit sweater with her jeans, and she carried a canvas bag in one hand.

She gave the bag a gentle pat. "I've brought fresh eggs for Rita."

"She'll be glad to get them," Harvey said. He introduced me and Brett. "Evie lives half a mile down the road," he explained to us. By then, his smile had faded and a worry line had appeared across his forehead. "You haven't seen or heard from Kevin today, have you?"

Evie seemed surprised by the question. "No. Why do you ask?"

Harvey brought her up to speed on Kevin's mysterious absence.

"Maybe he took off because he needed some time to himself." Evie gave Harvey a pointed look.

"You mean time to cool off?" I guessed, thinking I might know what they were saying to each other without words.

I could tell by their expressions that I'd guessed right.

"We overheard him arguing with Rita yesterday," Brett said. "I take it that's not an unusual occurrence?"

Harvey cleared his throat and shifted his gaze to Scout, who was now sitting at Evie's feet. "All couples have problems."

"But they've had more than their fair share lately," Evie said. "They're going through a rough patch. I think they can work through it, but things haven't been easy for either of them lately."

"So maybe they argued again," Brett said. "If that's the case, Kevin will probably come back when he's ready."

Harvey shook his head. "His truck's still here. Same with the ATV and the snowmobiles. And I just checked the skis and snowshoes. They're all accounted for. He wouldn't have gone off on foot. Not at this time of year."

The uneasiness in my stomach grew heavier. "Could someone have picked him up? A friend or neighbor, maybe?"

"Maybe." Harvey clearly wasn't convinced that was a real possibility.

"He'll probably turn up soon," Evie said, with a note of determined cheeriness in her voice. "I'd better get these eggs inside to Rita. Can Scout hang out with you for a bit, Harvey?"

"Of course."

Brett and I followed Evie in through the back door of the lodge. Once we reached the dining room, Evie disappeared into the kitchen in search of Rita while we poured ourselves glasses of ice water from a jug on the credenza. We both emptied our glasses quickly and decided to make ourselves mugs of hot chocolate next. As Brett was adding a healthy serving of mini marshmallows to each mug, I heard the front door of the lodge open. I hurried toward the lobby, hoping it was Kevin finally showing up.

A draft of cold air hit me as I heard the door shut. I peeked around the corner. A young woman dressed in winter gear darted toward a door opposite the staircase, one marked private. I'd never seen her before. The right side of her head was shaved, and six-inch dreadlocks swept down the other side. She carried a full backpack over her shoulder and she had a shopping bag with the logo of a popular Seattle boutique in one hand. She glanced behind her as she used a key to unlock the door. Then she quickly slipped out of sight, shutting the door firmly behind her.

"Not Kevin?" Brett had come up behind me, carrying both mugs.

I accepted the one he offered me. "No. It was a woman. She had a key to the Mannings' private quarters."

"A family member, maybe?"

"Probably."

I led the way up the stairs to our room. After shedding our outerwear, we settled in front of the gas fireplace to enjoy our hot chocolate. I tried to relax and clear my mind, to focus only on the present moment, but I couldn't stop the spinning of my thoughts. Kevin's ongoing absence was unsettling and I worried that he might have come to some sort of harm. Then there was the woman I'd seen down in the lobby. She had a key to the private quarters, so most likely she was allowed to go in there, but there'd been a furtive quality to her actions that had left me with the distinct impression that she hadn't wanted to be seen. If she was allowed to go into the private quarters and had the key legitimately, why did she need to be sneaky about it?

"Thinking about Kevin?" Brett guessed. He could always tell when my mind was elsewhere.

"Partly. Do you think something bad happened to him?"

"Could be." Brett set his mug on the coffee table and leaned back, settling an arm across my shoulders. "But if things aren't great between him and Rita, maybe he did need to get away for a while and was too angry to bother to tell anyone. Like you said, a friend or neighbor could have given him a ride."

"I hope that's all that's happened."

I took a sip of my hot chocolate and then pulled out my phone. I hadn't received any new text messages from my mom. Hopefully that meant all was well with the house and the animals. I did, however, have a message from my friend and neighbor Patricia Murray, asking for confirmation that I wanted to take part in Wildwood Cove's Festival of Trees in December.

The festival would run from early in the month right up until Christmas. The seniors' center had offered up its small gymnasium for the event. Local businesses and organizations taking part in the festival would each decorate a tree. The plan was to create an indoor holiday forest, with walkways winding among the evergreens. Visitors would get to vote on their favorite trees, and the participant with the most votes at the end of the festival would win a thousand dollars to donate to a charity of their choice. The businesses taking part would also provide a gift basket or other prize, and visitors could purchase tickets to enter raffles, with the money earned from ticket sales going to charity as well. It was the first time Wildwood Cove had put on the festival, but the organizers, who included Patricia, were hoping it would become an annual event. The customers I'd talked to recently at the pancake house were looking forward to it, so I figured there was a good chance that it would be popular.

I'd mentioned a couple of weeks earlier that I was interested in taking part on behalf of The Flip Side. That hadn't changed, so I sent Patricia a quick message, letting her know the pancake house would participate. I'd already purchased some cute ornaments that were perfect for decorating a tree with a breakfast theme.

I opened up my Internet browser and searched online for other suitable handcrafted ornaments while finishing off my hot chocolate. As I scrolled through an online store, I told Brett about the text message from Patricia.

"Do you want a tree too?" I asked him.

He stretched his arms over his head before reaching for his mug. "How about I help you with yours?"

I smiled. "I'd like that."

"And if Patricia could use my help with setting things up, I'm happy to lend a hand."

"I'll let her know."

I gave up on my search for ornaments for the time being and sent Patricia another quick message. After that, I put my phone away, not wanting to spend too much time on it while I was on vacation.

"Ready for some lunch?" Brett asked as he set his empty mug next to mine.

"I could eat." I wandered over to the window to take in the view of the lake again. The sky was a bolder shade of blue than it had been that morning, and the snow sparkled in the sunshine. The higher mountain peaks, all capped with snow, were fully visible now that the clouds had disappeared. The scene was beautiful enough to be featured on a postcard.

"But first I want to take another picture of the lake," I said. The sunny view was too gorgeous not to photograph.

Brett got up from the loveseat and grabbed our empty mugs. "Do you want to take your coat?"

"I don't think so. The sun has warmed things up out there, and I'll only be outside for a minute."

I tucked my phone in the pocket of my jeans and we left our room. As we descended the stairs, I heard voices in the lobby below us. We reached the ground floor in time to see Evie giving Rita a hug.

"Let me know what happens, okay?" she requested.

"I will," Rita said. "Thanks for coming by."

Evie sent a smile our way and then disappeared into the lounge on her way to the back door.

"No sign of Kevin yet?" I asked.

"No," Rita said with a frown. She drew in a deep breath and tried to smile. "Heading to the dining room for some lunch?"

"Soon," Brett said.

I detected some delicious smells coming from the dining room and my stomach growled in response. The enticing aromas provided good motivation to be quick with my photography.

I held up my phone. "We're going to go out and get a picture of the lake first."

The door marked private opened, drawing our attention. The young woman I'd spotted earlier emerged into the lobby, without her bags and winter gear this time.

Rita's eyes widened. "Zahra! I didn't know you were here!"

The young woman smiled. "I just got here a few minutes ago."

Rita hurried over to hug her, holding on tightly for a moment before releasing her. She kept an arm around the younger woman's shoulders as she addressed me and Brett. "This is my daughter, Zahra."

Now that I had a clear view of Zahra's face, and with her standing next to Rita, I could see the family resemblance. Zahra had the same high cheekbones and tall stature as her mother. I guessed her to be in her early twenties, and she had a silver stud in her nose that I hadn't noticed before.

"Brett and Marley are guests," Rita explained. She'd had a smile on her face, but now it slipped away. "You haven't heard from Kevin today, have you, Zahra?"

"No." Her daughter seemed confused. "Should I have?"

Rita's shoulders slumped as she let out a sigh. "I'd better call the sheriff."

Zahra's eyes widened with alarm. "The sheriff? What's going on?"

A phone chimed. Zahra pulled a smartphone from the pocket of her jeans and checked it.

Brett and I skirted around her and passed through the lounge to the back door, leaving Rita to talk to her daughter privately.

"This isn't Ray's jurisdiction, is it?" I asked Brett once we were out on the back deck. Ray Georgeson was the sheriff for Clallam County, where Wildwood Cove was located. He was also Brett's uncle. I was pretty sure we were well out of Clallam County.

"No," Brett said, confirming my thoughts. "I don't know the sheriff here."

"Whoever it is, I hope he or she can find Kevin safe and sound."

"I hope so too, but the sheriff might not be able to do much yet. Kevin's only been missing for about twelve hours."

Maybe an official investigation wouldn't start yet, but I couldn't help but think that twelve hours was plenty of time for something to go terribly wrong.

"Maybe we should organize a search party and start looking for Kevin," I suggested.

"It wouldn't be safe for anyone without the right skills and knowledge to head out into the woods up here," Brett said. "Especially at this time of year."

"True," I conceded, knowing he was right.

Brett gave me a quick hug. "We'll see what the sheriff tells Rita."

I nodded and returned his hug. After releasing him, I crossed the deck and stood by the railing, trying to push my troubling thoughts aside. It was chilly outside, especially without a jacket, but the bright sunshine was melting the snow off the roof and the trees. A steady *drip-drip-drip* provided a background soundtrack to the beautiful scenery.

I snapped a photo with my phone. "I'm going to go a bit closer to the lake." I took care going down the steps. I was wearing sneakers rather than my winter boots, and I didn't want to slip.

Brett accompanied me along the path that led to the lake. I stopped halfway along it and took another couple of photos. With that done, I tucked my phone into my pocket. A chilly breeze cut through my clothes, making me shiver.

"Ready to head in?" Brett guessed.

"Definitely."

I slipped my hand into Brett's and we made our way up the gentle hill toward the lodge. A few steps later, I drew to a sudden stop.

"Brett..." My voice cracked as I said his name. I pointed at the snowbank off to one side of the steps leading to the deck.

Brett swore and broke into a run. I raced after him, slipping but managing not to fall. A glove poked out from the middle of the pile of snow, along with a cuff of red and black fabric. Fabric that looked exactly like the jacket I'd seen Kevin wearing the day before.

Brett reached the snowbank and started digging with his bare hands. I skidded to a stop next to him and joined in, frantically shifting the snow away. I hoped desperately it was just the jacket and glove under the snow, but within seconds I knew that wasn't the case. I could feel an arm in the sleeve.

I barely noticed the tears stinging my eyes or the fact that I was losing the feeling in my hands.

"Did you lose something?" Harvey's voice startled me.

I kept digging as I glanced to the right. The groundskeeper strode towards us.

"Help!" I yelled.

The smile fell from Harvey's face. He charged over our way just as Brett shoved aside another handful of snow to reveal Kevin's face. His pale skin was tinged with blue and his eyes were closed. Brett brushed more snow away until he could place two fingers to Kevin's neck.

I already knew Kevin wasn't breathing, that he hadn't been for some time. One look at his face was enough to tell me that.

Even so, Brett's next words sent a terrible chill through my body.

"He's dead."

Chapter Five

"No." Harvey stared at Kevin's partially buried body. He took off his hat and gripped it tightly with both hands. His face was almost as pale as Kevin's, although without the tinge of death. "But how?"

We all stared at each other for a moment. Brett and Harvey were probably thinking the same thing that I was—Kevin couldn't have buried himself in the snowbank. There was too much snow on top of him for it to have accumulated naturally after his death. Someone must have shoveled it.

I didn't want to look at Kevin's lifeless face again, but I couldn't stop myself.

I swallowed against a wave of nausea as I spotted something I hadn't noticed before.

"Look." I pointed at the top of Kevin's head. A spot of red marred the bright whiteness of the snow.

Brett carefully brushed aside another handful of snow to reveal more red. *Blood.*

Brett took a quick step back and put an arm around me. I leaned into his side and closed my eyes.

He gave me a gentle squeeze. "We need to call the police. I don't have my phone on me."

I forced my eyes open and dug my phone out of my pocket with numb fingers. Brett took it and that brought me a hint of relief. I could have made the call, but I was glad I didn't have to.

Harvey still had his hat gripped in his hands. "I'd better go tell Rita."

A combination of grief, shock, and grim resignation showed on his face. I didn't envy him the job of breaking the news to Rita. Even though she and Kevin had their problems, his death would no doubt be a blow. And to learn that his death most likely wasn't natural…

It was no wonder that Harvey headed into the lodge with heavy steps.

As Brett spoke with the emergency operator, I turned my back on Kevin's body, unable to bear the sight of it any longer. I focused on the lake and the mountains instead, although I wasn't able to appreciate their beauty like I had just a short time ago.

Brett ended the phone call and wrapped his arms around me. "You should go inside. You're freezing."

It was only once he said those words that I realized I was shivering. "You should go in too," I said.

"It'll take a while for the sheriff to get here. I'll stay out here to make sure no one gets too close to the body."

For the first time it truly hit me that we were standing at a crime scene. I pulled back from Brett and looked around.

"He was probably killed hours ago," Brett said, as if reading my thoughts.

He was likely right about that. Whoever had killed Kevin probably wasn't lurking behind the snowbank, but he or she could still be nearby. In the lodge, even.

"I don't want to leave you out here by yourself," I said. Until I knew for sure that Kevin's killer was no longer around, I didn't want to take any risks.

"You're cold."

"So are you." I squeezed his hands, which were as icy as mine. "How about I go inside and grab our jackets?"

"Good idea."

I glanced up at the lodge. A shadowy figure stood by one of the windows, looking out at me and Brett. It took me a second to realize that it was Lily. I couldn't read her expression from this distance. I wondered if she'd already heard the grim news from Harvey.

"I'll be quick," I said to Brett.

I averted my gaze as I skirted around Kevin's body. I hurried up the steps to the deck, getting colder by the minute. The sun disappeared behind a cloud that hadn't been there just minutes ago. The diminishing light felt ominous. I glanced up at the sky. Gray clouds were rolling in from the north, moving swiftly. The sun wasn't likely to reappear today. The change seemed fitting, considering the circumstances.

By the time I stepped inside the lodge, Lily had disappeared. The lounge was empty and quiet. I thought I heard low murmurs coming from the dining room, but I didn't bother to check to see who was there. I didn't want

Brett to be outside on his own for long, so I took the stairs two at a time up to the second floor and fetched our jackets, as well as hats and gloves.

I shrugged into my own jacket on my way out of the room. I jogged back downstairs and reached the lobby just as Harvey came out of the Mannings' private quarters. He shut the door behind him.

"Did you talk to Rita?" I asked. From the stricken expression on his face, I could guess the answer.

He nodded and took a second to gather himself. "Her daughter is with her."

What a relief that Zahra had arrived that morning.

"I'll be outside with Brett," I said.

Harvey gestured toward the front door. "I'll wait out front for the sheriff."

We parted ways, and I wasted no more time getting back to Brett. He bundled up in the clothes I'd brought him and then we stood there together, waiting. Time ticked by slowly. More clouds rolled in, leaving very little blue sky left to be seen. The wind picked up a notch, and I was glad I'd retrieved our coats. Without them, the wait—already difficult—would have been unbearable.

I forced myself to take another look at Kevin to see if I could spot any further clues as to how he'd died, but with most of his body still buried there wasn't much chance of that. I widened my circle of observation, but there was no sign of a murder weapon nearby, or any other clue that I could see. I probably would have assumed that he'd fallen and hit his head, if not for the fact that he'd been buried in the snowbank. That was no accident.

I turned away again, not wanting to stare at the bloodstained snow or Kevin's eerily still, bluish face.

"He must have died last night," I said quietly. "Otherwise someone probably would have noticed the killer burying him in the snow."

"Most likely," Brett agreed.

My heart nearly tripped over itself as memories came rushing back to me. "Harvey was out here last night."

Brett took a second to absorb my words. "When you were up?"

I nodded, unable to say anything more at the moment. I didn't like thinking about what that could mean, but I also couldn't ignore what I'd seen.

"What time was that?" Brett asked.

I found my voice after another second. "Two o'clock, or a little later."

Brett's mouth set in a grim line. I knew what he was thinking. That very well could have been around the time Kevin was killed.

I remembered something more. "Someone else was up too. I heard a door close and footsteps out in the hall."

"Do you know which door?"

I thought back, desperately trying to find more detail hidden among my memories, but it was pointless. "No. Only that it was on the second floor."

Brett shoved his hands deep into his pockets. "Tell all that to the sheriff."

"I will," I assured him.

I didn't like to implicate anyone in Kevin's death, but I had to give the sheriff every scrap of information I had. Besides, as much as I didn't want anyone connected to the lodge to have had a hand in Kevin's death, what did I really know about anyone here except Brett? My gaze strayed to the lodge. I checked every window, but this time I couldn't see anyone looking out at us. Nevertheless, I felt exposed and uneasy standing near Kevin's body, even with Brett at my side.

When I caught the distant sound of a car engine, I hoped desperately that the sheriff had arrived. A moment later, the engine cut off and a car door slammed. Voices drew nearer and Harvey appeared from around the side of the lodge, a woman in uniform next to him.

Harvey drew to a stop and said something to the woman. She nodded and Harvey turned back the way he'd come.

"Sheriff Walczyk," the woman said by way of introduction as she approached me and Brett. "I understand you folks were the ones to find Kevin Manning."

"That's right," Brett confirmed.

The sheriff studied Kevin's mostly buried body for a moment and then asked us a few questions about how we'd found him and how much of the scene we'd disturbed.

I felt bad that we'd messed with the crime scene, but we'd had to check if Kevin was alive, and it hadn't occurred to us right away that he'd been murdered. Sheriff Walczyk didn't lecture us, so I figured she saw it the same way.

"Thank you," she said after we'd provided our answers. "I'll need to talk to you again, but you can wait inside the lodge."

I took Brett's hand and gladly left the sheriff to keep watch over Kevin. There was no one in the lounge. The first person we encountered in the lodge was a deputy in the lobby.

"Are you the guests who found the body?" he asked as soon as he saw us. We confirmed that we were.

"I'll need to take your statements. Mrs. Manning has allowed us the use of her office." He addressed me. "Ma'am, are you all right to give me your statement now?"

"Of course." I gave Brett's hand a squeeze before letting it go.

He waited in the lobby while I sat in the office with the deputy, who introduced himself as Reynolds. The small room contained a desk, two chairs, and a metal filing cabinet. A painting of Holly Lake hung on one wall while framed diplomas and certificates were displayed on another. I recounted to Deputy Reynolds how Brett and I had found Kevin in the snowbank, and how Harvey had appeared on the scene moments later. I also filled him in on the things I'd heard and seen during the night.

Once I'd told him everything I could think of, I traded places with Brett. There was a padded bench in the lobby, near the front door, so I slipped out of my jacket and took a seat. Aside from the low murmur of Brett's voice coming from the office behind the reception desk, the lodge was silent. I wondered where Harvey had gone and whether the other guests were somewhere in the lodge.

A minute or so later, I received a partial answer to my question. Hushed voices came from the direction of the stairway seconds before Lily and Ambrose appeared. Lily was speaking to Ambrose in an urgent whisper, but as soon as she spotted me, she stopped mid-sentence.

She quickly recovered from the surprise of seeing me sitting in the lobby. "Do you have any idea what's going on?" she asked me. "There are sheriff's department vehicles in the parking lot and I couldn't help noticing you and your husband gathered outside with Harvey a while ago."

The excited gleam in her eyes knocked me off kilter until I reminded myself that she didn't know someone had died.

I stood up slowly, not eager to be the one to deliver the news. "It's Kevin."

"He hasn't shown up yet?" Ambrose asked.

"He has, in a way," I said. "I'm afraid he's dead."

Lily's eyes widened and the color drained from Ambrose's face.

"Dead?" Lily echoed.

The door to the office opened and Brett emerged with his jacket over one arm, Deputy Reynolds right behind him. At almost the same time, the door to Rita and Kevin's private quarters opened and another deputy appeared, shutting the door behind him.

Lily and Ambrose still stood at the base of the stairs, staring at the deputies.

By unspoken agreement, Brett and I drifted toward the dining room. As we left the lobby, I heard Deputy Reynolds asking Lily and Ambrose if they were guests at the lodge. He likely wanted to interview everyone on the premises.

"No sign of Wilson," I said quietly when we reached the empty dining room.

I didn't know what to do. It would feel strange to lock ourselves away in our room, but I certainly wasn't in the mood for any outdoor activities. All my energy had drained away and my spirits drooped.

"Want me to make you a cup of tea?" Brett asked as I pulled out a chair at one of the tables and hung my jacket over the back of it.

"Yes, please," I said, realizing that I still wasn't quite warm after standing vigil over Kevin's body.

A woman in chef's whites popped her head out from the kitchen. "I can bring you drinks." She came farther into the room. "I've got a pot of coffee on in the kitchen. It's probably fresher than what's there." She nodded at the credenza where a small amount of coffee sat in the pot.

"That sounds great, thanks," Brett said. "I'll have coffee."

"And one cup of tea?" the woman said to me. "What kind do you prefer?"

"Orange pekoe, if you have it."

"Certainly. I'll be back in a minute."

She was true to her word. Brett and I had barely settled at the table when she reappeared with a mug of coffee and a tea cup and saucer, a teabag in the hot water.

"I'm the lodge chef, Cindy," she said once we'd thanked her for the drinks.

"Brett and Marley," Brett offered.

"I'm guessing you've heard the news," she said, her face solemn

I fished the teabag out of my cup, letting the water drip from it before I placed it on the saucer. "We were the ones who found Kevin."

"Oh, how terrible." She lowered her voice. "Harvey said Kevin was buried in a snowbank, that someone might have killed him." She shook her head. "I can't believe it."

I wanted to ask Cindy if she knew of anyone who might have wanted to harm Kevin, but Ambrose and Lily arrived in the dining room and headed our way.

"Would anyone like some lunch?" Cindy asked all of us.

It didn't seem quite right to have an appetite after what had happened, but my stomach grumbled, making my cheeks flush.

"We should probably eat something after all that snowshoeing," Brett said to me.

Lily pulled out a chair at the table next to ours. She seemed preoccupied, but said, "I could eat."

Ambrose murmured his agreement.

My embarrassment eased. At least I wasn't the only one who was hungry.

We all consulted the menus and Cindy took our orders before returning to the kitchen.

"Can you believe what's happening?" Lily asked me and Brett, her eyes wide. Wisps of hair had come loose from her bun, which had a pencil sticking through it. "We're right in the middle of a murder investigation."

"Suspicious death investigation," Ambrose corrected her. "They haven't said murder yet."

"True," Lily said. She returned her attention to me and Brett. "Did you find him out by the steps? Is that why you were standing there?" Before we had a chance to respond, she spoke again. "But if the body was in plain view, we would have seen it earlier."

"It wasn't in plain view," I said. "He was buried in a snowbank."

Lily's face paled. "To conceal the body?"

"It didn't snow enough for it to happen naturally," Brett said.

"What's going on out there now?" Ambrose had his gaze fixed on the back window.

Lily spun around in her seat. I turned more slowly. With the deck in the way, I could only see the heads of the people out near where we'd found Kevin's body, but it looked like Sheriff Walczyk was there with two of her deputies.

"Oh, my goodness!" Lily jumped up and hurried over to the window. She let out a gasp. "I think they found the murder weapon!"

I couldn't help myself. I joined Lily by the window. That gave me a better view of what was going on outside. Sure enough, Sheriff Walczyk was speaking with Deputy Reynolds and another deputy I hadn't seen before. Reynolds was holding a ski and all three had their attention fixed on it.

I stared at the white and blue ski, wishing I could see it better. I noticed a red mark near one end of it. "Is that…?"

"Blood," Lily said, finishing my sentence. "It's definitely blood."

Chapter Six

Even though my lunch was delicious, I wasn't able to enjoy it. I picked at the vegetable curry and didn't manage to finish the meal, despite all the snowshoeing Brett and I had done that morning. I was too on edge and preoccupied to focus on eating.

Brett finished his clubhouse sandwich and fries, but he wasn't his usual relaxed self either. We both stayed silent, though the inside of my head was anything but quiet. Thoughts about Kevin's death bounced around like ping-pong balls. I tried to settle my mind, to think about something—anything—else, but that was impossible, so I gave up and let myself think about the crime.

If the ski was the weapon Kevin's killer had used to strike him in the head, did that provide any clue to the murderer's identity?

I didn't think so. Harvey seemed to be in charge of all the outdoor equipment, but the door to the shed was left unlocked, at least during the day. Maybe it was locked at night. If so, and if that's where the ski had come from, I feared Harvey might well end up as the prime suspect.

Although I didn't really know Harvey at all, I didn't want him to be the murderer. I didn't want *anyone* at the lodge to be a killer. The thought of being in such close proximity to the murderer was enough to make my blood run cold. I wanted to ask Brett if we should go home. There wasn't much chance of us enjoying our vacation any longer. It wouldn't exactly be relaxing since we'd be constantly looking over our shoulders, wondering if someone down the hall or at the next table could be responsible for Kevin's death.

I didn't broach the subject yet, though. I wanted to wait until Brett and I were alone.

Over at the neighboring table, Lily and Ambrose were speculating about the murder. At least Lily was. Ambrose offered up sounds of apparent interest and agreement here and there, but it was hard to tell if he was really into the conversation. Much of what Lily was saying mirrored my own thoughts, although she didn't know about Harvey being outside in the middle of the night.

Cindy came out of the kitchen and cleared away Lily's and Ambrose's empty plates. After that, the two of them left the dining room together.

"You doing okay?" Brett asked me once we were alone.

I was about to answer when Cindy reappeared. With Rita out of commission, it seemed the chef had taken on the additional role of server.

"All finished?" she asked us.

"Yes, thanks," I said, nudging my half-empty plate toward the edge of the table. "It was delicious. My appetite just isn't what it usually is."

"Totally understandable," she said. "To be honest, I don't think it's quite sunk in for me yet. I keep expecting Kevin to show up." She picked up our plates. "I feel terrible for Rita."

"Do you live on-site?" I asked, wondering how much opportunity she had to see the comings and goings at the lodge at all hours.

"No. I live across the lake. Aside from the Mannings, the only person who lives on-site is Harvey. He's got a cabin in the woods, just a stone's throw from here."

"Has he worked here long?" I caught the way Brett was looking at me. He knew my questions arose from more than an attempt to make casual conversation.

"Three or four years, I think," Cindy said. "He's been here longer than I have, and it's almost two years for me."

My mind veered off in another direction.

"If you've lived around here for a while, I'm guessing you've heard the story about the local ghost," I said.

"Sure, I know the story." Cindy straightened the salt and pepper shakers on the neighboring table. "And I've seen her with my own eyes."

"The ghost?" I couldn't contain my surprise.

"Yep. I saw her out on the lake one time last spring. It was like she was walking on the water. That's how I knew it was Henrietta's ghost. That and the fact that she looked just like everyone else has described her."

I wasn't sure what to make of Cindy's account and I could tell Brett wasn't either. The chef seemed sincere, so she probably believed what she was saying, but did that mean she'd really seen the ghost of Henrietta Franklin?

"What does the ghost look like?" Brett asked. If he didn't believe the story, his voice didn't reveal that.

"Long, red hair," Cindy said. "And she's always wearing a green dress."

I froze at those words. Brett's gaze met mine from across the table.

Cindy continued, not noticing our reactions. "According to the story, it was her favorite dress."

I was too stunned to ask her more questions about Henrietta, even though several had bubbled up to the surface of my thoughts.

She glanced at Brett's empty mug and my teacup. "Can I get you anything else? More to drink, maybe?"

"I think we're done." Brett looked to me for confirmation, and I nodded. "Thank you."

Getting back to business, she collected our cups, adding them to the stacked plates. "I'll see you this evening," she said before returning to the kitchen.

"That's another thing I wasn't expecting on this trip," Brett said, a grin slowly taking shape on his face. "We saw a ghost."

"Maybe." I hesitated. "Do you really believe it?"

Brett shrugged, still grinning. "It was probably just an eccentric woman running through the woods, but it makes for a good story."

I tended to agree with him, although this was a small community. If there was an eccentric woman living in the area who liked to run through the snowy woods in a long dress, wouldn't the locals know about it? Harvey had said he didn't know of any redheads who lived nearby.

"Cindy said she'd see us this evening," I whispered as we got up from the table. "Will we really still be here then?"

"Do you want to go home?" Brett asked.

"Yes," I said without hesitation. Although I wanted to know more about Henrietta Franklin, I figured I could always look up information about her online, from the comfort and safety of our own home. "I don't see how we can enjoy ourselves now. What do you think?"

Brett took my hand as we left the dining room, our coats tucked under our arms. "I'd rather go home too. We'll need to check out."

"Maybe Cindy can help us with that," I said, hoping that was the case. The more time that passed, the less I wanted to spend another night at the lodge.

Out in the lobby, Wilson was finishing up a conversation with Deputy Reynolds. Wilson said something I couldn't hear and then strode away from Reynolds, nodding at me and Brett as he passed us by on his way to the dining room.

Deputy Reynolds also nodded at us, but then turned away and spoke quietly into his radio.

I tried to hear what he was saying, hoping for some news about Kevin's death, but all I heard was the indistinct murmur of the deputy's voice.

Upstairs, a wave of relief washed over me when Brett shut the door to our room. I hung up my coat, kicked off my shoes, and sank down onto the edge of the bed.

"Not exactly the vacation we hoped for, is it?" Brett asked, sitting down next to me.

"Not nearly. I feel terrible for Rita. And I can't help but look at the staff and other guests and wonder if one of them could be the killer."

Brett put an arm around me and gave me a squeeze. "I know. How about we get packed so we're ready to go? Then I'll ask Cindy if she can help with the checkout process. It should be easy since we already provided our credit card number. We'll have to check with the sheriff to make sure we're allowed to leave, though."

My heart dropped like a heavy stone. "Do you really think they'd make us stay here?"

"I doubt it. They've got our statements and our contact information. We should make sure, though."

I nodded as I leaned into him. "I hope we aren't suspects. We didn't have a motive to kill Kevin."

"I'm sure his family members and the lodge staff are of much more interest to the sheriff."

"Especially Harvey, since he was outside in the middle of the night. And he'd likely have access to the skis and other equipment, even if the shed was locked."

"I was thinking the same thing," Brett said. "Although, as Kevin's wife, I'm sure Rita will get scrutinized too."

"That's true."

We got up from the bed and started packing. It didn't take long to get all our belongings together. Brett was zipping the suitcase closed when a sharp knock on the door made me jump.

Brett and I shared a glance as he crossed the room to open the door. Maybe it was silly, but my heart was pounding. I breathed a sigh of relief when I saw that it was Deputy Reynolds who'd knocked on the door.

"Sorry to disturb you," he said, "but I'd like to ask you both a few more questions."

I couldn't mask my surprise. "Okay. I don't know what else we can tell you, though."

Brett stepped back to make space for the deputy to enter our room.

"I'd like to talk about how things have been here at the lodge since you arrived," Reynolds said as he stepped inside.

"Because you know more about Kevin's death now?" Brett closed the door. "Was it definitely murder?"

"Most likely, I'm afraid."

That didn't come as a surprise. Somehow, though, having the deputy confirm it set my nerves on edge even more than before.

We invited Deputy Reynolds into the sitting area. He took the armchair while Brett and I settled on the loveseat. Reynolds took out a notebook and pen and asked us to recount everything we'd seen and heard since our arrival. Brett told him about the conversation between Wilson and Kevin that we'd overheard while in the hot tub, and I shared what little I'd heard of Kevin and Rita's argument. Since we hadn't been at the lodge for long, we didn't have much else of interest to tell him. We told him everything we could remember, though, even if it didn't seem relevant.

"You said Evie is a neighbor?" Reynolds asked after I told him about Evie's arrival with the eggs that morning.

"That's what Harvey said," I confirmed. "And she seems to be a friend of Rita's." I explained how I'd seen the two women talking and hugging with the familiarity of friends.

"Do you know Evie's last name?" Reynolds asked.

"No. Sorry," I said.

Even though we couldn't help him with that, I knew the deputy would be able to find out the information easily enough.

Deputy Reynolds made a note in his book, and we continued to recount what we'd done before and after finding Kevin's body. By the time he snapped his notebook shut, much of the daylight had faded from the sky. The change surprised me when I glanced out the window. We'd had such a late lunch that it didn't feel like it should be dark yet. At the same time, it seemed like the day had stretched on forever.

"Is it all right if we head home?" Brett asked the deputy. "We were supposed to stay until Tuesday, but given the circumstances..."

"I understand." Reynolds stood up. "But you might want to consider waiting until morning."

I didn't like the sound of that idea.

"The temperature has dropped over the past couple of hours," Reynolds explained. "And with the melting that happened earlier in the day, the roads are like skating rinks."

"But we're allowed to leave?" Brett checked.

"Yes. We know how to get in touch if we need to speak with you further."
Reynolds rested a hand on the doorknob. "But I strongly recommend
staying put until morning."

Brett got up from the loveseat. "We'll keep that in mind."

He saw the deputy out the door before turning to face me.

"What do you think?" he asked.

I stood up and rubbed my arms. A tug-of-war was going on inside of
me. I wanted to get away from the lodge, to go home right away, but the
thought of navigating the icy mountain roads in the dark terrified me as
much as the idea of spending another night at Holly Lodge, possibly in
close proximity to a murderer.

"I don't like either option," I said.

Brett wrapped his arms around me and rubbed my back. He knew
why I was scared to take a chance on the road. I'd lost my stepfather and
stepsiblings in a mountain road accident.

"We'll be okay here tonight," he said. "As soon as the roads are safe,
we'll head home."

I hugged him back. "If Kevin's murder was targeted, we're probably
not in danger here."

I hoped that by saying those words out loud, I'd believe them. It didn't
quite work, mostly because of the big *if*. We really didn't know if the
murder was targeted or completely random.

Brett kissed me, and that helped to settle my nerves more than my
words had.

I reluctantly pulled back from him and got out my phone. "I'd better
text my mom and let her and Grant know we'll be home tomorrow instead
of Tuesday."

"Should we go downstairs?" Brett asked after I'd sent the text message.

"I don't know." I wasn't keen on hanging out with the other guests, not
knowing if one of them was a killer.

"I saw some board games in the lounge. Playing one or two could help
to pass the time."

He had a good point. Despite the encroaching darkness, it was still
just late in the afternoon. Even if it had been later, I didn't expect to sleep
well that night. Having something to focus on other than Kevin's murder
would probably be a good thing.

"Let's go see what games they've got," I said.

We set off downstairs, heading for the lounge. As we crossed the lobby,
the door to the Mannings' private quarters opened and Zahra appeared.

She smiled at us, although the expression didn't make the hint of sadness in her eyes disappear. "I'm sorry your vacation has taken such a terrible turn."

"Please don't apologize," I said. "Our vacation doesn't matter, not in the circumstances."

"We're so sorry about what happened," Brett added.

Zahra's smile was even sadder this time. "Thank you. I still can't believe it's real. I don't know why anyone would have wanted to hurt my stepfather."

"How's your mom doing?" I asked.

"She's hanging in there. She's a strong woman."

"I'm sure it's a comfort to her to have you here," I said. "Do you live here?"

"No, I live in Seattle, but I come to visit regularly. I decided to drive up this morning, and now I'm glad I did. I wouldn't want my mom to be on her own right now."

The phone on the reception desk rang.

Zahra eyed it. "I'd better get that. If there's anything you need during the rest of your stay, just let me know."

We thanked her and left her to answer the phone.

I was relieved to find that the lounge was empty, but we didn't have the room to ourselves for long. We decided to try a game called Cathedral, since it was meant for two players, and we were in the process of taking the pieces out of the box when Ambrose, Lily, and Wilson all arrived. Lily had a cotton tote bag with her and Ambrose had a notebook in his hand.

"You're still here too," Wilson observed when he saw us seated at a small table. "I thought you might have left."

"We're waiting until the roads are safer," Brett said.

"Same idea as the rest of us." Wilson wandered over to a set of floor-to-ceiling bookshelves and began perusing the titles.

"It's creepy to think of spending the night here," Lily said quietly as she sat down in an armchair and pulled a knitting project out of her bag. "But at the same time, I'm getting all kinds of ideas for my next book. I just spent an hour jotting them down before I could forget them."

I detected an excited energy coming from her. I wasn't too sure what to think about the fact that she was, at least in some way, enjoying this experience. I tried not to judge her too harshly, though. Maybe it was her next book that had her excited. She might still feel badly about Kevin beneath the surface. *Unless she'd killed him.*

Suppressing a shudder, I picked up the game's instructions and quickly scanned them before handing them to Brett. The game wasn't complicated, so I figured we could pretty much jump right in.

"Ambrose has a treat for us," Lily said as she untangled some yarn that had wound around her knitting needles. "He's going to read us one of his poems."

Ambrose cleared his throat and shifted on the couch where he'd taken a seat. "Only if everyone wants me to."

A fire burned in the fireplace and the lenses of his glasses glinted with the reflection of the flames.

"Of course we want you to." Lily gave the rest of us a pointed look. "Right?"

"Sure," Brett said. "That would be great."

I nodded in agreement, glad for almost any distraction.

Wilson grabbed a book off the shelf. "Sure, sure," he said, as he read the description on the back cover.

I didn't know if he was even aware of what he was agreeing to.

Ambrose cleared his throat again and stood up. "All right." He positioned himself by the fireplace and opened the slim notebook he'd brought with him. "This one's called *Garden*." He pushed his glasses farther up his nose before starting to read.

> "Where once only weeds took root
> A thing of beauty sprouted
> Magical with a burst of color
> A smell so sweet, my heart filled and shouted
>
> Flower of my heart
> Every petal that makes you unique
> Every sigh, every touch of yours
> Helps me forget all that is bleak."

Ambrose kept his eyes on the page as he recited the poem, but when I glanced over Lily's way, I noticed that she was blushing furiously as she tried to contain a pleased smile.

Ambrose continued on, reading the final verse.

> "No more weeds in this garden
> That grows with love for you
> Forever will I cherish and nurture

Always I will be true."

It was subtle, but as Ambrose read the last line of his poem, I was sure I detected a slight dreamy look in his eyes. He closed the notebook and looked up, first at Lily, and then at the rest of us, an uncertain smile on his face

Lily dropped her knitting and applauded enthusiastically. Ambrose's smile grew in size and confidence. I suspected that the poem was Ambrose's way of expressing his love for Lily—the flower of his heart, as he'd put it—and she was clearly charmed by it. The rest of us joined her in applauding.

"That was great, Ambrose," I said. "Thank you for sharing it with us."

"My pleasure." With flushed cheeks, he set his notebook on the coffee table and turned toward the bookshelves, scanning the titles.

"How about reading one more?" Lily suggested.

"Perhaps another time." Ambrose chose a book off the shelf and wasted no time settling on the couch and opening the novel.

For a moment it seemed like Lily was going to press the issue, but with Ambrose's attention already elsewhere, she stayed quiet and refocused on her knitting.

In the cozy room with the fire crackling and popping, it was almost possible to forget that someone had died violently just outside the back door. Almost.

Even as I focused on the game, a sense of unease never quite left me.

Brett and I played three rounds of Cathedral, with him winning two, and then we said good night to the other guests. As we headed upstairs to our room, I wondered if we'd get any sleep at all that night.

Chapter Seven

I slept better than I'd expected, although I did wake up a few times listening for the sound of someone creeping about in the hallway. Each time, the lodge remained still and silent. Maybe it was partly the stress of the day that helped me sleep, but I knew I would have stayed awake for hours without Brett next to me. He spent much of the night with an arm around me. Together with the locked door, that allowed me to feel relatively safe.

Daylight had yet to make an appearance when we got up, so we knew we'd have to wait a while yet before the ice would melt from the roads. We weren't exactly eager to spend too much time downstairs with the others before we could leave, so we whiled away the first part of the morning drinking tea and coffee while snuggled up on the loveseat in front of the gas fireplace in our room.

When we did venture downstairs, the sky had lightened and the rising sun was tingeing the few clouds with pink. If not for the murder, I would have been looking forward to another beautiful day spent in the mountains.

On our way downstairs, voices floated up toward us. I recognized Zahra's right away, but it took me a moment to realize that the other woman speaking was the Mannings' neighbor, Evie. I paused part of the way down the stairs and Brett stopped at my side. I wasn't sure if we should interrupt the conversation happening below us.

"Things weren't right between them," Zahra was saying. "And I know mom talked about separating, but they did love each other."

"I know they did, honey," Evie said.

"But the police don't know that. And now my mom is the sole owner of the lodge. She inherits *everything* from Kevin. What if the cops think she killed him?"

"Even if they think that, nothing will come of it, because they won't find any evidence. They need more than just an apparent motive to arrest someone."

"I hope you're right," Zahra said. She sounded weary and worried.

My heart went out to her. I hoped Rita hadn't killed Kevin. It was bad enough that Zahra had already lost her stepfather to a violent crime.

As Zahra's and Evie's voices faded away, I glanced at Brett and we continued down the stairs. By the time we reached the lobby, the two women had disappeared. I could still hear voices in the distance, but different ones this time.

When we entered the dining room, I was surprised to see Rita there. She sat at a table with Wilson, both of them with a cup of coffee in front of them.

"I think we can come up with an agreement we'll both be happy with," Wilson was saying.

"We can sort out the details once things settle down around here." Rita glanced up and spotted me and Brett. She pushed back her chair and stood up. "Good morning." She tried to smile at us, but didn't manage to banish the sadness and fatigue from her face.

Brett and I returned her greeting.

"We're so sorry for your loss," I said.

"Thank you." She blinked away tears. "And I'm sorry your vacation has been spoiled."

"Please don't worry about that," I said.

"Nevertheless, anyone who wants to leave early will receive a refund for the rest of the time they planned to stay."

"That's not necessary," Brett said.

She tried to smile again. "I insist." She picked up two menus from a nearby table. "Would you like some breakfast?"

"Please." I accepted one of the menus, and Brett did the same.

We didn't spend much time looking at them. Brett ordered french toast and bacon while I requested an omelet. Rita took the menus back and disappeared into the kitchen. I hoped she wasn't forcing herself to work when she wasn't up to it, but maybe keeping busy was helping her cope.

Ordering breakfast made me miss The Flip Side. The pancake house wouldn't open again for another three days, even though we were leaving Holly Lodge early, but I craved the familiarity of my work there, as well as everything else about home.

It seemed silly to be homesick while on a brief trip just a short distance away, but I knew it was more the circumstances than time or geographical location that had me longing to be back in Wildwood Cove. I'd feel so much better, far more relaxed, once we were back in the comfort of our own home, close to our friends and family instead of hanging out with near-strangers and wondering if one of them was a murderer.

Rita brought us our food a short time later. As with all the other meals we'd had at Holly Lodge, breakfast was delicious. My appetite had returned full force, so I was able to appreciate the scrumptious flavors this time, unlike the last meal I'd had. Brett and I were halfway through our food when Ambrose and Lily arrived in the dining room. We exchanged greetings with them, and Rita took their orders before disappearing into the kitchen once again.

To my relief, Lily and Ambrose spoke quietly with each other. I didn't want to get drawn into a conversation with anyone if I could help it. Although my appetite had returned, I remained uneasy. I wished I could will the sun to melt the ice on the roads. I tried to be patient, but I could almost hear each second ticking sluggishly by, even though there was no clock in the room. I kept glancing out the window to check for any signs of melting snow or icicles. Brett caught my eye and reached over to squeeze my hand. The gesture helped me to relax, at least a little bit.

A minute or two after Rita left for the kitchen, Harvey appeared. He held his hat in his hands, and his winter coat was unbuttoned. He looked a bit ill at ease, standing there at the entrance to the dining room. His gaze bounced around the tables before landing on me and Brett.

He headed our way. "Have you seen Rita this morning?" he asked in a low voice.

"She's in the kitchen," I said.

He nodded his thanks and crossed the room to the kitchen door. Ambrose and Lily's murmured conversation died off. For a minute, the only sounds in the room were the rustling of newspaper pages as Wilson turned them and the occasional clacking of cutlery against plates as Brett and I ate.

"You know," Lily said, breaking the near-silence, "Harvey and Kevin weren't on good terms." Although she seemed to be talking to Ambrose, she spoke loudly enough for the rest of us to hear.

Wilson lowered his newspaper so he could see Lily. "What makes you think that?"

"They argued the other day. I heard them with my own ears." Excitement glittered in her eyes. "Harvey was hopping mad. He even threatened Kevin!"

"That's a lie!"

I nearly jumped out of my chair when Harvey's voice boomed across the room. He stood near the kitchen door, his hat crumpled in his large fist as he glared at Lily.

She shrank back in her seat. "I heard you." Her voice had lost some of its confidence.

Harvey glowered at her. "And what did I say?"

Lily glanced around at the rest of us, but we all waited for her to speak.

She sat up straighter and met Harvey's eyes. "Kevin said he intended to go ahead with something. I'm not sure what. Then you said if he went through with it, you wouldn't put up with it."

Harvey's glare hadn't lost any of its intensity. "That wasn't a threat. It was a statement of fact."

Rita appeared behind him. "What's going on?"

"This lady's making accusations," Harvey said, pointing at Lily. "Unfounded and untrue ones."

Lily frowned. "You *did* argue with Kevin."

"He wanted to expand the lodge to at least four times its current capacity," Harvey said, his voice almost trembling with barely controlled emotion. "I was telling him that if he went through with that, I'd leave. I like peace and quiet. Crowds aren't for me. Kevin was my friend, and he wanted me to stay, but I had to let him know that I couldn't if things changed that much. That's it. I never would have hurt him."

Tears shone in Rita's eyes. "Of course you wouldn't, Harvey."

Ambrose surprised me by speaking up. "We're all on edge after what happened to Kevin. It's easy to let our suspicions run wild, but that won't help matters. And none of this is fair to Rita."

Lily stared at her hands, folded in her lap.

The storminess faded from Harvey's eyes. He put a hand on Rita's arm. "He's right. I'm sorry, Rita."

"No, I'm the one who should apologize," Lily said, raising her gaze, her expression contrite. "It was insensitive of me to bring up the subject. I'm sorry."

Rita patted the hand Harvey had rested on her arm. "It's all right, both of you. It's a trying time for all of us." She attempted a smile. "I'll go check on the food."

She returned to the kitchen and a few seconds of awkward silence ticked by before Harvey crammed his hat on his head and strode out of the room.

I realized I hadn't touched my food for several minutes. I exchanged a glance with Brett, and then got back to eating. I'd only taken one bite when Wilson spoke up.

"Since we're pointing fingers"—he stared hard at Lily—"you were up and about the night Kevin was killed."

Lily sputtered, her eyes wide, but she didn't get any coherent words out before Wilson continued.

"I heard the floorboards creak out in the hall. When I took a look, there you were, fully dressed, heading for the stairs. At ten past two in the morning."

"I couldn't sleep!" Lily said. "Getting up and moving around for a while helps me when I'm having trouble sleeping."

"And where did you go while you were 'moving around'?" Wilson asked.

My stomach twisted when I saw that he was almost grinning. He was taking pleasure in making Lily squirm.

Brett cut in before Lily could respond to the question. "Like Ambrose said, this sort of talk isn't helping matters."

This time Wilson really did grin. He picked up his newspaper and gave the pages a shake to straighten them out. "Just thought it was worth mentioning."

He went back to reading, or at least pretended that he did. He'd clearly enjoyed stirring the pot and I sensed that he was waiting to see what would now rise to the surface.

"I came downstairs and read a book for a while," Lily said, still on the defensive. "Then I went right back to bed. I didn't kill Kevin. Why would I?"

Ambrose reached across the table and took her hand. "It's all right, Lily. I know you didn't kill him."

Lily relaxed. "Thank you, Ambrose."

Wilson turned the page of his newspaper. "Of course," he said casually, his eyes still on the paper, "they do say it's the quiet ones you have to watch out for." He sent a brief glance and a smirk at Ambrose before returning his attention to the newspaper once again.

Lily's back stiffened. "What a ridiculous insinuation! Ambrose wouldn't hurt a fly!"

"Ignore him," Ambrose advised her. "He's just trying to rile us up."

The kitchen door opened and Rita appeared, carrying two plates. Everyone fell quiet. I was glad the bickering hadn't continued in Rita's presence.

Still smirking, Wilson got up and dropped the newspaper on the table before walking away. I suspected he enjoyed stirring up trouble for his own amusement, and I couldn't help but dislike him for it.

Rita set the plates before Ambrose and Lily. They both thanked her, and Lily smiled at her, even though her eyes still danced with indignation.

I took one last bite of my food and pushed the plate aside, my appetite gone.

"All done?" Brett asked. He'd polished off his french toast and bacon.

I nodded, and we left the dining room without another word.

As soon as we were out in the lobby, I let out a whoosh of air.

"I could hardly breathe in there with all that tension," I whispered.

"It was a bit much." Brett pulled his phone out of his pocket. "Hopefully we can be on our way soon."

He consulted the weather app on his phone and I leaned in close to get a look for myself. Never before had I been so desperate for warm temperatures.

"I think we should be fine now," he said. "The temperature is above freezing."

"Thank goodness," I said, taking his hand and heading for the stairs. We took them two at a time. "Let's go get our things."

Since we'd mostly packed the day before, we only had to add a few items to the suitcase. Within ten minutes, we were back down in the lobby, itching to get on our way. I wondered if we'd have to go in search of Rita, since there was no one at the reception desk, but I really didn't want to bother her. Fortunately, Zahra appeared and handled the checkout process.

Once that was settled, we loaded the suitcase into the truck and got on the road. The sun shone brightly and the ice had melted, leaving the roads damp but no longer treacherous. Out on the highway, we picked up speed, and I relaxed against my seat, relieved to leave Holly Lodge behind us.

I looked forward to spending the coming night in our own bed, without any worries about being under the same roof as Kevin's killer. I closed my eyes, relaxing even further.

Something pinged against the side of the truck. My eyes shot open. I sat up straight as several other pings followed. Brett slowed the truck, but not before something small struck the windshield.

Brett swore. "Someone must have had a load of gravel that wasn't secured properly."

I looked out the side window. Sure enough, gravel was scattered over the road. We passed safely over the rest of it, thanks to Brett slowing the truck, and he picked up speed again once the road was clear.

The damage was already done, though. There was a chip in the windshield, almost the size of a penny.

"That'll have to get fixed," Brett said.

I sank back against the seat again. "I hope we can get home without any more problems. We've already had enough."

"You can say that again." Brett glanced my way. "Maybe next time we should just take a staycation."

I let out a long sigh, feeling more homesick than ever. "That sounds like a good idea to me."

Chapter Eight

Brett and I spent the next day at home, hanging out with my mom and Grant, and showering Bentley and Flapjack with attention. The following morning, my mom and Grant set off for Seattle. I was sorry to see them go, but they'd be back for a visit in the new year. That wasn't far away now. December had arrived, and Wildwood Cove's Festival of Trees would begin in a few days. Preparing for the festival and for Christmas would keep me plenty busy for the next while. I figured time would probably fly by.

"I think I'll head over to the seniors' center and get to work on our tree," I said to Brett as we cleaned up the breakfast dishes after my mom and Grant had left.

"I'll come too," he said. "I can lend a hand with the tree, and whatever else needs to be done."

As soon as we'd finished tidying up, I grabbed the box of ornaments I'd purchased specially for the festival tree while Brett loaded some tools into his truck.

"What about the windshield?" I asked as I buckled up my seatbelt a few minutes later. We hadn't had the ding in the glass fixed yet.

Brett backed the truck out of its parking spot next to my car. "I called the garage yesterday. Zach is fully booked for the next couple of days and Lonny is off sick. I've got an appointment for Thursday. Lonny's hoping to be back by then."

"That's too bad that he's sick," I said. "We should have him and Hope over for dinner one night when he's better."

In addition to being a mechanic, Lonny Barron owned the Wildwood Inn with his wife, Hope. I'd first met the couple back in the spring, and since then Brett and I had hung out with them a couple of times.

"They're having that holiday open house just before Christmas," Brett reminded me.

"Oh, right." I had been looking forward to the open house at the inn, but recent events had pushed it to the back of my mind. "They might be too busy for anything else over the next few weeks then. There's always the new year, though."

"We'll work something out."

The drive to the seniors' center took only a few minutes. Brett found a parking spot just down the street from our destination, and we both climbed out. I shivered as I grabbed my box of ornaments. The temperature was hovering around the freezing mark. There was no snow down here on the coast, but the grass was white with frost, and the breeze carried a sharp chill with it.

I hurried into the seniors' center, with Brett right behind me carrying his toolbox. As we stepped into the building's anteroom, I smiled. The small space had already been decorated for the holidays. A Christmas tree stood in one corner, with letters hanging from garlands spelling out "Welcome to the Festival of Trees." It was also decked out with silver and blue baubles. In another corner was a beautiful wicker reindeer. Paper snowflakes hung from the ceiling, and fairy lights had been strung around the double doors leading into the next room.

Those doors stood open and Patricia Murray appeared in the doorway. She smiled when she saw me and Brett.

"Hey, you two. Good to see you! Ready to get to work on your tree?"

"Definitely," I said.

"And anything else you need a hand with," Brett added, holding up his toolbox.

"Fantastic. Brett, I'll take you up on that. We've still got several decorations to hang, and we've got a big wooden sleigh to put together."

"Just point me in the right direction," Brett said.

"Head for the back of the room. You'll see John there with the sleigh," Patricia said, referring to her husband. "Or at least what *will* be the sleigh."

She grabbed a placard from several leaning against the wall of the anteroom. The sign had "The Flip Side Pancake House" written across it in black letters. She handed it to me. "Here you go, Marley. You can claim a tree from the ones that don't already have a sign."

"Patricia!" a woman's voice called from somewhere in the next room.

"I'll check in with you guys in a bit," Patricia said before dashing out of sight.

"Thank you!" I called after her.

Brett took my box of ornaments, leaving me with just the sign to hold. "Let's find you a tree."

When we stepped into the next room, I stopped to take in the sight before me. Clearly, there was much left to be done, as several trees remained undecorated and boxes of garlands, baubles, and other decorations sat here and there on the floor. Despite that, simply walking into the room infused me with holiday spirit. There had to be at least a dozen trees within my line of sight and they filled the room with their delicious scent.

I breathed in deeply. "It smells like Christmas."

"It does," Brett agreed.

The room typically served as a small gym and meeting space, but now it was on its way to becoming a magical indoor forest. From the way the trees were set up, it looked as though there would be two curving pathways, one on either side of the long room, and a straight one down the middle. Each one was lined with trees. The straight path led to an open door at the far end of the room. I couldn't see much beyond the door from where we stood, but I thought I saw at least one other tree set up behind a man and woman who were consulting a clipboard.

"Which way?" Brett asked.

"Maybe left." I set off along that path.

The first several trees we passed already had placards propped up next to them, displaying the name of the business sponsoring the tree. Several of them were already adorned with at least some decorations. A few looked complete, ready for the festival's opening. Seeing those trees made me even more eager to get to work on mine. I hoped that focusing on something fun and holiday-related would help to chase away the somber cloud that had followed me and Brett home from Holly Lodge.

I continued along the path until I reached its last bend, where it curved to meet up with the straight path at the end of the room. A Douglas fir caught my eye. It stood at least six feet tall and had beautiful, full branches. I was glad to see that it hadn't yet been claimed.

"This one," I said, stopping before it.

"Good choice." Brett set my box of decorations down next to the tree. "Do you want me to help you get started?"

"That's okay, thanks. You go ahead and help John with the sleigh."

Brett kissed me. "Just holler if you need me."

As he disappeared from sight, I stood back to get a good look at my tree. It really was beautiful. I decided to start by wrapping a garland around it. I'd brought a blue and silver one that I thought would look great. Normally I liked to put lights on Christmas trees, but Patricia had told me days ago that there would be twinkle lights decorating the room, but not the individual trees. The organizing committee wanted to avoid the nightmare of dozens of electrical cords snaking across the floor. Judging by the trees that had already been decorated, they'd all look amazing even without lights.

I pulled the garland out of the box and held it piled in my arms. Maybe I should have taken Brett up on his offer of help. The tree stood several inches taller than I did, so reaching the top branches would be a bit of a stretch. I decided to try my best on my own and see how it went. If I needed help, I'd go fetch Brett for a few minutes.

I tried tossing one end of the garland up into the top branches, but it fell short. I tugged it down to try again.

In the background, I could hear voices and the occasional round of hammering. Two of the voices drew closer.

"I'm so sorry," a woman said.

I glanced toward the back of the room as a blond woman came into sight between the trees, heading down the middle pathway with Patricia.

"Don't be," Patricia said. "I completely understand."

Two little girls, one blond and the other with dark hair, dashed past Patricia and the other woman, giggling as they ran by. I saw them in flashes between the trees.

"Emily!" the blond woman yelled. "No running inside!"

Both girls slowed to a walk, still giggling as they disappeared behind some trees.

"We have plenty of volunteers," Patricia said, "so we'll be fine."

They were farther away from me now, so the woman's response was just a murmur to my ears.

I tossed the garland up toward the top of my tree again, and this time had more success. Standing on tiptoes, I tried to wrap the garland around the tree, but I couldn't get it to sit where I wanted. I struggled with it for another minute or so without much luck.

I was still wrestling with the garland when Patricia reappeared, this time on the same path as me.

"Hold on, Marley. I'll grab you a stool." She dashed out of sight and then came back a few seconds later, carrying a step stool. "This should help."

"Thank you. It'll help a lot." I made sure the stool was steady before climbing onto it. "Is there a problem with one of the volunteers?" I couldn't help my curiosity.

"Not really a problem," Patricia said. "Johanna Jessen had planned to help out with decorating the room, but she was offered extra hours at her job. She's a single mother. She went through a nasty divorce and moved out here from Idaho last year. I know it's a struggle for her to make ends meet, so she couldn't turn down the extra work."

"Do you really have enough volunteers without her?" I asked as I tucked the garland in among the upper branches. "Because if you need me for anything, just let me know."

"I appreciate that. I think we'll be okay, especially now that Brett's helping John with the sleigh."

I hopped down from the stool and shifted it around the tree before climbing on it again.

"Here, let me help you with that." Patricia grabbed the end of the garland as I tossed it around the tree.

"Thanks." I jumped down from the stool again. The garland was now well within reach when I stood on the floor, so I nudged the stool aside.

"It's too bad you and Brett didn't get the vacation you were hoping for," Patricia said as we worked.

"You heard about what happened?" I wasn't all that surprised. Patricia always seemed to know what was going on around the peninsula.

"I talked to one of the friends Rita and I have in common." She shook her head sadly. "Such terrible news."

"It really was terrible," I agreed. "And our vacation definitely didn't go as planned." I tucked the garland in among the branches. "But it seems like a minor inconvenience compared to what happened to Kevin."

"I know." She took the garland from me and settled it in place on her side of the tree before passing the end to me. "I still can't believe he was murdered!"

"How well did you know him?" I asked.

"Not all that well, but he used to live here in Wildwood Cove."

"Really?" That was news to me.

"I know Rita better, even though she didn't live here in town as long as Kevin did. About a year or so after they married, they bought Holly Lodge and they've lived up there ever since. John, Sienna, and I have only gone up there twice, but while Rita was here in Wildwood Cove, she was in a book club I belonged to at the time."

I tucked the end of the garland into place and stood back to admire our work. "I feel terrible for Rita, but she seemed to be holding up okay. Her daughter is with her."

"That's good to know," Patricia said with relief. "I've been worried about her."

I couldn't stop myself from asking my next question. "Do you have any idea who might have wanted to kill Kevin?"

"None at all. He always seemed like a nice man. I can't believe someone murdered him and buried him in a snowbank. It's awful."

"How did you hear about the snowbank?" I asked, surprised that she knew about that detail.

"A woman who was staying at Holly Lodge booked into the B&B yesterday," Patricia explained. "She told me more than my friend was able to tell me." She grimaced. "Maybe a bit more than I really wanted to know."

It wasn't hard to guess the identity of that woman. "Lily Spitz is staying in Wildwood Cove?"

"For a few days, anyway. She's a romance and mystery writer, which you probably already know." When I nodded, she continued. "Apparently she wants to set a book here on the Olympic Peninsula so she's checking out various locations, getting to know the area."

"A romance or a mystery?" I asked.

"A mystery, I believe, though I'm not a hundred percent sure."

"I'll have to get a copy of the book when it comes out," I said. "It would be cool to read one set around here."

"And we know how you can't resist a mystery," Patricia said with a smile.

I laughed. "I think all of Wildwood Cove knows that by now."

I knelt down next to my box, carefully lifting out a few of the decorations.

"I'd better go check out what's happening in the next room," Patricia said. "We're putting together Santa's workshop back there."

"That sounds fun."

"Hopefully it will be. Just let me know if you need any more help."

I called out my thanks as she hurried off.

I spent the next while hanging my decorations on the branches of my tree. I'd found a seller on Etsy who made cute food-themed ornaments by hand. I'd bought several, including a miniature stack of pancakes with butter melting on the top, a waffle sprinkled with sparkly fake cinnamon and sugar, and others in the shape of toast, one topped with jam and the other with slices of avocado. I'd also purchased a miniature frying pan with bacon and eggs in it, and several tiny teacups in different colors.

It didn't take long to get all the ornaments on the tree. When I stood back to see how everything looked, I immediately noticed a problem. The tree was still quite bare. I didn't have nearly enough ornaments to decorate it fully. I briefly considered choosing a smaller tree, but I didn't want to undo the work I'd already put into this one, and the other available trees weren't much different in size. I'd have to come up with another solution, but I couldn't do much else with the tree at the moment.

After tucking my empty box out of the way, I wandered off in search of Brett. I found him not far from the entrance to the back room. He and Patricia's husband, John, were using cordless drills to put the life-sized wooden sleigh together. From the looks of it, they were almost done with the job.

Brett fastened a screw into place and then glanced up and noticed me. He set down his drill. "How's the tree?"

"Good, except for the fact that I need way more decorations."

Brett held out an arm and I stepped closer to him so he could wrap it around me. "I'm sure we can come up with more."

Hopefully he was right. I didn't know of any stores in Wildwood Cove that sold food-themed Christmas tree ornaments, but I could take another look online and place a rush order.

Patricia appeared between two trees, looking around. A tall woman with spiky dark hair hurried toward us from another direction.

"No luck?" the dark-haired woman asked Patricia.

"Not yet."

"What's wrong?" I asked, noting the confusion on Patricia's face.

"We're looking for some ornaments," she replied.

"Stars and acorns," the other woman said. "Sparkly silver ones."

"Where did you last see them, Annette?" John asked her.

"On my tree."

"Someone took the decorations off your tree?" I didn't know why anyone would have done such a thing.

"Not all of them," Annette said, "but a few."

"And we haven't been able to find them anywhere," Patricia added.

"I can't believe it." Annette rested her hands on her hips. "Who the heck steals Christmas decorations?"

Chapter Nine

John, Brett, and I helped Patricia and Annette search for the missing ornaments, without success. Eventually, we had to give up and accept that the decorations were truly gone. It was hard to imagine how that could have happened without someone stealing them.

"I'll check with everyone else who's already put up decorations, to make sure nothing else has gone missing," Patricia said once we'd finished searching.

Annette thanked us all for our help and then shifted some of the decorations still on her tree, trying to make the gaps less obvious.

"Somebody's lacking holiday spirit," I said to Patricia as Brett and John returned to working on the sleigh.

"Let's hope it's an isolated occurrence." She had a worry line across her forehead.

I couldn't blame her for being concerned. She and the other volunteers had put a lot of work into the event and wanted it to become an annual town tradition. If the festival didn't run smoothly, its first year could end up being its last.

We decided to focus on something more positive. We couldn't do anything about the missing ornaments, but we could put up other decorations. Since I couldn't work on my tree anymore at the moment, I helped Patricia with stringing lights around the room.

Brett and John finished with the sleigh a short time later and came over to help us out. When all the lights were up, we decided to call it a day. I fetched the empty box I'd stashed next to my tree and the four of us left the seniors' center together. A couple of volunteers stayed behind to keep working, and others would join them later in the day. I had no doubt that the place would look incredible by the time the festival started. Hopefully my tree would too.

As we stepped out into the cool afternoon, my stomach grumbled, reminding me that I hadn't eaten lunch. I was about to suggest to Brett that we stop by the bakery for sandwiches, when I spotted a familiar figure walking along the opposite side of the street.

I put a hand on Brett's arm. "Isn't that Ambrose?"

"You've met him?" Patricia asked as she zipped up her jacket.

"He was staying at Holly Lodge on the weekend," Brett replied. "He's not from Wildwood Cove, is he?"

Brett had grown up in town and knew most of the long-time residents, at least by sight.

"Not originally," John said.

"He moved here a couple months ago," Patricia added. "He's a poet, and I've heard him speak at the library. He draws a lot of his inspiration from nature. Maybe that's why he was up in the mountains, to get closer to the wilderness."

And maybe the fact that he lived in Wildwood Cove was another reason why Lily had come to town.

Ambrose was out of sight now, and he slipped from my mind too. Brett and I exchanged a few more words with Patricia and John, and then we climbed into Brett's truck.

Once we had arrived home and greeted our animals, we sat down to eat sandwiches we'd picked up at the bakery after leaving the seniors' center. I was about to take a bite out of my veggie sandwich when I stopped, my gaze settling on a mason jar full of seashells that sat on the kitchen windowsill. I had a habit of picking up pretty shells when out walking on the beach, and I'd managed to build up quite a collection. I had two other jars filled to the brim, those sitting on a windowsill in the family room.

I set down my sandwich. "I wasn't sure what to do about The Flip Side's festival tree, because I don't think it'll be all that easy to find enough breakfast-themed ornaments to make it look fully decorated, at least not in the next couple of days."

"But now you've got an idea?" Brett guessed before taking a bite of his turkey sandwich.

"The Flip Side is a seaside pancake house, so maybe I could use decorations with an ocean theme. I could probably even make them myself." I was already picturing how I could use the shells.

Brett took a drink of water. "Maybe some of them. You don't have much time before the festival starts, remember."

"Good point," I conceded. I probably wouldn't be able to make more than a handful of ornaments in the amount of time I had, and it would take more than a handful to fully decorate the tree. "I'll see what I can find online."

After eating, I did just that. Fortunately, I found some online shops with what I needed. My purchases included colorful glass sea creatures and seagulls. I placed a couple of rush orders that would hopefully arrive within forty-eight hours. I hadn't entirely nixed the idea of making some decorations myself, so I also spent some time sorting through my seashells and washing the ones I thought would make good tree ornaments. I still had plenty of work to do to make my new vision come together, but I was determined to make The Flip Side's festival tree look spectacular.

* * * *

It would have been so easy to stay in bed the next morning. When I woke up, the world was still pitch black outside the windows and a chill had settled over the bedroom. Brett was sound asleep and the temptation to stay curled up next to him was almost too great to resist. If not for Flapjack standing on my shoulder and staring into my eyes with his amber ones, I might have gone right back to sleep.

After I showered and dressed, I headed downstairs, Flapjack and Bentley leading the way. I let Bentley out into the yard for a few minutes and dished out some food for Flapjack while he purred and rubbed against my ankles. I was about to make myself a smoothie when my phone chimed across the room. I grabbed it from the table and read the text message I'd just received.

Don't eat breakfast.

That's all it said, and no further text messages followed. That didn't surprise me. The Flip Side's chef, Ivan, had sent the text, and he was a man of few words.

I knew I wasn't likely to regret following his instructions, so I skipped my smoothie and bundled up in preparation for heading out into the frosty morning. Brett was still sleeping and I decided not to wake him. He had another day off work and there was no reason for him to be up before dawn, even if he hoped to work on our home renovations, which he probably would. He didn't like leaving projects unfinished, and the new master bathroom was a long way from being done. Brett had gutted the old storage closet and had put in the door to our bedroom, but that was as much as he'd had a chance to do before we'd set off for our brief getaway.

After giving Flapjack a cuddle and kissing Bentley on the top of his curly head, I left the house. Much of the year I walked to and from work, but in the cold and darkness of the winter mornings, I relied much more on my car.

The drive to the pancake house took only a few minutes. The Flip Side had a prime location in Wildwood Cove—right on the beach and not far from Main Street. In the summer months, I put a few tables out front of the restaurant so diners could enjoy the fresh sea air with a perfect view of the ocean. At this time of year, however, the view had to be enjoyed through the large front windows, with a toasty fire burning in the stone fireplace.

I parked in the small lot behind the restaurant, happy to see the warm light that glowed in the kitchen window. I hurried inside and stopped in my office long enough to shed my coat and drop off my tote bag. From there, I went straight to the blissfully warm kitchen.

Ivan and his assistant, Tommy Park, were both there. Ivan was filling muffin tins with what looked like batter for gingerbread muffins, and Tommy was drizzling maple glaze over a batch of pumpkin scones. Pie plates full of baked apple pie and pumpkin pie filling sat cooling on one of the countertops, ready to be used to fill crêpes. The kitchen smelled heavenly. My mouth watered and my stomach gave a loud rumble.

Tommy dropped what he was doing as soon as he saw me. "Happy birthday, Marley!"

I accepted his bearhug with a big smile on my face. "Thank you, Tommy."

Ivan set down the large bowl of muffin batter. "Happy birthday." He scowled at me. "Did you eat breakfast?"

"Not a single bite."

"Good." He pointed at a stool. "Sit down."

My smile remained as bright as ever. I was used to Ivan's gruff personality and I had nothing but respect and affection for him.

I pulled the stool up to the counter and took a seat.

Ivan poured some batter into a crêpe pan. "Apple or pumpkin?"

I eyed the pie plates across the room. "Hmmm."

It wasn't an easy choice to make. Ivan's apple pie crêpes and pumpkin pie crêpes were both among my absolute favorite seasonal items from The Flip Side's menu.

"One of each," Ivan declared.

I smiled again. "There can't be such a thing as a better breakfast than that."

"Are you having a party?" Tommy asked as he finished glazing the pumpkin scones.

"No," I replied. "Originally, we weren't supposed to get back home until yesterday afternoon, so we haven't planned anything. But that's okay. I'm happy to spend a quiet evening with Brett."

Tommy started glazing a second batch of scones. "I heard your vacation got interrupted."

"Another murder." Ivan practically growled the words, his dark eyes staring me down from across the worktop.

"Not my fault," I said in my defense. "I wish I hadn't been anywhere near the lodge when it happened."

Ivan still glared at me. "You found the body." It sounded like an accusation.

"You know about that?"

Ivan glanced at Tommy.

"Everyone knows about the murder," Tommy said, "but I got that tidbit from Rob."

I should have guessed. Tommy sometimes took photos for the local paper, the *Wildwood Cove Weekly*, and he'd become friends with reporter Rob Mazzoli.

"He wants to interview you, by the way," Tommy added.

I probably shouldn't have been surprised about that either. I'd been mixed up in several murder investigations in the past. Although my name had appeared in the paper on occasion, I hadn't been asked for more than a quote or two. Rob was fairly new to town, and had already proven that he was intent on getting eyewitness accounts to add to his stories.

"I'm not sure I want to go over it in detail," I said. "It wasn't a pleasant experience, and I don't want to be disrespectful to the victim's family."

"Rob's a good guy," Tommy assured me. "If you don't want to answer some of his questions, he won't hold it against you."

"I'll think about it." I didn't want to commit to anything right then.

Ivan had two crêpes prepared now. He scooped apple pie filling onto one and pumpkin pie filling onto the other. Then he rolled them up and topped them with a very generous dollop of whipped cream.

He slid the plate toward me. "Eat up."

"Ivan, you're the best." I took the knife and fork he offered me and dug in.

I didn't speak for the next couple of minutes. I was far too busy enjoying the scrumptious flavors of apple, pumpkin, and cream. Only once I'd eaten half of each crêpe did I pause long enough to ask Tommy a question.

"What else does Rob know about the murder?"

Ivan stopped in the midst of chopping up asparagus. "Why are you asking?"

"I'm just curious." When Ivan didn't stop glaring at me, I added, "And I want to know if the killer's been caught. Finding Kevin's body was unsettling, to say the least. So was staying at the lodge after the murder. It's hard to get it off my mind."

Ivan pointed his knife at me. "You need to stay out of this murder investigation."

I held up my hands in surrender. "It happened in another county. I doubt I'll have the chance to get mixed up in it." I didn't bother to mention that two of the other guests from Holly Lodge were now in Wildwood Cove, giving me an opportunity to talk to them about the crime if I decided that was something I wanted to do.

Ivan grunted and got back to chopping. I wasn't sure if I'd appeased him or not.

Tommy had listened to us with a grin on his face. Now that Ivan had said his piece, Tommy spoke up.

"I talked to Rob yesterday afternoon. At that point, no one had been arrested. The cops haven't even said if they've got any suspects, although I'm sure they're taking a good look at the wife, since she inherits everything. As for the details, I know the murder weapon was a ski, the victim died of blunt force trauma to his head, and the killer tried hiding the body in a snowbank."

A shudder ran through my body as I recalled the moment when Brett and I had uncovered Kevin's lifeless face. I set down my knife and fork.

"Talking about murder isn't good for your appetite," Ivan grumbled.

I tried to push the unpleasant memories out of my mind. "Don't worry, Ivan," I said, picking up my cutlery again. "Nothing can stop me from finishing these crêpes."

I fell quiet again, not saying a word until I'd cleaned my plate. Even after that, we only talked about the pancake house. Slipping into that normalcy made me feel better. After a while, I made myself a cup of tea and then left Ivan and Tommy to their work in the kitchen.

Out in the dining room, I knelt in front of the large stone fireplace and struck a match, holding it to the pile of kindling I'd set out. As the tiny flames grew larger, I added more wood until I had a good blaze going. The room immediately had a cheerier, cozier atmosphere. It was still dark outside, and I'd had to scrape frost off my windshield before leaving home that morning. I knew The Flip Side's earliest customers would appreciate the warmth and comfort of the crackling fire.

The place would be even cheerier once I had a chance to deck it out for the upcoming holidays. At the moment, the mantel over the fireplace displayed a few Thanksgiving decorations, including a small cornucopia and a wicker turkey basket that held some fake leaves and acorns. I needed to take those down and replace them with Christmas and winter decorations. I didn't have a tree for the pancake house yet, but I planned to get one soon. Hopefully Brett and I would have a chance to visit a nearby Christmas tree farm in the coming days. We needed a tree for our house as well.

I collected all the Thanksgiving decorations and put them away in a storage cupboard near the office. Then I checked over everything to make sure the restaurant was ready for customers. Leigh Hunter, The Flip Side's full-time waitress, arrived and greeted me with a hug, the fresh scent of frosty air still clinging to her.

"Happy birthday, Marley!" she said as she released me. "Is your day off to a good start?"

"Definitely," I assured her, remembering my delicious breakfast.

Her bright smile faded. "On another note, I heard you found another body."

I wasn't surprised that she'd heard the news.

"You can't seem to get away from them," she said as she unzipped her puffy winter jacket.

"I know." I sighed. "I really wish I could. I'd love to never find one again."

"At least your honeymoon wasn't interrupted by a murder."

"That was definitely a blessing," I agreed. I had nothing but good memories from the few days Brett and I had spent in Victoria, British Columbia after our summer wedding.

As Leigh disappeared into the break room to put away her purse and coat, I smiled at the empty dining area. Even though The Flip Side had been closed for just a week, I'd missed my staff, who were like family to me, and our regular customers.

When the first diners arrived shortly after seven o'clock, I still had a smile on my face. It didn't take long for the place to fill up. I happily helped Leigh with taking orders and serving meals. Chatting with customers was one of the many things I loved about working at the pancake house.

Ed and Gary, two of The Flip Side's most faithful customers, arrived in the middle of the breakfast rush. Their favorite table was already occupied, but they didn't mind sitting elsewhere. They always ordered the same breakfast—blueberry pancakes with bacon and sausages—so I relayed their orders to the kitchen before heading over to their table.

"We hear you had an eventful vacation," Ed said as I filled their mugs with coffee.

Gary added cream to his cup. "And not in a good way."

"I guess eventful is one word for it," I said.

Ed shook his head. "It must have been awful for you and Brett."

"It was," I agreed, "but far worse for the victim's family."

"Bah!" A gray-haired man at the next table swatted the air with his hand, as if batting away my words. "They're better off without that blockhead."

I stared at him, shocked.

"Come on now, Dwight," Gary admonished. "That's no way to talk."

Dwight pointed his fork at Gary. "You didn't have to live next door to the man. It was a glorious day when he moved up that mountain."

"You might not have liked Kevin," Ed said, "but he didn't deserve to get killed."

"That's what you think." Dwight dropped his fork onto his empty plate and pushed back his chair. "But I know differently. Kevin Manning finally got what he deserved."

Chapter Ten

I stared in shocked silence as Dwight dropped some bills on the table and stomped out of the pancake house. Several customers watched him go, having heard his last words. A few whispered to each other once he was gone.

"What the...?" I was still at a loss for words.

"Don't mind him, Marley," Gary advised. "Nobody in Wildwood Cove holds a grudge quite like Dwight Zalecki."

"But why does he have a grudge against Kevin?" I asked, still stunned.

Even though I'd overheard Kevin arguing with Rita and Wilson at the lodge, he hadn't seemed like a bad guy. I didn't really know Kevin, of course, but Dwight's attitude shocked me nonetheless. I'd seen him at The Flip Side before, always eating alone, but he'd never said much of anything during his previous visits.

"They were neighbors for years," Ed explained. "And Dwight's the kind of guy who can find fault with anything and everything. He complained about how many cars Kevin had in his driveway, noise, the state of Kevin's front lawn, you name it."

Gary picked up his mug. "But things really came to a head when a windstorm knocked a tree from Kevin's property onto Dwight's garage." He paused for a sip of coffee. "They exchanged a few choice words. Dwight never got over that."

Ed fought a grin. "I believe Kevin called him an irascible old geezer."

Gary let out a short chuckle. "I'd forgotten about that. And Dwight gave as good as he got. I won't repeat what he called Kevin." The smile faded from Gary's face. "Things really went downhill after that."

I glanced around the pancake house. I needed to get back to helping Leigh, but my curiosity kept me in place. "How so?"

Leigh stopped on her way past us, her arms full of dirty dishes. "Kevin dated Dwight's niece." She'd clearly been keeping tabs on our conversation. "The poor woman ended up moving to Seattle with a broken heart."

Ed and Gary nodded as Leigh whisked off to the kitchen.

"Some say Kevin only dated Calista to annoy Dwight," Ed said.

"And there might be some truth to that." Gary took another sip of coffee. "But true or not, he ended up dumping her a few months later when Rita moved to town. Kevin couldn't take his eyes off Rita from the moment he first saw her."

As much as I wanted to stay and hear more, I really had to get back to work. A group of four customers was waiting to order and two tables needed to be cleaned. I should have been offering coffee refills as well.

I reluctantly left Gary and Ed's table and attended to the other customers. As the breakfast rush wound down, I retreated to the office to catch up on some administrative tasks. Gary and Ed had left by then, so I didn't have another chance to talk to them. Maybe there wasn't anything else they could have told me about Dwight's grudge against Kevin anyway.

In the office, I sank down into the chair behind the desk, but jumped back up almost immediately. Brett stood in the doorway, holding a bright bouquet of flowers.

"Happy birthday," he said, taking my hand as we met in the middle of the office. He pulled me close for a lingering kiss. "Sorry I missed you earlier. You should have woken me."

"I wanted to let you sleep." I took the flowers from him. "These are beautiful. Thank you."

I gently set the bouquet on the desk so I could put my arms around Brett. "I'm glad you stopped by."

"Looks like I timed it well. I was hoping you wouldn't be too busy."

"Perfect timing," I said. "Are you hungry?"

"I just ate, but that probably wasn't good thinking on my part."

I patted his flat stomach. "You should always leave room for Ivan's cooking."

"Next time I'll remember to do that."

I kissed him, and he ran a hand down my hair.

"Are you coming home after work?" he asked as he tucked a curl behind my ear.

"I want to put up some Christmas decorations, but after that I'll come home. I can't do anything more to my tree at the festival yet, so that will have to wait another day or two." I eyed him suspiciously. "Why?"

"Just wondering."

I didn't miss the twinkle in his blue eyes. "Do you have something planned?"

"Maybe." His grin told me his maybe was a definite yes.

"You're not going to share?"

"Nope."

"Not even a clue?" I pressed.

He laughed. "One clue would never satisfy you."

I narrowed my eyes. "You're going to make me wait all day to find out? Torturing me on my birthday shouldn't be allowed."

He grinned and tugged me closer. "I promise I'll make it up to you."

I could feel myself getting lost in his eyes. "I'll hold you to that promise."

"Please do."

After another kiss, Brett headed home to work on the master bathroom. I would have liked him to stay longer, but I wouldn't have got any work done if he had. He was very good at distracting me.

I fetched a vase from the storage room and filled it with water for the bouquet. At first, I left the flowers in the office, but later I moved them out next to the cash register so everyone could enjoy their beauty and bright colors.

Once the last customers of the day had left, I hauled a box of Christmas decorations into the dining room. Then I stoked the fire, enjoying the cozy atmosphere it created. Outside, the day had grown dark and rain pelted down from gloomy clouds, the occasional bit of hail or slush mixed in. The front windows of the pancake house gave me a great view of the choppy ocean. Whitecaps topped the waves and, from what I could see, the beach was deserted. It was a good day to stay indoors.

With rain pelting against the windows and the fire popping and crackling, I opened the box and set some decorations out on a nearby table. I'd barely started emptying the box when someone tapped on the front door. I hurried over to open it when I saw Patricia's seventeen-year-old daughter, Sienna, huddled inside her jacket.

She darted inside as soon as I had the door open. "Happy birthday, Marley!" She quickly shed her wet jacket and gave me a hug.

"Thank you." I returned the hug. "What made you brave this weather to come over here?"

Sienna worked at The Flip Side part-time, but during the school year she was scheduled to work only on weekends.

She scooted closer to the fire and held out her hands to warm them. "I wanted to wish you a happy birthday in person. Plus, I heard about the murder."

I should have known. Sienna's love for mysteries matched my own.

"Do you have any suspects yet?" she asked.

"Not really."

She didn't hide her skepticism. "Seriously?"

I removed bubble wrap from a lantern filled with red and gold baubles.

"Ooh! I love those lanterns!" Sienna hurried over. "Can I help you decorate?"

"I won't say no to that offer."

She unwrapped another lantern. "But, come on, you must have suspects."

"Maybe I've thought about it a little bit," I admitted.

"I knew it!"

She glanced toward the kitchen, where Ivan and Tommy were still working. Ivan didn't like either of us getting mixed up in potentially dangerous mysteries.

Sienna leaned closer and lowered her voice. "We've got a guest at the B&B who was at Holly Lodge when the murder happened."

I set the lantern I'd unwrapped on one end of the mantel. "Lily Spitz. Your mom mentioned that."

Sienna put the other lantern on the opposite end of the mantel. "I know she's a mystery writer and all, but she seems a little bit *too* excited about the whole murder thing. Is she one of your suspects?"

"I know what you mean about her excitement. And everyone who was at the lodge is a suspect in my mind." I pulled a cute snowman ornament out of the box. "Well, except Brett."

"And you."

I smiled. "Yes, I'm pretty sure I don't need to add my own name to the list."

Ivan emerged from the kitchen then, so we abruptly cut off our conversation about the murder. I knew Ivan objected to our tendency to get involved in mysteries because he didn't want either of us ending up in danger, but I preferred to avoid any extra-intimidating scowls and glares from him, if possible.

Ivan got his coat from his locker and then said goodbye to us. Tommy left a minute or two later, leaving me and Sienna alone at the pancake house.

Sienna set a couple of the snowmen on the windowsill and then fetched her phone from her coat pocket. "I'm going to look up Lily's books. I love reading mysteries."

"Me too."

She smiled at me. "That doesn't surprise me."

I returned her smile. "Right back at you."

Once all the snowmen were on display, I pulled two strings of lights out of the box and started untangling them.

"This sounds like so much fun!" Sienna said, her gaze fixed on the screen of her phone. "One of Lily's books is a winter mystery set on Mount Baker."

"Really?" I finally got the lights untangled. "Maybe I'll buy that one."

"Me too." She tapped her phone. "Hold on…Yes! I have enough left on my gift card balance to buy the e-book." She tapped the screen a couple more times. "There. I got it. I'll start reading it this weekend."

"Let me know if it's good."

Sienna assured me that she would. She put away her phone and we spent another half hour decorating the pancake house. When we were done, we admired our work.

"All we're missing now is a tree," Sienna declared.

She was right. We'd created a festive atmosphere, but a tree would make the dining room look even better.

"I'm hoping to get one soon," I said. "I'll have three trees to decorate this year."

"Here, home, and…at the festival?" she guessed.

"Yes. Speaking of which…" I grabbed my phone and checked the tracking information for the ornaments I'd ordered the day before. The packages had been shipped and were supposed to arrive by the end of the next day.

I showed Sienna pictures of the decorations I'd ordered, and she enthusiastically approved. By then, the fire had died down and it was getting darker outside. Rain still lashed against the windows and I was glad I'd driven my car to work.

"Did you walk here?" I asked Sienna as we pulled on our jackets.

"Yes, but I regretted it almost as soon as I was out the door." She peered out the window with obvious reluctance.

"Don't worry," I told her. "I've got my car. I'll give you a ride home."

"You're a lifesaver," she said with relief.

We dashed out the back door and ran for the shelter of my car. The windshield wipers had to work vigorously, and I drove slowly because of the poor visibility. I dropped Sienna off at her place and then backtracked down the road. When I pulled into my driveway, I noticed right away that there were two extra cars parked in front of the house.

I smiled, recognizing the vehicles. Lisa Morales and Brett's only sibling, Chloe, were here. They were my best friends, and Chloe was also my sister-in-law now.

I locked my car and ran up to the front porch. Despite my best efforts to avoid getting wet, water dripped from my hair and my jacket.

The front door opened before I had a chance to put my key in the lock. I caught a brief glimpse of Brett before a golden blur zoomed past him. Bentley let out a woof of excitement, his whole body wagging along with his tail. I crouched down to give him a hug, and received sloppy kisses in return.

I got an entirely different sort of kiss from Brett before I slipped out of my damp jacket and he shut the door on the wet and blustery evening. I followed the sound of laughter to the family room at the back of the house, where the room was lit by warm light and a fire crackled in the fireplace.

"Surprise!" Lisa barreled toward me and squeezed me in a hug. "Happy birthday!"

"*Maybe* a surprise." Chloe moved in for a one-armed hug, since she was holding a purring Flapjack in the other. "But definitely happy birthday."

"Thank you." I smiled at both of them and gave Flapjack a pat on the head. "I knew Brett had something planned, but I didn't know what."

Brett came up behind me and wrapped his arms around me. "A quiet evening in with a couple of your closest friends. I thought you'd like that. Is it all right?"

"Better than all right. It's perfect." I turned in his arms so I could give him a kiss.

"He probably had an ulterior motive," Chloe said. "With just two guests, it'll be easier to kick us out later so you can have some alone time."

"Nobody's going to get kicked out," I said.

Brett grinned. "Don't be so sure about that."

I gave him a playful shove that failed to knock him off balance.

Lisa took my arm and tugged me farther into the family room. "Come on. Open your presents."

"You didn't need to get me presents," I said.

Lisa waved off my protest. "*Of course* we got you presents."

I dropped down onto the couch. Lisa took the spot next to me while Chloe settled in an armchair with Flapjack on her lap. Bentley dashed over to his bed beneath one of the windows, turning around twice before lying down.

Over in the kitchen, Brett held up a few takeout menus. "What do you want for dinner, Marley?"

"What do you all feel like?" I asked everyone.

"Whatever you want," Chloe said. "Your birthday, your choice."

I thought for a second. "Pizza?" I glanced at the others.

"We won't argue," Lisa said. "Here." She placed a present on my lap, wrapped in shiny purple paper. "This one's from me."

I tore off the paper, already knowing that the best present was having the company of my husband and my two closest friends.

Chapter Eleven

After a delicious dinner delivered from Wildwood Cove's pizza parlor, we got comfy in the family room with slices of chocolate cake from the local bakery. At Chloe and Lisa's request, Brett and I had already recounted the story of Kevin's murder and how we'd discovered his body. Like most of the town, they'd heard about the murder, but wanted to know how much of what they'd heard was fact and how much had turned into fiction as it got passed along the grapevine.

"I'm glad Zahra's with Rita," Chloe said as she balanced her plate on her knee.

"You know her?" I asked with surprise. I hadn't mentioned Zahra by name.

Chloe licked chocolate ganache off her fork. "We took a yoga class together a few years back, when she lived in Wildwood Cove. She was in her senior year of high school at the time, so now she must be...what, twenty-three, maybe?"

"That sounds about right." I sank my fork into the heavenly piece of chocolate cake on my plate. "She's living in Seattle now."

Chloe nodded as she savored a bite of cake. "We've kept in touch online. She's a graphic designer for an advertising company."

"Is Kevin her father?" Lisa asked.

"Stepfather," Chloe replied. "Rita and Kevin married when Zahra was in high school. I think it was a bit of a whirlwind romance. Rita and Zahra had only lived here a few months when the wedding happened. Before that, the two of them lived in Los Angeles."

Lisa directed her next question my way. "Who do you think killed him, Marley?"

"I really don't know. I hate to think that it could have been someone who was sleeping down the hall from us at the lodge, but it could have been."

Chloe shuddered. "That's way too creepy."

"Maybe we shouldn't be talking about murder on your birthday," Lisa said. "Is The Flip Side decorating a tree for the festival?"

I was glad for the change in subject. As much as I enjoyed mulling over mysteries and putting mental puzzle pieces together, at the moment I was far more interested in having a good time with Brett and my friends. I told Lisa and Chloe about how I'd run out of breakfast-themed decorations and what I had planned for the tree.

When I mentioned my idea of using some seashells from my collection, Chloe sat up straight.

"Ooh!" She clapped her hands together. "I'd love to help you make decorations out of shells."

"Me too," Lisa chimed in.

"We can start tonight." Chloe set her empty plate on the coffee table and gently shifted a sleeping Flapjack from her lap. She stood up and settled him on the chair she'd just vacated. "After all, the festival starts in two days."

"You guys really don't have to do that," I said.

Lisa was on her feet now too. "We want to."

"You wouldn't rather watch a movie?" I asked, wanting to be sure.

Chloe waved off the question. "We can watch a movie another night."

"Like maybe Friday night," Lisa said.

"Well, not this Friday." Chloe carried her plate into the kitchen. "I've already got plans. But any other night."

"Plans?" I asked, intrigued.

Lisa waggled her eyebrows at Chloe. "As in a date?"

"She's not allowed to date until she's forty," Brett spoke up from the kitchen, where he was loading the dishwasher.

Chloe rolled her eyes. "A bit late for that. As if you'd get a say, anyway."

"Supplies," I said quickly, before Brett could retort. "We need supplies."

I fetched the shells I'd already cleaned while Brett went off in search of my paints and other craft supplies that I'd stored in the main floor tower room. Lisa, Chloe, and I gathered at the kitchen table. After he brought me my craft supplies, Brett took Bentley out for a short nighttime walk. Flapjack continued to snooze away on the armchair, no doubt enjoying the warmth from the fire.

"I have an idea." Chloe sorted through the shells, picking out clamshells of different sizes. "How about this?" She set a medium-sized clamshell on top of a large one, and then added a smaller one to the top of the stack.

Next, she grabbed a marker and drew two dots for eyes, and several more to make a smiling mouth.

"A snowman," I said as I realized what she was doing. "That's so cute."

"Adorable," Lisa agreed.

Chloe used an orange marker to draw a carrot nose. "We can even add little hats." She used a blue pen to do just that. To finish it off, she added three red buttons on the middle shell.

"It's perfect," I told her with a smile.

Chloe set down the red marker. "Now we just have to stick the shells together and add a loop of string for hanging it."

I rummaged around in my craft box and pulled out a glue gun. With all the necessary supplies out on the table, the three of us got to work.

* * * *

Although the next day was gloomy and cold, the rain had stopped. I still drove to work because of the darkness and the damp, bone-chilling wind, but it was nice to stay dry when going to and from my car. Once again, I was glad for The Flip Side's fireplace, and so were the customers. Several of them mentioned how cozy it was with the warmth and crackling of the fire.

An hour after the pancake house had opened, I took a moment to look out the front window. One glance was enough to make me even more glad that I'd brought my car to work. The break from the pouring rain had ended. It came down in sheets now, and the steely gray ocean looked angry and tumultuous. Even the seabirds I'd seen out there earlier had disappeared, probably to take shelter in the trees.

Brett had started back to work that morning. He was helping Pedro's crew remodel a kitchen and bathroom in an old Victorian across town. He'd arranged to take a break midmorning so he could drop his truck off at the local garage. Lonny was over the flu that had kept him home for days, so we could finally get the windshield fixed.

After receiving a text from Brett saying that he was on the way to the garage, I left Leigh to look after The Flip Side's customers and drove to meet him so I could give him a ride back to his worksite. He'd told me he could walk—it would only take him ten minutes or so—but in this weather, I didn't want him to have to head back to work on foot.

When I pulled into the small parking lot next to the garage, I spotted Lonny, dressed in gray coveralls, talking with Brett just inside one of the open bay doors. I pulled the hood of my jacket over my head and jogged over to them.

"Hey, Lonny," I said after giving Brett a quick kiss. "I'm glad you're feeling better."

"Thanks," he said. "So am I." He ran a hand through his brown hair. "That was a nasty flu. I hope you guys can avoid getting it."

Brett put an arm around my shoulders. "We got our flu shots. Hopefully they'll be effective."

"Next year I'll be getting one of those," Lonny said.

"So, what's the verdict on our windshield?" I asked, noting that Brett's silver pickup truck was already inside the garage, parked next to a dark green one.

"Shouldn't be a problem to fix," Lonny said. "I can have it ready for you by the end of the day."

"Sounds good," Brett said. "How's Hope doing these days?"

"Crazy busy, but good. The inn was fully booked over the weekend."

"I'm glad things have been going so well with the inn," I said. Lonny and Hope had worked so hard to make it a success. They were such a nice couple, and I hoped business would continue to be good for them.

My gaze zeroed in on the green truck's windshield. "Looks like this truck has the same problem as ours."

It had a chip in the glass, a bit bigger than the one in Brett's windshield.

"Yep." Lonny stuck his hands in the pockets of his coveralls. "That's not its only problem—the truck has seen better days—but the windshield crack might have happened in the same place as yours."

"Up near Holly Lodge?" Brett asked.

Lonny nodded. "Dwight Zalecki was up in that area over the weekend. He came down on Sunday and hit a patch of loose gravel."

"Definitely sounds like it could have happened in the same place then," Brett said.

I barely heard him. I was too busy thinking that Dwight—the customer with a grudge against Kevin Manning—had been in the vicinity of Holly Lodge when Kevin was killed.

Chapter Twelve

I shared my thoughts with Brett as I drove the short distance to his worksite. I pulled my car up to a free space by the curb two houses down from the Victorian where Pedro's crew was busy with renovations. It was a beautiful house, dark red with white trim and a three-story tower. It was bigger than our house, but I wasn't envious in the least. Ours was plenty big enough, and this one didn't have a beachfront location.

"So Dwight had motive and possibly means," Brett said once I'd told him what I was thinking. "But why wait all this time to kill Kevin? It sounds like Dwight's held a grudge against him for years. Wouldn't he have been more likely to kill Kevin back when they were neighbors?"

"Possibly. But who knows what's been going on in Dwight's head for the past few years?"

"Good point." Brett kissed me and unfastened his seatbelt. "I guess we can't rule him out yet." He opened the passenger door. "See you tonight." He got out of the car, but then leaned back in. "I love you."

"I love you too."

He jogged through the rain to the red Victorian.

When he'd disappeared inside, I drove back to The Flip Side, arriving just in time for the start of the lunch rush. I tied my red apron around my waist and got to work. Although I scanned the room for Dwight, he wasn't there. That wasn't surprising, since he only showed up at the pancake house once in a while.

I did, however, see many other familiar faces, and time flew by as I took orders, delivered meals to tables, and chatted with several regular customers as well as a couple of new ones. Everyone was in a good mood, and many diners were chatting about their plans for the holidays and the town's upcoming events, including the Festival of Trees and the town light-up. Many people were also looking forward to the holiday open house at the Wildwood Inn.

The rush was tapering off when Ambrose came in the door. I stopped in my tracks when I saw him, but then gave myself a mental kick and got moving toward the kitchen again. Ambrose paused inside the door and removed his fogged up glasses.

On my way past, I smiled at him. "Hi, Ambrose. Welcome to The Flip Side. Sit anywhere you like."

I got the impression that he was almost as surprised to see me as I was to see him. As far as I could remember, Brett and I had never told him that we were from Wildwood Cove.

When I emerged from the kitchen, Ambrose was seated at a small table near the back of the room. I grabbed the coffee pot and headed his way.

"Coffee?" I asked when I reached his table.

He nodded. "I didn't realize you worked here."

I filled his mug. "I'm the owner, but I don't think it ever came up that we were both from Wildwood Cove."

"No. I suppose it might have, if things had gone…differently."

"It's terrible what happened," I said.

"Yes, it is." Ambrose cleared his throat and removed his glasses, blinking as he touched a finger to the corner of one eye.

He was on the verge of tears, I realized.

I set the coffee pot on the table, my heart squeezing with sympathy for him. "Did you know Kevin well? Or was that your first visit to Holly Lodge?"

"Not my first by far." He put his glasses back on, appearing more in control of his emotions now. "I've been to Holly Lodge several times over the past couple of years. The first time I stayed there, my heart was captured." He tugged his coffee mug closer to him, but didn't take a drink. "It's so beautiful and peaceful up there in the mountains. I was filled with inspiration and had to go back."

I could understand that. I was no poet, but if not for the murder, Brett and I would likely have wanted to visit Holly Lodge again in the future.

"Then I guess you know the family quite well," I said.

"I'd say so, yes. Although, really, I know Rita better than I knew Kevin. She tends to spend more time with the guests."

"Ambrose!"

I turned at the sound of a woman's voice.

Lily brushed past me and dropped into the seat across from Ambrose. "You haven't eaten yet, have you?" She glanced at me and did a double take. "Oh, hi! You live in Wildwood Cove?"

"For more than a year and a half now," I said. "Coffee?"

"Earl Grey tea, please," she requested.

"Coming right up." I left them to read over the menu.

When I was on my way back to their table with Lily's tea, she put a hand over Ambrose's as he reached for his coffee mug. As I got closer, Ambrose slid his hand away from hers and shifted in his seat. Although his eyes were clear of tears now, he seemed subdued.

I set Lily's tea on the table and took out my order pad. Ambrose asked for the cinnamon pancakes and, after a brief moment of consideration, Lily did the same. As I headed for the kitchen once again, I heard Lily chatting away brightly, her bubbly mood providing a stark contrast to Ambrose's somber one.

* * * *

When I arrived home later that afternoon, two packages waited for me on the front porch. I opened them with excitement and a small hint of apprehension. Some of the ornaments I'd ordered were fragile, and I hoped they hadn't broken in transit.

Fortunately, every piece was intact, and I loved each one. The sea creatures were adorable, their colors bright. They would look amazing on the tree.

I let Bentley outside to run around the yard in the rain while I held Flapjack in my arms and watched from the shelter of the covered front porch. Flapjack enjoyed spending time out in the yard, but he didn't like getting rained on. Bentley, on the other hand, never minded the weather. Rain or shine, he was always excited to get outside.

He moseyed around the yard for a few minutes, checking out the scents and looking for the perfect spot to lift his leg before returning to the porch. After drying Bentley off and giving him and Flapjack each a treat, I gathered up my packages and drove over to the seniors' center, eager to get back to decorating my tree.

A lot had been done in my absence. When I stepped into the main room, it was like walking into an indoor winter wonderland. Almost all of the trees were now fully decked out, red and green lights twinkled overhead, and artificial snow had been liberally dusted around the trees. The pathways had been demarcated with red and white ropes reminiscent of candy canes, and decorations like three foot tall wooden nutcrackers, cute woodland animals, and wicker reindeer filled in the previously empty spaces.

All of the sponsors had done a great job with their trees. Lonny and Zach's garage had a tree decorated with classic car ornaments. My favorite was an old red truck with a Christmas tree in the back. The tree sponsored by Marielle's Bakery featured cute cupcake ornaments as well as pink and white bows that matched the colors of the logo on Marielle's bakery boxes.

The local coffee shop, the Beach and Bean, had opted to go with more traditional decorations rather than themed ones. The tree was decked out in blue and silver, with baubles, stars, and sparkly snowflakes. The local birdwatchers' society had festooned its tree with bird ornaments and gold and silver pinecones. There was also a mermaid-themed tree and one with decorations all in shades of purple.

Of all the trees I admired on my way down the path, my favorite was the one sponsored by Wildwood Cove's public library. Miniature books hung from the branches, all with covers from real novels. I spotted classics like *A Christmas Carol* and *Pride and Prejudice*, as well as newer books by authors like Louise Penny and Stephen King.

I'd almost reached my tree when I stopped short, staring with surprise at the one next to mine. I couldn't help but smile. According to the sign, the local toy store had decorated the tree. That made perfect sense. Black and silver decorations hung from the branches, but what really made the tree stand out was the Darth Vader helmet topping the tree and the lightsaber sticking out from the middle branches. A black cape hung over the back half of the tree and black boots showed from beneath the lowest branches. I didn't doubt that Darth Vader would get plenty of votes, especially from Wildwood Cove's younger citizens.

Still smiling, I stepped over the rope to get to my tree, ready to get to work. I hoped I'd be able to make my tree look as good as all the others. I set down my boxes and then straightened as I heard Patricia's voice.

"Hi, Marley. How's everything? Are any of your decorations missing?" She sounded stressed and she had worry lines across her forehead.

I studied my tree. "As far as I know all of my decorations are here." I did a quick check of my breakfast-themed ornaments. All seemed to be accounted for. "Why? Have more gone missing?"

"Unfortunately. Several people came by this morning to finish decorating their trees. Four of them reported missing decorations." She consulted her phone. "Three snowflakes were taken from the Beach and Bean tree, two cupcakes from Marielle's, some purple baubles from the general store's, and a couple of red ones from the Windward Pub's tree."

"That's a lot," I said, puzzled. "Why would anyone do this?"

Patricia sighed. "I wish I knew. The thefts are putting a damper on the festival, and it hasn't even officially started yet."

I felt bad for her, and for everyone else who'd worked so hard to organize the event.

I glanced around the room. "No surveillance cameras in here?"

"No," Patricia confirmed. "And not outside either."

That was unfortunate, but not surprising. Most buildings in Wildwood Cove didn't have surveillance cameras. I'd installed some outside The Flip Side only after the pancake house had been the target of some vandalism.

"Have there been a lot of people around the past couple of days?"

"Several, but mostly just the volunteers and sponsors. And Letty Campbell. She's the chair of the center's board of directors."

"Maybe one of the sponsors is trying to sabotage their competition?" Even as I voiced the theory, I had trouble believing it. The individuals and businesses sponsoring the trees didn't have anything to gain personally by winning. The prize money would go to a charity of their choice.

"I really don't know what's going on." Patricia sounded weary. "At least this won't stop the festival from going forward. The trees still look great. It's just been adding unneeded stress."

"Do you know when the latest missing ornaments disappeared?" I asked. I had trouble shrugging off mysteries, no matter how small.

"Between the time I left yesterday and when I opened this morning. Marielle started decorating her tree yesterday afternoon and left just minutes before I locked up. She popped by again first thing this morning to add a few more bows. That's when she realized some of the cupcake ornaments were gone."

"Was anyone else here when you left, or when you first arrived today?" I asked.

Patricia thought for a second. "Annette left when Marielle did. Aside from me, Marielle was the first to arrive this morning."

"Who has keys to the seniors' center?" I knew I was asking a lot of questions, but Patricia didn't seem to mind.

"I have one for the duration of the festival. Letty Campbell and the other board members. And the maintenance guy, Chuck Banfield. But he's out of town for a couple of days and, anyway, I can't imagine any of them stealing Christmas decorations."

"Patricia?" a woman called from the next room.

"Excuse me, Marley." With a brief smile weighed down by stress, she rushed off to find the woman who'd called her.

Someone else hurried down the central pathway. Annette, I realized a moment later.

She stopped between two trees and peered over a large nutcracker at me. "Hi! Have you fallen victim to the thief?"

"Not yet," I said. I noticed that she had a small box in her arms. "Replacement decorations?"

"Yep. Hopefully these ones won't get taken. I'm determined to win this competition!" She flashed me a brief smile and then hurried off.

I got busy decorating my tree, carefully hanging the beautiful glass sea creatures as well as the snowmen that Lisa, Chloe, and I had made out of shells. Chloe had also made a couple of angels, using clamshells for the dresses and mussel shells for the wings. Store-bought or handmade, they all looked great on the tree. It wouldn't be the end of the world if someone stole my decorations, but I hoped it wouldn't happen.

I wished there was a way to identify the thief, but without surveillance cameras, the chances of that happening were slim. In the end, I decided I'd simply have to be vigilant while at the seniors' center, in case the thief was operating in plain view. Other than that, all I could do was cross my fingers and hope that he or she wouldn't strike again.

Chapter Thirteen

I texted Patricia around noon the next day, asking if any further ornaments had disappeared from the festival trees.

So far nothing more has been reported missing, she wrote back. *Thank goodness!*

I shared her relief. Maybe the thief was satisfied with what he or she had already taken. It was still unfortunate that some items had been stolen, but hopefully the festival would run smoothly from now on. It would officially open the next morning, and I was looking forward to stopping by after work tomorrow so I could take in the entire display.

Brett and I planned to go together, but we also had more immediate plans. After he finished work today, we were heading out to a nearby Christmas tree farm to pick up trees for The Flip Side and our house. We'd gone to the same farm the year before, for our first Christmas together, and I hoped the trip would become an annual tradition.

The thought of establishing traditions with Brett, ones we could enjoy together for years and years, filled me with happiness. We'd been married for more than three months now, but sometimes I still had to pinch myself to make sure that my life was real and not just a beautiful dream. Before Brett, I'd never dared to imagine that I'd find a man as amazing as him.

After closing the pancake house and giving it a good clean, I locked up and headed home, looking forward to the evening I'd be spending with Brett. Although we finally had a clear and sunny day, without a drop of rain, I'd still driven to work. I knew I wouldn't have wanted to make my way along the beach in the pitch darkness of the early winter morning, but I missed spending time by the ocean. I could see it from my house and from The Flip Side, but that wasn't quite the same as spending time on the beach.

When I arrived home, I had some time to kill before Brett would finish work. I got together all the ingredients I'd need to make a batch of spaghetti sauce, but before starting to cook, I took Bentley out for a walk along the shore.

Bentley was as happy as I was to spend some time by the water. He galloped and bounded around, even splashing in the shallows for a few seconds here and there. I wasn't crazy enough to dip so much as a toe into the cold waters. Even Bentley didn't go in beyond the depth of a couple of inches.

We walked all the way to the eastern end of the cove, enjoying the fresh air despite the chill. It was quiet out that way, with only a few seagulls sharing the beach with us. The sun shone brightly, though I couldn't feel much of its warmth through the cold wind. I was glad I'd bundled up in a winter jacket, hat, and gloves before setting out. Wildwood Cove might not have been in the mountains, and we might not have had any snow, but it still felt like winter.

On the way back home, I spotted a lone figure standing on the beach out in front of Patricia's bed-and-breakfast. As I drew closer, I realized that the person was Lily. Bentley wasn't quite as exuberant as when we'd first set out, but he was still wagging his tail and enjoying the outing. He trotted over to Lily and she gave him a pat on the head.

"What a cute dog!" She smiled at me. "We meet again."

"I live nearby," I explained.

I didn't tell her exactly where, even though I could have pointed out my house from where we stood. There were a few people out on the beach closer to town, a couple of them with dogs, but out this way we were alone. I wasn't too worried, but I couldn't help but recall what Wilson had said about Lily during our last breakfast at Holly Lodge. On the night that Kevin had died, Lily had been up and about just after two in the morning. I didn't know for sure when Kevin had been killed, but I also didn't know for sure that I wasn't talking to his murderer.

"Have you heard anything more about Kevin's murder?" I asked, watching Lily's face for any clues as to her guilt or innocence.

"Not a thing." She buried her gloved hands in the pockets of her knee-length coat. Her expression revealed nothing.

I changed tack. "I hear you're planning to write a book set here on the Olympic Peninsula."

She brightened at the change of subject. "That's right. Wildwood Cove might even make an appearance."

"That would be cool," I said, meaning it. "Will it be another murder mystery? That's my favorite genre."

"Yes, it'll be a mystery, probably with a dash of romance. I love combining my two favorite genres." She huddled deeper into her coat as a gust of wind swirled around us. "I wanted to have the murder take place at Holly Lodge. It's fun for my readers if they can visit—or think of visiting—the places where my books are set. I thought it would have benefitted me *and* the Mannings."

"But you changed your mind?" I guessed, judging by her frown.

"I had to. I make a practice of getting permission if I'm going to set a murder at a real place of business. This time it wasn't forthcoming."

"I can see why Rita wouldn't agree now."

"So can I, but I had to change my plans before Kevin died. I never even got a chance to talk to Rita about it. Kevin was adamant that he didn't want a fictional murder taking place at his lodge." She shrugged. "Now he's got a real one instead."

The cool way she said that sent a chill skittering down my spine.

"Anyway," she continued, "I'll probably still use Holly Lodge as my inspiration, but I'll use a different name. I might even incorporate a ghost story, like the one about Henrietta Franklin."

"That sounds great." I didn't have to feign my enthusiasm. "I look forward to reading the book."

The afternoon was morphing into evening, daylight quickly fading from the sky. I needed to get home so I could start cooking the spaghetti sauce, but I wasn't quite ready to give up on digging for information.

"Was it your first visit to Holly Lodge last week?" I asked.

"It was. I heard about it through Ambrose. He's been there several times. I can see why he finds it great for inspiration." Her expression grew somber. "Poor Ambrose."

"Why do you say that?" I asked.

"I don't know if you've heard, but Kevin was hoping to expand the lodge. He told Ambrose he could run writing retreats there once it had meeting rooms and more space for guests. Ambrose was really looking forward to that. Rita was never on board with the expansion, so there's no chance of it going ahead now."

"Hopefully Ambrose will find a way to have his retreats, whether at Holly Lodge or somewhere else," I said.

"Hopefully."

I took a step back. "I'd better run. Enjoy the rest of your time in Wildwood Cove."

She smiled. "I plan to."

Bentley had wandered off to sniff at one of the logs on the beach. I called to him and he came running. As we walked the rest of the way home, I thought over everything Lily had said. It seemed like Ambrose didn't have a motive to kill Kevin. In fact, if what Lily said was true, Kevin's death may have thwarted his plans, especially if Rita didn't want to expand the lodge.

Lily, on the other hand, I couldn't rule out as a suspect. Maybe Kevin's refusal to agree to have a fictional murder set at Holly Lodge wasn't a strong motive for the author to kill him, but I wasn't quite sure what to make of Lily. She seemed mostly unaffected by Kevin's death. That could have been because she didn't know him, or maybe she kept her emotions to herself. Nevertheless, something about her made me uneasy, and I decided that I needed to learn more about her before drawing any final conclusions.

* * * *

While the spaghetti sauce simmered on the stove, I got comfortable on the couch with Flapjack by my side and my laptop on my knees. Lily's mention of Henrietta Franklin had brought the ghost story to the front of my mind and had piqued my curiosity. I'd learned a little bit about Henrietta while at Holly Lodge, but I wanted to know more. How had she died and why was she thought to haunt the lake? Those were the questions I hoped to answer.

Fortunately, I had no trouble finding information about Henrietta, even though there wasn't a huge number of websites with hits. A non-fiction author and history buff who lived on the Olympic Peninsula had written a lengthy blog post on the subject, and a historical society had a write-up about Henrietta on its site. I read both accounts of Henrietta's back story and found that they didn't differ in substance.

According to both sources, Henrietta Langford was born in Colorado in 1902. At the age of twenty-three, she moved to the Pacific Northwest with her sister and cousin. Henrietta found work as a barmaid at a tavern on the peninsula, and that's where she met her future husband, Billy Franklin, a regular patron at the tavern. Henrietta and Billy married in 1926, and their marriage marked the start of a downward spiral in Henrietta's life. It was no secret that Billy was violent toward Henrietta, and she often showed up for work bruised and battered.

Then, one day in September 1929, Henrietta failed to show up at the tavern for her shift. She was never seen again.

Friends of the Franklins reported that the couple had gone up to Billy's cabin at Holly Lake, ostensibly so Billy could do some hunting and fishing, but only Billy returned. He claimed that Henrietta had run off with another man, but few accepted that story as the truth.

Nothing was ever proven, but Henrietta's friends and family firmly believed that Billy had killed her at the cabin and sent her body to the bottom of the lake. The first sighting of Henrietta's ghost—with her long red locks and wearing her best dress—was reported in 1931. Since then, many people had claimed to see Henrietta's ghost out on the lake or on the shore.

Billy had been questioned by the police after Henrietta's disappearance, but he was never arrested or tried. He had died in 1939 as a result of injuries sustained in a tavern brawl.

I sat back, stroking Flapjack's fur as I digested the story. I wished there'd been some evidence that concretely established what had happened to Henrietta, but I didn't see any reason to doubt that Billy had killed her. He certainly hadn't been much of a husband. It was too bad he'd never had to pay for what he'd done to Henrietta, but maybe karma had caught up to him at the tavern in 1939.

Now I knew Henrietta's connection to Holly Lake—it was most likely her final resting place. I still didn't know if I believed that people had seen her ghost. I didn't know if *I'd* seen her ghost.

Unsettled, I shut down my laptop and got up from the couch to finish making dinner, more appreciative than ever that I'd lucked out when it came to finding my husband.

* * * *

After our dinner of spaghetti and garlic bread, Brett and I drove to the local tree farm in Brett's truck, its windshield now fixed. On the way, I told him what I'd learned about Henrietta Franklin. Brett's thoughts mirrored my own—it was an interesting and tragic tale, but he still wasn't convinced that there was a real ghost haunting the lake. By the time I'd finished telling him Henrietta's story, we'd reached our destination.

Since we arrived at the farm after dark, we couldn't head out to cut down a tree. Instead, we had to choose from the pre-cut ones in the lot near the entrance. That area was lit with bright lights, and Christmas music played through outdoor speakers. A few people stood by a fire pit, enjoying the warmth of the flames while chatting and sipping hot drinks.

A small building known as the Santa Shack operated as a seasonal café of sorts. It had hot drinks and sugar cookies for sale, with a few tables and chairs inside. I knew from the year before that the Santa Shack served delicious hot apple cider. Even though we'd just had dinner, Brett and I planned to make a stop at the Shack before leaving the farm.

First, however, we focused on the trees. We took our time, assessing each tree before deciding if it was in the running. After we'd looked at a dozen or so, Brett stood up a five-foot Douglas fir with full branches.

"How about this one for The Flip Side?" he asked.

I held off on judgement until I'd walked all the way around the tree, studying it from all sides. "It's perfect," I declared.

"One down, one to go."

"Let's make that two to go," I said. "One for the living room and a smaller one for the family room."

Brett had no objection.

One of the farm's employees took the tree to shake off the loose needles and wrap it while we continued our search. After another half hour, we'd picked out a six-foot tree for the living room at the front of our house, where we had our family gatherings on Christmas Eve and Christmas Day, and a cute four-foot tree for the family room at the back of the house, where we spent most of our time.

I'd end up decorating four trees this year, but I didn't mind. I loved decorating for the holidays.

By the time we'd paid for the trees, we were more than ready for something hot to drink. The temperature hovered around the freezing mark and the breeze, while slight, had me shivering.

"Do you want me to go grab us drinks while you finish up?" I asked.

Brett was in the process of loading the trees into the back of his truck. "Sure."

I rubbed my gloved hands together, hoping to work some warmth into my fingers. "Hot chocolate or apple cider?"

"I think I'll go with hot chocolate this year."

I jogged over to the Santa Shack and stepped inside, the warmth of the interior and the smell of spices from the cider hitting me right away. Christmas music played in here as well, and twinkle lights had been strung overhead. Evergreen wreaths and swags hung on one wall, available for sale. I stopped to admire them, and ended up picking out two, one for the front door of our house and the other for The Flip Side.

Over at the counter, I ordered hot chocolate for Brett, apple cider for me, and two snowmen sugar cookies that looked far too good to resist. I paid for the food and drinks, as well as the wreaths. While I waited for the woman behind the counter to get the drinks ready, my gaze strayed to the few tables off to my right, where a handful of people sat enjoying drinks and cookies.

My gaze snapped back to the first table I saw. Chloe sat there, a mug of something hot on the table before her. It came as a surprise to see Deputy Kyle Rutowski with her. I'd met the deputy several times and I knew he'd grown up in Wildwood Cove. He was out of uniform and also had a drink in front of him. I almost called out to them, but then I realized with another jolt of surprise that they were holding hands.

I remembered that Chloe had never confirmed or denied that she had a date planned. I wondered if that had been on purpose.

The lady behind the counter handed over the drinks I'd bought, along with a small paper bag holding our cookies. I glanced Chloe's way again, debating whether I should stop and say hi. When I saw the way she and Kyle had their heads close together, talking softly and still holding hands, I quietly slipped out the door without saying anything.

As I walked past the nearest row of pre-cut trees, I noticed two girls gazing up at a tall one with awe. They appeared to be about eight years old, and I recognized them as the girls who'd been at the seniors' center the first day I'd gone to pick a tree. I remembered the fair-haired one was named Emily.

"I wish I could have a big Christmas tree like this one," Emily said to her friend as I passed them. "We always used to have a tall one, but my mom says we can only have a small one this year."

She looked so sad, but hopefully she'd end up with a beautiful tree, no matter how tall or short.

Brett jogged over to greet me, relieving me of his hot chocolate and the wreaths. "Looks like we're buying the place out."

"Almost," I said with a smile, knowing he was teasing.

I climbed into the truck and set my apple cider in the cup holder while I fastened my seatbelt. Brett climbed in too and started the engine, cranking up the heat in an attempt to dispel the chill that had seeped into the vehicle in our absence. As we drove along the farm's driveway, heading for the highway, we passed a green pickup truck going in the opposite direction. The driver was a young man, but the truck reminded me of Dwight and his dinged windshield.

Thinking about Dwight led me to consider another one of my suspects—Rita. When I'd seen Lily on the beach, she'd mentioned that Rita had never wanted to expand Holly Lodge like Kevin had. Zahra had said that Rita was now the sole owner of the lodge, so its future was completely in her hands. Could that have been what she wanted all along?

There was no denying that Rita and Kevin's relationship wasn't perfect. Zahra claimed that they'd still loved each other, and maybe they had, but was Kevin's hope to expand Holly Lodge a major point of contention between them? If so, could Rita have killed her husband to gain full control of the business and property?

It was a chilling thought, but one I couldn't ignore. There didn't seem to be a way to prove or disprove that theory, though. No one had mentioned seeing Rita after she'd supposedly gone to bed on Friday night. And since she'd been alone in the lodge's private quarters, no one could confirm that she'd stayed in bed until morning.

I needed more information about my suspects if I was ever going to rule any of them out. That would have to wait, however. At the moment, I had something to tell Brett.

"You'll never guess who I saw in the Santa Shack…"

Chapter Fourteen

"Chloe and Kyle Rutowski?" Brett said as we drove along the highway. He sounded like he was having trouble believing me. "Are you sure they were on a date?"

"Positive. They were holding hands and looking very cozy."

"Holding hands on their first date?"

I tried to suppress a grin. "It's not like Kyle was proposing. And…I have a feeling it might not be their first date."

Brett frowned. "Our whole family knows Kyle. Why wouldn't Chloe mention it if she's been out with him before?"

"Probably because she didn't want everyone sticking their nose in her business."

"I wouldn't do that," he protested.

I nearly choked when I tried to hold back a laugh.

Brett sent me a sidelong glance. "What's so funny?"

"You're a great brother, Brett, but sometimes you do go into full-on big brother mode."

He opened his mouth to retort, but then seemed to change his mind and shut it.

"Besides," I continued, "it's not easy to have any privacy in a small town. Maybe they just want to see where things go between them before all of Wildwood Cove knows they're dating."

I figured that might be why they'd gone to an out-of-the-way place like the Santa Shack. Obviously, doing that didn't guarantee that they wouldn't be seen by someone who recognized them, but if they'd met up somewhere in town, it was pretty much a sure thing that at least half of Wildwood Cove would have known about it by the next morning.

"Okay," Brett said after a moment. "I guess I can understand that."

I patted his knee. "Kyle's a good guy."

"I know."

"So you won't give him or Chloe the third-degree next time you see them?"

"I don't know about that," he said.

"Brett…"

One corner of his mouth quirked upwards, and I knew he wasn't as worried as he'd pretended to be. "I'll do my best to play it cool." He glanced my way, a full-fledged grin now on his face. "So, you're not going to grill Chloe either?"

"I won't grill her." My smile matched his. "But I fully intend to request details the next time I see her."

Brett laughed. "That's my Marley."

* * * *

We'd just arrived home when Patricia texted me with the news that the festival thief had struck yet again. More baubles and snowflakes had disappeared, but from trees that hadn't been hit before. Whoever was behind the thefts was taking care not to steal too much from any single tree. Maybe the person responsible didn't want to victimize any one sponsor too much, or perhaps the culprit's method had more to do with the hope that the disappearances would go unnoticed if only a few decorations were taken from each tree.

I wondered what the thief's motive might be. The ornaments weren't particularly valuable, aside from possible sentimental value. Maybe the decorations had simply caught the thief's fancy, or perhaps the culprit was trying to derail the festival for some reason. I didn't see how anyone would think that a few missing ornaments would put a stop to the event, though.

While helping Brett unload the trees, I mulled over the problem, wondering if there was a way to catch the thief. Either the missing decorations would have to be found in someone's possession, or the thief would have to get caught while striking again. Now that there'd been three separate incidents, I figured there was a good chance that there would be a fourth.

I texted Patricia back, asking for more details. She responded, letting me know that the theft had again taken place after she'd locked up for the evening and before she arrived in the morning. There were no signs of forced entry and nobody's key had gone missing.

Patricia knew all of the board members and strongly believed that none of them were involved. She was probably right, but I didn't think it was possible to know that for sure. Sometimes people did things that seemed wildly out of character.

A plan formed in my head. I shared it with Brett as he set the last of the three trees in a bucket of water on the front porch, where they would stay until we set them up in a day or two.

"You want to go over to the seniors' center now?" Brett checked his phone. "It's nearly nine o'clock."

"I know, but the ornaments are most likely disappearing after hours. I want to see if I can catch the thief in the act."

Brett didn't seem convinced by my plan. "Were there any signs of forced entry into the building?"

"No."

"Then it seems more likely that the thefts are happening during the day, maybe right when everyone's leaving, or first thing."

"That's a possibility," I agreed. "But maybe the thief got hold of a key to the center somehow and had a copy made. That's possible too." I unlocked my car. "I won't be gone too long."

"Hold on," Brett said as he opened the front door to the house. "Let's give Bentley a minute outside first."

"You're coming with me? You don't have to."

"Of course I'm coming with you." Brett opened the door. "How else can I make sure you stay out of trouble?"

The illumination from the porch light allowed me to see his grin.

"Very funny," I said, but I didn't protest further. I was glad he'd offered to go with me. Sitting alone in my car in the dark and cold wasn't a particularly appealing activity. Having Brett's company would make it more bearable.

As I locked up my car again, Bentley came barreling out of the house. He greeted us with his usual enthusiasm and then spent some time sniffing at the bushes along the fence. He did what he needed to do, and then Brett ushered him back inside. A minute later, we were back in Brett's truck and driving into the heart of Wildwood Cove. The street where the seniors' center was located was deserted, all the shops and businesses closed for the night.

Brett parked across the road from the center and cut the truck's lights and engine. Far too soon, the warmth inside the truck faded away, replaced by the cold air seeping in from outside. Nothing moved out on the street. That didn't change over the next several minutes.

"What if the thief goes in through the back door?" Brett asked. "We'll miss him sitting here."

"The same thought was just going through my mind." I reached for the door. "I'll go have a look around back."

Brett was faster at getting his door open. "I'll go. You stay here where it's warm."

He was gone before I had a chance to protest. It wasn't exactly warm in the truck now, especially since he'd opened his door, but I was glad I didn't have to go creeping around the back alley in the dark. Maybe Brett should have taken a flashlight, I realized. Although, he had a flashlight app on his phone, and we didn't want to alert the thief to our presence.

I knew there wasn't much chance of Brett encountering anything dangerous while he checked out the back of the seniors' center, but even so I remained tense while he was gone. The minutes passed by slowly. I zipped my jacket up higher, on the verge of shivering. The interior of the truck was probably the same temperature as outside now. I wished I had another cup of hot apple cider to warm me up.

A few more minutes passed. I wondered if I should go looking for Brett. Maybe something had happened. If he'd interrupted the thief...

I reached for the door, my worries escalating. I was about to open it when Brett emerged from the gap between the seniors' center and the neighboring building. He jogged across the street and climbed into the truck. I breathed a sigh of relief.

"Anything?" I asked.

"Not even a rat."

I shuddered. "Thank goodness."

"We could sit here all night and most likely not see anything."

"You're right," I conceded. "And we'll turn into popsicles if we stay here much longer."

"What this place needs is security cameras," Brett said.

"Maybe if Patricia talks to the board, they'll invest in some." I decided to ask her about that soon.

Brett was about to start the truck's engine when I put a hand on his arm.

"Hold on. Someone's coming." I'd spotted the figure in the rearview mirror.

A man walked along the sidewalk, on the other side of the street, heading toward the seniors' center. I watched him through the mirror with tense anticipation. When he got closer, I twisted in my seat until I could see him through the driver's side window.

"Isn't that—" Brett started.

"Ambrose," I finished for him. *"Ambrose* is our thief?"

"Or not," Brett said as Ambrose walked right past the front entrance to the center.

We waited to see if he'd turn down the narrow pathway between buildings, but he stayed on the sidewalk. When he reached the corner, he crossed the side street and kept going in the same direction.

"Okay, so he's not the thief," I said. "That would have been really weird."

He'd disappeared from sight now. With nothing else to focus on, I was suddenly aware of just how cold I'd become. My fingers and toes felt as though they'd turned to ice.

"Let's go home," I said, failing to stifle a small sigh of disappointment.

Brett started the engine. "Cameras are probably the best bet for catching the thief."

I held my gloved hands up to the heating vent. "I'll talk to Patricia about that."

Brett pulled away from the curb and drove toward home. As we turned right onto Wildwood Road, I spotted Ambrose again as he passed beneath a streetlamp.

"Maybe I can talk to Ambrose for a second," I said.

Brett slowed down and pulled over to the curb. I thought about asking Brett to lower his window, but decided it would be better to slip out of the truck quickly to prevent as little heat loss as possible from the interior. I shut the door as soon as I was on the sidewalk.

"Ambrose!"

He stopped in his tracks and looked in my direction, his stance wary.

"It's Marley," I called out as I crossed the street toward him.

He immediately relaxed.

"Brett and I were driving by and thought we'd stop to say hi," I said.

Brett had followed me out of the truck and now joined us across the road.

"It's a bit chilly to be out walking, isn't it?" I asked with a shiver.

"It's cold," Ambrose agreed, "but I like fresh, crisp air. I'm heading down to the beach. There's something about the ocean at night that sings to my soul."

"I can understand that," I said. And I could, although I wouldn't have chosen such a cold night to hang out at the beach.

"What are you two doing out and about?" Ambrose asked.

"We stopped by the seniors' center for a few minutes," Brett replied.

I was glad he'd come up with a succinct answer. I wasn't sure what Ambrose would think if I'd given him the full explanation. He might have found it odd that we'd chosen to sit around in the cold on the off chance we could catch a thief.

Maybe it *was* odd. It wasn't something Brett would have done on his own. He'd likely decided to humor me, not wanting me to go by myself and knowing I'd have trouble settling if I didn't at least try to catch the thief.

"Any news about the murder investigation?" I asked, getting to the reason why I'd stopped to talk to Ambrose.

"Not really," he said. "I called Rita yesterday to see how she was holding up. The police have been giving her a hard time."

"Do they think she killed Kevin?" Brett asked.

Ambrose shrugged. "They sure asked her a lot of questions."

"That might just be routine," I said.

"They have to look at the family members," Brett added.

Ambrose frowned. "I get that, but they're wasting their time."

"You think she's innocent?" I surmised.

"I think others are far more likely to be guilty."

"Such as?" I hoped he'd say more.

"Harvey," Ambrose said. "Remember what Lily told us about him?"

"He argued with Kevin," Brett said.

Ambrose nodded. "Exactly. And I've heard a rumor that he was seen outside in the middle of the night."

"That's true," I said, wondering how he'd found out about that. "It was me who saw him. I looked out the window just after two. He was out on snowshoes."

Ambrose shoved his hands in the pockets of his jacket. "Sounds suspicious to me."

"How well do you know Harvey?" I asked, remembering that Ambrose had been to Holly Lodge several times. "Do you really think he could be a killer?"

"I don't know him very well. I've seen him around every time I've stayed at the lodge, but he mostly keeps to himself. It seems weird that he was out on snowshoes in the middle of the night."

"Maybe he couldn't sleep," I suggested. "Just like Lily."

"Lily wouldn't hurt anyone," Ambrose said quickly, jumping to her defense.

"I wasn't suggesting that she would." I didn't add that I hadn't discounted the idea entirely. I wasn't surprised that Ambrose believed in her innocence, though. "I heard you were hoping to hold writing retreats at the lodge."

Ambrose frowned. "That's not likely to happen now. Unless it's a really small one."

"Rita didn't share Kevin's intention to expand the lodge?" Brett asked.

"She was against it from the start," Ambrose replied.

I wondered if I should ask if him if he knew what Rita might have been talking to Wilson about shortly before Brett and I had left Holly Lodge. He didn't give me the chance.

"Sorry. I've got to get moving. It's too cold to stand around."

"It is," I agreed. "Sorry to keep you. Will you be at the town light up tomorrow night?"

"No, that's not my kind of thing. I don't like crowds." He was already turning away from us.

"Enjoy your time at the beach," I said.

Ambrose mumbled his thanks and then strode off down the road. A moment later he flicked on a flashlight and turned onto a pathway that would take him to the beach.

Brett and I wasted no time getting back into the truck. It was cold in the cab again, but not as cold as outside. This time, we drove home without stopping. We left the icy air behind when we got into the house, but I wasn't able to do the same with all my questions about Kevin's death.

Chapter Fifteen

Before any customers arrived at The Flip Side the next morning, I parked myself at the desk in the office and did a quick Internet search on Wilson Gerrard. I'd dreamed about him during the night, although I wished I hadn't. All I could remember from the dream was Wilson laughing maniacally while looming over Lily, who was trying—without much success—to write a book despite the distraction of the unnerving laughter. I didn't know if the dream had any deep meaning, but it left me thinking about the unpleasant man and I wanted to find out more about him.

Both Lily and Ambrose had said that the plans for Holly Lodge's expansion had died along with Kevin. Maybe they believed that to be true, but I couldn't shake the memory of Rita's discussion with Wilson in the lodge's dining room. It had sounded like it was business-related, like they were working on a deal of some sort, and I wasn't yet completely convinced that Rita hadn't changed her mind about expanding. It was also possible that she wanted to sell Holly Lodge now that Kevin was gone.

Rita certainly seemed like the one with the most to gain from Kevin's death. Whether she kept the lodge, enjoying full control over it, or sold it for what would probably be a good price, she had a motive for wanting her husband out of the way, especially since they'd had their troubles. Wilson also had a motive, though. Kevin had refused to sell the lodge to him. Whether it was true or not, maybe the real estate developer believed he'd have a better chance of buying Holly Lodge with Kevin dead.

It was easy to find Wilson's website as well as several other mentions of him online. None of what I read gave me much insight into his character or the likelihood that he could be a killer. I scoured the Internet for more information, but all I really learned was that he already owned a couple of chalets up in the mountains, which he rented out to people on vacation.

I gave up, fighting back a sense of frustration at how little progress I'd made toward figuring out who'd killed Kevin. In theory, I could have minded my own business and left the crime-solving to Sheriff Walczyk. Anyone who knew me would have laughed at that idea, though. It was pointless for me to try to forget about an unsolved mystery.

I had to push Kevin's murder to the back of my mind for the time being, however. The pancake house was packed during the breakfast rush, so I helped out Leigh and Sienna with serving customers.

I was happy to see that many diners had ordered the newest menu items that had been added on a seasonal basis. The gingerbread muffins, pumpkin scones, and cinnamon pancakes received great reviews and I had to promise several people that I'd pass on their praise to Ivan and Tommy. The compliments got a grin out of Tommy and a slightly eased scowl out of Ivan.

"Hey," I said to Sienna when our paths crossed in the kitchen, "how's Lily's book?"

She set a load of dirty dishes on the counter. "I haven't had a chance to read it yet. I forgot I had a book to read for English class. It's almost five hundred pages!" She made a face. "And I have to write an essay on it for next Friday. I probably won't get a chance to read Lily's book till then."

If we hadn't been so busy, I would have asked which book she had to read for class. Even without knowing, I sympathized with her. I'd always been an avid reader, but I hadn't always enjoyed the books I'd had to read in school.

The breakfast rush finally slowed around midmorning, shortly before Chloe showed up. I'd texted her the night before, asking if she could meet up with me today. I hoped she wouldn't mind too much when I asked her about Kyle.

"It's chilly out there," Chloe said as she shrugged out of her jacket when we reached the office.

I figured it was better to chat in there, out of earshot of anyone else.

"Let's get you something to warm you up." I hung her jacket on the coat stand in the corner. "Coffee?"

"Please." She rubbed her hands together.

"What about food?"

She considered the question for a second. "Those cinnamon pancakes I had a couple of weeks ago were amazing."

I took a step toward the door, intending to head for the kitchen.

"But," Chloe continued, "the pumpkin scones are incredible too. How do I decide?"

"I think I have a solution," I said with a smile.

I left her there in the office and made a quick trip to the kitchen. When I returned, I was carrying a mug of hot coffee with added cream and sugar for Chloe, a cup of tea for myself, and a small paper bag. Once I'd set my tea on the desk, I handed the coffee and the bag to Chloe.

"Two pumpkin scones to go. Ivan's cooking the pancakes as I speak."

A smile lit up her face. "You're the best, Marley."

"I hope your opinion's not about to change." I sat in one of the chairs in front of the desk and invited Chloe to take the other.

"Uh oh. What does that mean?" she asked, eyeing me with a mixture of curiosity and apprehension.

I decided not to beat around the bush. "I saw you and Kyle together at the Santa Shack last night."

Understanding dawned on her face. "I see. And now you want all the juicy details."

I was glad to see she was smiling, her eyes bright. "Guilty as charged."

"But why didn't you say hi?"

"I didn't want to interrupt you guys. You looked very...cozy."

A hint of pink showed on Chloe's cheeks. "That's not a bad way to describe it." She blew on her coffee before taking a sip.

"You know I'm dying here, right?" I said.

She gave me a wicked smile before taking another sip of coffee. "It was our third date," she said at last.

Words tumbled out of my mouth. "When was the first? How did this even happen? Have there always been sparks between you?"

Chloe laughed again. "Don't hold back with the questions or anything, Marley."

"Sorry," I said, only slightly contrite. "You know I can't help myself. I'm nosy by nature."

"To be fair, I'd be doing the same to you if our positions were reversed."

My gaze strayed to the door. "As much as I want to hear the answers to my questions, I'd better go check on our pancakes first."

I hurried to the kitchen, eager to get back to my conversation with Chloe. Within a couple of minutes, I'd returned to the office with a plate of cinnamon pancakes for each of us.

We immediately dug in. Chloe cut off a piece of pancake and sighed with happiness as she bit into it. I savored the first bite of my own pancakes, trying to be patient.

"To answer your questions," Chloe said finally, "we had our first date two weeks ago. I ended up on the side of the highway with a flat tire on my way home from work one day. Kyle was patrolling the area and stopped to help. He changed the tire for me and he called me later that day to make sure I'd made it home without any further mishaps."

"That was nice of him. Is that when he asked you out?" I considered another possibility. "Or did you ask him out?"

"He asked. And yes, it was during the phone call. It took me by surprise a bit, but I didn't hesitate when I said yes. To be honest, I'd never really thought about him in that way before."

"But now that you do...?"

Her cheeks turned pink again. "I don't want to jinx things, but so far things have been great."

I jumped up from my chair and gave her a one-armed hug while trying to keep my pancakes from sliding off the plate.

"I'm so happy for you."

Chloe hadn't always had the best relationships in the past, so I was glad she was seeing Kyle, who I knew was a really good guy. Chloe was one of the nicest people I'd ever met. She deserved someone who appreciated her.

"Don't get too carried away," she warned. "We've only had three dates."

"I know." I sat down again. "But I like that you're happy."

"So do I." She eyed me over her coffee cup as she took another sip. "I'm guessing Brett saw me with Kyle too."

"He didn't, but he knows that I did."

"He's not going to go all big brother on me, is he?" she asked with apprehension.

"I think I talked him out of that."

"Thank you," she said, relieved. "I love him, but I don't need him getting all overprotective."

I bit down on my lower lip. "Do you mind that we know?"

"Not at all. It's impossible to keep a secret for long in this town. And it's not like Kyle and I want to keep it a secret. We just wanted a chance to spend some time with each other before the whole town started gossiping about us."

"I understand completely. I'll keep my lips sealed." I pretended to zip them shut.

"You probably don't need to. If you saw me with Kyle, someone else who knows me probably did too. I'll tell my parents tonight. I'm sure they'd rather hear it from me than through the grapevine."

"They like Kyle, right?"

"I think so. They don't have any reason not to. They get along well with his parents too." She cut another piece off her stack of pancakes. "But enough about me. Have you solved the murder yet?"

"Not even close." I remembered something. "You said you know Rita's daughter, Zahra."

"Mmhmm," Chloe confirmed as she enjoyed a bite of pancake.

"Have you been in touch with her since Kevin's death?"

"Only to express my condolences, but I was planning to check in on her this weekend." She gave me a knowing look. "You're wondering if she knows anything about her stepfather's murder."

I gave her a sheepish smile. "I'm really predictable, aren't I?"

Laughter shone in her blue eyes. "When it comes to mysteries, anyway."

"So, do you think it's possible?" I asked after I finished off my tea. "I know she doesn't live at Holly Lodge full-time, and she arrived after we found Kevin's body, but could there still be a chance that she'd know something?"

Chloe thought for a second. "I guess she might know if Kevin had any trouble with someone."

"How did Zahra get along with Kevin?"

Chloe's gaze sharpened. "You don't think she could have killed him, do you? Zahra's not a killer, and you said yourself that she didn't arrive at Holly Lodge until after Kevin was dead."

"That's true." I hesitated, wondering if I should voice my thoughts. In the end, I went ahead. "I'm not saying Zahra did kill Kevin, but I saw her arrive at Holly Lodge, and she was acting like she didn't want anyone to see her."

Chloe set her empty plate on the desk and held her coffee mug in both hands. "I'm sure there's an innocent explanation. Besides, why would she not want to be seen arriving at the lodge after Kevin's death if she killed him? Wouldn't she want people to notice, so she'd look innocent?"

"Good point," I conceded.

Chloe was most likely right that Zahra had nothing to do with the murder, but I still couldn't help wondering why she'd acted sneaky when she arrived at Holly Lodge. I knew I might never find out, though. I tried not to let that irk me too much. I wasn't always good at letting go of unanswered questions.

"Do you have any plans to see Zahra soon?" I asked.

"Let me guess, you'd like a chance to talk to her."

"Not to accuse her of anything," I said quickly. "Just to see if she knows anything helpful. But I wouldn't want to upset her in any way."

"I know you wouldn't," Chloe said. "I think if we were straight with her, and told her you have a knack for solving mysteries, she'd probably be happy to talk to you."

"Really?" My hopes rose.

"I'll get in touch with her this weekend," Chloe promised. "Maybe she'll be willing to come down to Wildwood Cove. But I'm going to be completely honest about why I'm asking."

"That's a good idea. And if she doesn't want to talk to me, I totally understand."

Chloe took one last sip of coffee before setting her mug on her plate. "I'll text you as soon as I talk to her." She stood up. "Thanks for the food, Marley, and the company."

I got up and gave her a hug. "I'm glad you were able to come by. Any plans for the rest of the weekend?"

"Maybe," she said with a smile.

"Another date?" I figured that was a good guess.

"Kyle and I are going to the Festival of Trees later this afternoon." She paused for a second. "I guess that means I should go straight over to see my parents and tell them I'm dating him. Once we show up at the festival together, the whole town's going to know."

"That's true. The cat will definitely be out of the bag. And I might see you there. I'm hoping to stop by later."

I walked Chloe out and then returned to work, wondering if Zahra had some valuable information and if she'd be willing to share it.

Chapter Sixteen

After The Flip Side had closed for the day, I texted Brett to see if he was interested in going to the Festival of Trees with me. It was the first official day of the event, and although I'd already seen most of the trees, I still wanted to take in the holiday atmosphere and check out how everything had come together. Brett was working with Pedro's crew again, but he responded to my message within an hour. He wanted to go with me, so we arranged to meet at home shortly after five.

That gave me some time to kill, but I didn't mind. Bentley needed a walk, and I was craving some time on the beach. The weather was chilly once again, frost still visible in places, but I needed to breathe in some fresh air and listen to the waves breaking on shore. Sometimes I wondered how I'd managed to live so many years in the city, without spending time by the ocean on a daily basis. Living on the beach made me feel much more settled, more at peace. Of course, Brett and all the other great people in my life contributed to that as well. Moving to Wildwood Cove was the best thing I could have done. I'd never regretted the decision, not even for a second.

As soon as I got home, I let Bentley out the back door. He zoomed out onto the porch and down the steps to the yard, his tail wagging. Flapjack and I followed close behind him. Flapjack jumped up onto the porch railing and settled in to watch whatever birds might fly past. I tugged my hat down farther over my ears and zipped my jacket right up to the top. The tall, dry grass at the top of the beach bent and swayed in the cold breeze. Whitecaps topped the waves, although the ocean wasn't as turbulent as it could get sometimes. I couldn't see any boats out on the water. It wasn't exactly good weather for a pleasure cruise.

The tide was all the way in, so Bentley and I didn't have far to go to reach the water's edge. Once there, we headed east, Bentley switching between galloping along and stopping to sniff interesting smells. Every so often, I hopped up onto one of the logs that had been washed up on shore, balancing my way along it before jumping down again.

My eyes watered in the cold wind, and I was glad I'd remembered to wear a hat and gloves, but I had no desire to turn back and head home. Bentley and I walked almost all the way out to the eastern end of the cove. We remained there for a while as I tossed a stick to Bentley, making sure not to throw it into the water. He'd splashed in the shallows a couple of times, but even he seemed to find the water too cold.

Eventually, we headed back toward home, in no hurry. When we passed by the yellow and white Victorian where Patricia lived with her husband and Sienna, I slowed my steps. Rob Mazzoli was leaving the B&B through the back door, Patricia with him. They exchanged a few words that I couldn't hear, and then Patricia stepped back inside and shut the french doors. Rob jogged down the steps from the porch and strode across the yard toward the beach.

Rob was fairly new to Wildwood Cove, having moved here less than a year ago. He'd worked for a newspaper in Seattle until he'd decided he wanted a slower pace of life somewhere he could enjoy plenty of outdoor activities. Now he was the lead reporter for the local paper, the *Wildwood Cove Weekly.*

"Hey, Marley," he greeted when he saw me. "How's it going?"

"Things are good," I said. "How about you?"

Rob patted Bentley when the dog trotted up to greet him. "I can't complain, especially since I've got a new story to write."

"Something about the B&B?" I asked, wondering if that was why he'd paid Patricia a visit.

"A guest."

"Lily Spitz, the writer?" I figured that was a good guess, even though I didn't know anything about the other B&B guests—if there were any others at the moment.

"You know about her?" He didn't give me a chance to respond. "Right. Of course you do. You were both up at Holly Lodge when Kevin Manning was killed. Speaking of which…" He produced his phone from his pocket. "I was hoping to ask you a few questions about that. We reported the murder in this week's paper, and I'm working on a follow-up article for next week. I know you and Brett found the body," he continued, "so I was planning to pay you a visit anyway."

"Ask away," I said.

Although I wasn't eager to relive the details of finding Kevin's body, I wanted to cooperate with Rob. He was often a good source of information and I'd always known him to be respectful when interviewing me or any other locals.

He asked me several standard questions, and I answered as best I could while he recorded the conversation on his phone.

None of his questions took me by surprise until he asked, "Do you know of any reason why someone would target both Kevin Manning and Lily Spitz?"

"What?" I asked, shocked. "Is Lily okay?"

"She's fine. A little shaken up, maybe. That's the new story I'm working on. She received a threatening letter."

"From Kevin's killer?" I still hadn't recovered from my shock, although I was relieved to know that Lily hadn't been harmed.

"That hasn't been confirmed," Rob said. "But it seems likely."

"When did she receive the letter and what did it say?" I wasn't sure if he'd tell me, but I was glad when he did.

"She found it in her bag today after doing some shopping here in town. I guess you'd call it a note rather than a letter. All it said was, 'you're next.'"

I shivered, and not because of the cold wind. "That's scary." I thought over his words again. "But that really muddies the waters. I can think of a few people who might have had something against Kevin, but Kevin *and* Lily?"

"I know. It complicates things," Rob agreed. "That's why I was hoping you might have some insights."

"I wish I did. But as far as I know, the only person at the lodge who knew both Kevin and Lily before last week was Ambrose."

"That's what Lily said, and she was adamant that Ambrose would never hurt anyone, least of all her."

"They do seem to be in love with each other," I said.

"There's got to be another explanation then." Rob checked the time on his phone. "But for now, I've got to put together a story with what I do know. Good talking to you, Marley."

"You too," I said as he set off along the beach toward downtown Wildwood Cove.

I stayed put for a moment, wondering if I should head up to the B&B to talk with Lily and Patricia. Bentley sniffed around the base of a log while I considered my next move. In the end, I decided to head home. I definitely wanted to talk to Lily about the threatening note, but it would be better to go by the B&B when I didn't have Bentley with me, especially since his paws were currently covered with wet sand.

I let Bentley explore the interesting smells for another minute or two, and then we made our way home. I rinsed and dried Bentley's sandy paws before letting him into the house. Living on the beach meant it was inevitable that some sand would get tracked indoors, but I tried my best to keep it to a minimum. That wasn't always an easy task with a dog in the family.

Flapjack had remained on the porch the whole time we were gone, and he was more than happy to get back inside. Although he enjoyed getting some outdoor time each day, he wasn't a fan of cold weather.

I fed the animals their dinners and they were licking their dishes clean when Brett arrived home from work. He took a quick shower, and then we were off to the Festival of Trees.

It wasn't easy to find a parking spot in the center of town. We had to circle the block before we were able to nab a free space not too far down the street from the seniors' center. I figured the tree festival had drawn a lot of people into town that evening, but the light up was also happening that night. No doubt many people had decided to take in both events.

All of the hours that Patricia and the other volunteers had put into the festival had clearly paid off. With all the decorations now up, the twinkle lights on, and Christmas music playing softly in the background, there was a magical quality to the transformed seniors' center. It was easy to pretend that we were outdoors in a magical forest, except for the fact that it was nice and warm.

Several other people wandered the pathways, admiring the trees, but the room wasn't so crowded that we couldn't enjoy ourselves.

Brett and I held hands as we strolled through the room, taking time to appreciate each and every tree.

"I'm definitely voting for this one," Brett said when we stopped in front of The Flip Side's tree. "It's the best by far."

I smiled at him. "I think you're biased, but I won't stop you from voting."

"I might be biased, but I've also got good taste." He kissed me. "After all, I married you."

"Biased, but charming," I said, giving him a kiss in return.

"Hey, is this your tree, Marley?"

Brett and I turned around to find Chloe approaching us. Kyle was with her, his hand holding hers. They looked cute together, something I intended to tell Chloe the next time we were alone.

Brett and Kyle greeted each other as if nothing had changed. Even though Brett could get protective of Chloe now and then, I knew he didn't have a problem with her dating Kyle. In fact, he'd admitted to me just before we'd gone to sleep the night before that he was glad she was seeing someone we knew was a good guy.

"This is The Flip Side's tree," I confirmed.

"It's fantastic! The ornaments we made look super cute." Chloe fingered one of the glass sea creatures. "And these are beautiful."

"They were a good find," I said, pleased she liked the finished tree.

"You can count on my vote," she promised.

"I hear the two of you were in the middle of everything that happened up at Holly Lodge," Kyle said to me and Brett after I'd thanked Chloe.

"It wasn't quite the vacation we'd planned," Brett said. "We feel terrible for Kevin's family."

"Have you heard anything about the murder investigation?" I asked Kyle.

Kyle was a deputy here in Clallam County, but I figured he probably had an idea of what was going on in the other counties on the peninsula.

"I know there haven't been any arrests yet," Kyle said, "but these things take time."

"They're looking into several possible suspects," Chloe added, "but Kyle won't tell me who their prime suspect is." She tried to frown at him but didn't do a very good job of it.

Kyle grinned at her, and I could see in his eyes how much he liked Chloe.

"I don't know that they have one yet," he said.

"It sounds like Rita had the most to gain," Chloe said, keeping her voice low so no one would overhear. "But for Zahra's sake, I hope she had nothing to do with it." She fixed her gaze on me. "Any closer to figuring out whodunit, Marley?"

"I don't know what you're talking about," I said with feigned innocence. "I'm not one to speculate about murder investigations."

Brett and Kyle both laughed at that.

I jabbed an elbow into Brett's ribs. "You're not supposed to laugh *that* hard."

"Sorry." He didn't look very sorry as he slid an arm around my waist. "But you'll never fool anyone in this town."

"I know." I leaned into him. "But I really don't have a clue who the killer is."

"Sheriff Walczyk and her deputies will figure it out." There was only the slightest stern edge to Kyle's voice.

I wanted to ask him if he'd heard about the threatening note Lily had received, but we were all distracted by two boys and a little girl who barreled past us, heading for Santa's workshop in the next room.

The next second, an older couple caught Kyle's attention and drew him into a conversation with them.

Brett and I said goodbye to Chloe and continued on our circuit of the room. Once we'd checked out every single tree, Brett purchased some tickets from Sienna, who was dressed as an elf, and then we made our way around the room again as he chose which giveaways to enter. After he'd slipped all his tickets into giveaway boxes, he cast his vote for his favorite tree, making no secret of what he was writing on his ballot.

People were still arriving at the seniors' center, even though the festival would be shutting down for the night in another hour. Brett and I made our way through the growing crowd and out onto the street, where brisk, frosty air greeted us. We walked hand-in-hand over to Main Street, our breath forming white clouds in the night air. The crowds were even bigger in this part of town. Dozens of people had gathered on the sidewalks, waiting for the moment when all the lights on the streetlamps and trees would get switched on.

My stomach rumbled, reminding me that we hadn't yet eaten dinner. We planned to head over to the local pizza parlor after the light up, but to tide us over we bought cups of hot chocolate from a vendor on the street corner.

We waved at familiar faces and greeted friends and neighbors, but soon a hush fell over the crowd and Wildwood Cove's mayor led the countdown.

"Three, two, one!" everyone in the crowd counted together.

Then the lights flicked on and the street transformed from ordinary to beautiful.

Despite all that had happened at Holly Lodge the week before, in that moment I was filled with nothing but happiness and holiday spirit.

Chapter Seventeen

I left the pancake house shortly after closing the next day, after taking a moment to admire the Christmas tree in the corner. Brett had brought it over first thing in the morning and had helped me decorate it before The Flip Side opened. We'd had to decorate quickly, but I thought we'd still done a good job.

Lonny and Hope's open house was taking place that afternoon and evening, and Brett and I didn't want to miss it. Brett had the day off and had already taken Bentley for a long walk, so I didn't have to worry about that when I got home. Instead, I changed into a skirt and sweater and tidied up my hair. Brett was looking handsome in a dark blue suit and a brighter blue tie that matched the color of his eyes. It amazed me how he could still give me butterflies.

When we drove up the long driveway toward the Wildwood Inn, I admired the scenery. The inn was housed in a white Victorian mansion with covered porches and bay windows. Hope had grown up there, and she and Lonny had recently purchased the property from Hope's aunt. Brett had worked on the gardens back in the spring, getting them ready for the inn's grand opening and garden party. The gardens weren't in bloom at the moment, but the setting was still gorgeous, with the lawn stretching back to the woods.

Some of the daylight had already faded from the sky and the mansion's windows glowed with light. Several cars were parked next to the inn and I didn't doubt that more people would arrive over the next couple of hours. Lonny and Hope had many good friends in Wildwood Cove, and I knew I wasn't the only one who'd been looking forward to their holiday open house.

I admired the Victorian again after we climbed out of the truck and followed the path to the front steps. White lights outlined the windows and had been wrapped around the porch railing. A flocked pine wreath adorned the front door and small flames flickered inside candleholders made of ice that decorated the small tables on the porch.

Brett and I greeted Lonny and Hope in the spacious foyer. We handed over the box of chocolates we'd brought as a gift, and Lonny took our coats while Hope walked with us to the dining room, situated to the left of the foyer. The chairs had been removed from beneath the long dining table, which held an impressive spread of finger foods.

I waved to Marielle, who owned the local bakery. She looked festive in a red dress with holly earrings as she added a mini quiche to her plate. A middle-aged man and woman were also in the dining room.

"Hope, this is incredible," I said. "Did you make all the food?"

"Most of it. I bought the sausage rolls, and the macarons and the butter tarts are courtesy of Marielle."

Marielle smiled and tucked a lock of dark hair behind her ear. "Make sure you try Hope's artichoke dip," she said to me and Brett. "It's divine."

The front door opened, heralding the arrival of more guests. Hope excused herself and went to greet them.

I hadn't realized I was hungry until I took in the sight of all the tempting food. Brett and I each took a small plate from the stack at one end of the table. Then we slowly made our way around it, adding things to our plates here and there while we chatted with Marielle.

Once we had our plates filled, we drifted across the foyer to the parlor. I dipped a cracker in the scoop of artichoke dip I'd put on my plate and took a bite.

"Wow. This dip really is amazing." I swiped another cracker through it.

"I need to get the recipe from Hope," Marielle said. "I'm crossing my fingers that it's not a family secret."

"I'd like the recipe too." I'd already finished most of the dip on my plate and I knew I'd be heading back for seconds before long.

"Check out that tree," Brett said.

Now that we were in the parlor, we could see a large Christmas tree standing in one corner. It had to be at least ten feet tall, and it almost reached the high ceiling. It was decked out in vintage Christmas ornaments and red and green lights.

"I love it," I said, impressed. "Hope," I called, grabbing her attention as she came into the room. "You should have entered a tree in the festival. This one is gorgeous."

She smiled, clearly pleased. "Thank you. Maybe I'll have a chance to enter one next Christmas. I didn't have the time this year."

"I can understand that," I said, thinking of all the work she must have done to get ready for this party while also looking after the guests staying at the inn.

She and Lonny had opened the place for business less than a year ago, but the inn had already proven popular with tourists, even during the quieter seasons.

Brett and I wandered around, chatting with people we knew as we munched on our finger foods, all of which were delicious. The guests were spread out over three rooms—the dining room, the front parlor, and the library. Leigh was there with her husband, Greg, having left their three daughters in the care of their grandmother, and I made sure to say hello to them.

After I'd finished all the food on my plate, I left Brett chatting with someone he knew through his work with Pedro and returned to the dining room. I was hoping to get more of the artichoke dip and to sample a few other goodies I hadn't yet tried. There were about half a dozen people in the dining room now, mostly standing and chatting around the edges of the room.

One man was at the table, adding food to his plate.

"Hi, Mr. Teeves," I said as I joined him by the table. "How are you doing?"

Gerald Teeves lived next door to me, with his teenage son, Logan. We weren't exactly friends, but we'd become more neighborly with each other over time.

"Can't complain," he said as he added two mini sausage rolls to his plate. "How's business at the pancake house?"

"It's going well, thanks," I said. I spooned some artichoke dip onto my plate and added a few crackers.

Teeves was in the real estate business, and I wondered if he knew anything about Wilson. I figured there was a good chance that he did.

"Do you know Wilson Gerrard?" I asked casually as I selected a red macaron from a plate.

"Sure," he said. "How do you know him?"

"Brett and I met him last week when we were on vacation up in the mountains."

Teeves nodded as he chewed on a sausage roll. "I know he's done some work up there, tearing down ratty old cabins and putting up chalets for vacationers. That's what he's into, mostly—building vacation rentals."

I sampled a mini cheese ball on a pretzel stick. It was loaded with delicious flavor. "I think he was hoping to buy the lodge where we were staying, but the owners weren't interested in selling."

Teeves spooned a generous dollop of dip onto his plate. "I bet Wilson was a thorn in their side then."

"Why do you say that?" I asked with interest.

"Wilson doesn't like not getting what he wants. It's good to be tenacious in our line of business, but he takes it a bit farther than most."

I thought the same could have been said of Teeves, although I didn't voice that opinion. As soon as he'd found out that I'd inherited my cousin Jimmy's Victorian, he'd hounded me to sell it, even though my grief was still fresh and raw at that point. It hadn't endeared me to him.

Teeves moved down the table and added an assortment of gingerbread, shortbread, and thumbprint cookies to his plate. "You don't by any chance mean that lodge where the owner was killed, do you?"

"Holly Lodge," I said with a nod. "It's very sad."

"I know the place." He seemed to have heard only the first part of what I'd said. "Nice parcel of land right on the lake. Underutilized. I can see why Wilson wants it."

I didn't exactly agree that it was underutilized. For those who wanted peace and quiet without crowds, Holly Lodge was perfect in its current state. It didn't surprise me that Teeves didn't view it that way, though.

"I think he's going to continue to be disappointed," I said. "Rita, the surviving owner, has no intention of selling, as I understand it."

"I wouldn't be so sure." Teeves bit into a cookie. "Wilson has a habit of doing whatever it takes to get his way."

Chapter Eighteen

Teeves headed out of the dining room, his plate full. It took me a moment to shake off the conversation. It had upset me when Teeves had bugged me about selling my house right after Jimmy's death. If Wilson intended to hound Rita so soon after Kevin's murder, I couldn't help but feel that was disrespectful. Although, he hadn't seemed to be hounding her the morning Brett and I left the lodge. In fact, Rita had appeared to be equally involved in their conversation.

I still wanted to know what they'd been discussing. Maybe Zahra would know. Chloe had texted me earlier to let me know that Zahra had agreed to accompany her to the open house. After I'd filled my plate with more crackers and some gingerbread, I wandered down the hall to the library. When I poked my head in the room, I waved at a couple of familiar faces, but Chloe and Zahra weren't among them. Hopefully they'd arrive before too long.

I retraced my steps to the foyer, where I met up with Brett.

"I need a refill," he said, holding up his empty plate.

I followed him into the dining room. I had enough food on my plate, but I was getting thirsty. While Brett selected several items from the buffet, I filled two glasses with cranberry punch. I handed one to Brett when he reached my side, and we headed back to the parlor together.

Four young girls, ranging in age from about eight to eleven, stood by the big Christmas tree, admiring it with wide eyes. I recognized two of the girls from the first day I'd worked on my tree at the seniors' center. They'd also been at the Christmas tree farm the other night. One was Emily, but I didn't know the name of her dark-haired friend.

Brett and I spent several minutes chatting with Leigh and Greg before they got involved in a conversation with one of their neighbors. The front door opened and I heard a familiar voice out in the foyer.

I wandered over that way in time to see Hope taking Chloe's and Zahra's coats. I hung back, not wanting to pounce on them as soon as they'd come in the door. As Hope disappeared with their coats, Chloe and Zahra moved into the dining room. A few minutes later, they arrived in the parlor. Chloe had a plate of food, but Zahra had only a glass of cranberry punch.

"Oh my gosh. This food is amazing!" Chloe gushed as they met up with us by the green-tiled Victorian fireplace. She had several items on her plate, including a macaron with a bite out of it, a cheese ball, and some crackers and artichoke dip. "You should try some, Zahra."

"I will later," Zahra said. "I made the mistake of eating a late lunch, so I'm not hungry at the moment."

I smiled at her. "Definitely a mistake. How are you doing?"

"Not too bad, considering. It's been a difficult week, but I'm glad I've been able to stay at the lodge with my mom. I took a couple of weeks off work, so I don't need to head back to Seattle for a while yet."

"How's Rita holding up?" Brett asked.

Zahra swirled the punch in her half-filled glass. "She's devastated, but she's also very strong. I know she'll pull through okay."

"Do you have guests at the lodge right now?" I thought it would be extra stressful for Rita if she had to deal with that. Ambrose and Lily had left shortly after we had, and Wilson had planned to check out soon, but I didn't know if new guests had arrived since our departure.

"Not now," Zahra replied, "but we did up until yesterday because we couldn't give them enough notice to cancel. We had to offer refunds to the ones we canceled on for this coming week. Starting next Monday we'll be back to normal operations, but we wanted some time to ourselves."

"That's good that you did that," Chloe said. "You both need time."

Zahra looked down at her glass for a second. She'd yet to take a sip of her punch. "We're having a memorial next weekend. You're all welcome to attend, but I totally understand if you can't. It's not the most convenient location for everyone."

"Is it at Holly Lodge?" Chloe asked.

Zahra nodded. "It seemed right to do that. We'll have a short service and a reception inside, but we thought the best way to honor Kevin was to do something he loved—play hockey out on the lake."

"He was a hockey player?" Brett asked with interest.

"He started when he was five and played all the way through college," Zahra said, a faint smile appearing on her face. "Every winter he'd get friends together and have games on the lake. It'll be weather permitting this time, of course, but the forecast looks promising."

Brett sent an unspoken question my way. Understanding just by meeting his gaze, I nodded.

"Marley and I will come," Brett said. "And I'd love to join the hockey game."

Zahra's face brightened. "Thank you. My mom and I would love for you guys to be there."

"I'd like to come too," Chloe said. "When will it be?"

"Next Saturday, starting at eleven in the morning."

Chloe nudged Brett's arm. "Can I get a ride up with you guys?"

"For a price," Brett said.

This time Chloe jabbed him with her elbow. All that did was make Brett grin.

"Of course you can," I told her.

"I'm not much of a hockey player," Chloe said to Zahra. "But I can skate. I took figure skating lessons for a few years when I was growing up."

"Really?" I said with surprise. "I didn't know that." I knew Brett had played hockey while in elementary and middle school, but I'd never heard about Chloe's figure skating.

Chloe shrugged. "I wasn't very good, and I stopped taking lessons once I got to high school."

"She was better than she's letting on," Brett said.

"Well, I definitely won't be any use in the hockey game," I said. "I can stay on my feet on skates—most of the time—but that's about the best I can do."

"Don't worry," Zahra assured me. "Playing in the hockey game isn't required. With the other friends and neighbors who will be there, I think we'll be able to get two teams together."

Zahra finally took a drink of her punch, draining most of it in one go. When she spoke again, she'd lowered her voice. "Marley, Chloe tells me you've solved murders in the past."

"I might have had a hand in solving a couple," I said.

Chloe shook her head. "Don't listen to her. She's downplaying her accomplishments. She's been instrumental in closing several cases."

Brett put a hand to my lower back. "It's true."

"I think you're both biased," I said to Chloe and Brett before addressing Zahra. "But I'll do my best to figure out who killed Kevin, if you don't mind."

"I don't mind at all," Zahra assured me. "All I know is that my mom didn't kill him. The cops grilled her, and I get that they had to, but it's made a tough situation even more difficult for her."

"Is Rita getting out and about at all?" I asked, thinking about the threatening note and wondering if Rita had an opportunity to deliver it to Lily here in Wildwood Cove.

"No," Zahra replied. "I invited her to come here, but she wanted to stay home. Aside from a trip to the sheriff's office, she hasn't left the lodge." She paused to drink the last of her punch. "I hope the sheriff won't question her again. Mom and Kevin had their problems, but she never would have hurt him. She's really torn up about his death. She doesn't let on in front of others, but when it's just the two of us, she breaks down."

Zahra's eyes had become misty. She blinked away the threatening tears.

Chloe put a hand on her arm. "I'm so sorry, Zahra."

Zahra nodded and cleared her throat as she leveled her gaze at me. "Chloe said you might have some questions."

I was glad she'd been the one to take the conversation in that direction.

I considered where to start. "Do you know of anyone who might have wanted to hurt Kevin? Anyone he had trouble with?"

"Sheriff Walczyk asked me that too," Zahra said. "I've been thinking and thinking about it. I know Kevin didn't like the real estate developer, Wilson Gerrard, hounding him about selling Holly Lodge, and he had problems with a neighbor when he lived here in Wildwood Cove."

"Dwight Zalecki," I supplied.

"That's right. But I don't know that either man would have wanted to kill Kevin. It's just so...extreme. But who else could it have been if not one of those two?"

"One of the guests?" I suggested. "Or someone who works at the lodge?"

"I don't see why any of the guests would have had a motive to kill him. Same with Cindy, the lodge's chef. And Harvey...I've known him for years. I really hope it wasn't him." Zahra stared into her empty punch glass.

"But you don't know for sure?" Chloe asked, picking up on the same hint of uncertainty as I had.

Zahra bit down on her lower lip. "Up until recently I would have said no way, because Harvey and Kevin were friends. But lately...things were a bit strained between them."

I recalled what Harvey had told us. "Because Harvey said he'd leave if Kevin went ahead with expanding the lodge?"

"Yes," Zahra confirmed. "But Harvey loves Holly Lodge as much as we do. I don't think he'd really leave."

If that was true, maybe it strengthened Harvey's motive. If he loved Holly Lodge that much, he really could have been willing to kill Kevin to stop the expansion.

"Who does your mom think killed Kevin?" I asked.

"Someone not connected to the lodge. Like Dwight, or some transient. I hope she's right. It's bad enough that Kevin was murdered. If the killer is someone we know, that'll be another blow."

I wondered how Zahra would react to my next question. "I saw you when you arrived at Holly Lodge last weekend. I got the sense you were trying to get inside unseen. Is that true?"

Zahra seemed surprised at first, but to my relief, she smiled a second later. "You're right. I didn't want my mom to see me because I had her birthday present still in the bag from her favorite store in Seattle."

It was an innocent explanation, and I thought she was telling the truth.

"She's a great amateur detective, but that means she has a suspicious nature," Chloe said with a smile.

"Sorry," I apologized to Zahra.

"Don't worry about it." She didn't seem bothered.

My thoughts circled back to Harvey.

"I don't suppose I'll have a chance to talk with Harvey anytime soon," I said, more to myself than the others.

"He comes down to Port Angeles once a week," Zahra said. "He picks up supplies and he always has lunch at the same fish and chips place. Do you know The Codfather?"

It was impossible to forget that name. "I've been there a couple of times."

"They have some of the best fish and chips on the peninsula," Brett added.

"And the coleslaw!" Chloe sighed happily. "So good!"

"The coleslaw's my favorite," Zahra agreed. "Anyway, Harvey goes there every Tuesday at one o'clock. That's his day off, and he's a predictable man."

Maybe not entirely predictable, if he'd snapped in anger and had killed Kevin.

More guests had arrived while we talked, and it was getting harder to keep our conversation private.

I decided to get in another question while I still could. "On our last morning at the lodge, your mom was talking with Wilson Gerrard. It sounded like a business discussion, but I thought your mom wasn't interested in selling Holly Lodge."

"She's not." Zahra sounded completely certain. "My mom owns another piece of property farther up the mountain. It's lakefront property too. She's been thinking about selling it, possibly to Wilson."

A woman with gray hair came over and put an arm around Zahra's shoulders. "Zahra, honey, I was so sorry to hear about Kevin."

Chloe, Brett, and I shifted away to give them some privacy. I side-stepped to make way for Emily and her dark-haired friend as they darted past us, giggling and heading for the dining room.

"What do you think?" Chloe whispered to me once the two young girls were gone.

"She'll be having fish and chips on Tuesday," Brett said with a grin.

"That's the plan," I agreed.

Brett put an arm around my waist. "I'll come with you. I don't like the idea of you meeting up with a potential killer on your own."

I kissed him on the cheek. "I'm not about to turn down your company."

Brett took my empty glass from me. "More punch?"

"Please."

He disappeared into the growing crowd.

I hooked my arm through Chloe's. "No Kyle today?"

"He's working, but we're having dinner together sometime this week."

"How did your parents react when you told them about the two of you?"

Chloe's smile lit up her whole face. "My dad was good about it, and my mom was really excited. She thinks Kyle's great."

"And so do you."

Her smile grew even brighter. "I can't deny it."

Brett returned with our refilled glasses and Chloe slipped away to get some more food. Brett and I chatted with a few of the other guests and time passed quickly. Eventually, we made another trip to the dining room. Brett took a butter tart while I made a beeline for the crackers and artichoke dip. This time, I also took some brie cheese to eat with my crackers.

It was completely dark outside now, and the Christmas lights glowed cheerily around the windows and along the porch railing. As I wandered back into the parlor again, a miniature Christmas village caught my eye. It was set out on the top of an antique barrister's bookcase, near the Christmas tree. I made my way around a group of guests chatting in the middle of the room, hoping to get a closer look at the village.

Before I got there, something else stole my attention.

Emily stood by the Christmas tree, on her own now. As I drew closer, she unhooked a small nutcracker ornament from a branch and tucked it into the pocket of her dress.

Chapter Nineteen

Emily slipped out of the room and disappeared from sight. I hesitated, not knowing what to do. Brett was chatting with one of the clients of his lawn and garden business, so I didn't interrupt him to ask for his input. I decided I needed to do *something*, but I hoped I could tread carefully.

I stopped by the dining room to set my empty glass on a tray that had been set out for that purpose. I left my empty plate behind as well, after munching on my remaining crackers and brie cheese. Not seeing Emily in the parlor or dining room, I set off down the hall to the library.

On my way, I tried to remember Emily's last name. Jensen? No, that wasn't quite right. A second later it came to me—Jessen. And her mother's name was Johanna.

The library wasn't as crowded as the parlor and dining room. Lonny was there, chatting with a young couple I'd seen around town but didn't know. The other occupants of the room were all children, seated around two small tables playing board games. Emily sat at one of the tables, watching three other girls playing Snakes and Ladders. All four girls appeared to be about eight years old.

"Emily?" I said as I approached the table. "My name's Marley. Can I talk to you for a moment?"

She hesitated, and I couldn't blame her since I was a stranger to her.

"It's about the nutcracker," I added.

Her blue eyes widened with fear.

"You're not in trouble," I rushed to assure her. "I just want to talk about it."

Emily slid off her chair with reluctance, darting a glance at the other girls. They were so engrossed in their game that they didn't pay us any attention.

We stayed in the library, but I kept my voice low so no one would overhear me.

"That nutcracker isn't yours, is it?"

Emily shook her head, tears pooling in her eyes. "Please don't tell my mom."

"I don't think that will be necessary," I said with a pang of sympathy for the girl. "But you need to put the ornament back on the tree, okay?"

She took the small nutcracker from her pocket and stared down at it as she nodded.

"Have you taken any other decorations?" I asked.

She wouldn't meet my gaze. "Just this one."

"What about from other trees?" I prodded, pretty sure I knew the answer.

A tear escaped from her eye. "A few others," she whispered.

"Emily?" Johanna Jessen appeared so suddenly that Emily and I were both startled.

"Hi, Mrs. Jessen. I'm Marley Collins," I said when Johanna focused on me.

I was about to say more when the woman's gaze latched onto the nutcracker in her daughter's hand.

"Where did you get that?" she asked.

Emily stared at her shiny black shoes. "I took it from Mr. and Mrs. Baron's tree," she confessed before I had a chance to intervene.

The color drained from Johanna's already pale complexion. "Why? Please tell me you weren't planning to keep it."

Emily's face crumpled and more tears trickled down her face.

Johanna took Emily's arm and steered her out into the hall. I followed after them.

"I'm sorry," I said, feeling terrible even though I knew it was wrong for Emily to take what wasn't hers. "I saw Emily take the ornament and was hoping to get her to put it back."

"It's not your fault. She knows better," Johanna said before speaking to her daughter again. "Did you take anything else?"

"Not from this tree," Emily whispered.

"You mean you've taken things from *other* trees?" Johanna closed her eyes briefly. "Oh no. I heard about the thefts at the Festival of Trees. Please tell me you weren't behind them."

Emily gripped the nutcracker more tightly, crying silently.

Johanna drew in a deep breath.

"Put it back *exactly* where you found it," Johanna said.

Emily was still crying, but without making a sound. She did as she was told, heading along the hall to the parlor. We followed and watched from the foyer as Emily hung the nutcracker on the same branch she'd taken it from.

"You know it's wrong to steal," Johanna said in a low voice when Emily had rejoined us. "What were you thinking?"

Emily sniffed and wiped at the tears that continued to fall down her cheeks. My heart went out to her. Luckily, no one else seemed to have noticed what was going on. All the other guests were too engrossed in their conversations.

"Daddy didn't let us take our Christmas decorations when we moved," Emily said in a small voice. "Not even my favorite nutcrackers."

Johanna's face fell and her shoulders slumped. "Oh, honey."

"We didn't have anything to put on our tree this year," Emily continued. "I wanted to decorate it, to surprise you. I thought if I borrowed some ornaments, maybe no one would notice, and I could put them back later."

"How would you return them without anyone noticing?" Johanna asked.

Emily shrugged and stared at her feet.

Johanna crouched down so she was on Emily's level. "Honey, I'm so sorry about everything that happened between me and your daddy. It wasn't you he was trying to keep the decorations and everything else from, it was me."

Emily didn't raise her head. "It was still mean."

Johanna sighed heavily, and I suspected that the fallout from her divorce weighed heavily on her.

"I appreciate that you wanted to surprise me," she told her daughter, "but stealing is wrong."

Emily nodded. "I'm sorry."

"How did you get the ornaments from the festival?" I asked, unable to keep my curiosity in check. "Patricia Murray thought they were taken after hours."

Johanna's gaze sharpened as she refocused on her daughter. "Emily?"

"Those times I said I was playing with my friends?" she said. "I really went to get the ornaments. After I saw Mrs. Murray leave each day, I went in through a basement window."

"Did you break the window?" Johanna's tone was stern.

Emily's eyes widened and she shook her head vigorously. "No! I swear! It wasn't locked." She drew her hands up inside the sleeves of her dress. "It was really scary, but I had that flashlight that's hooked onto the zipper of my coat."

Johanna nodded, somewhat absently. I could tell she had a lot of thoughts swirling about in her head.

Worry practically radiated from Emily's wide eyes. "Will I go to jail?"

Johanna let out another sigh and straightened up, resting a hand on Emily's shoulder. "You won't go to jail," she assured her daughter. "But you're going to return every single ornament that you took and you'll apologize to each person you stole from. Understand?"

Emily nodded, lowering her gaze again.

Johanna turned to me. "Thank you so much for bringing this to light."

"I'm sorry for spoiling your evening," I said.

"Please, don't be." She took Emily's hand. "Let's go home and you can show me where you hid the ornaments."

As she and Emily headed down the hall to fetch their coats, I hung back, my heart aching.

"There you are," Brett said as he emerged from the parlor. "You okay?" He put an arm around me and rubbed my back.

I leaned into him. "I'm all right."

Several people passed us on their way to the dining room, so I didn't say anything more. I didn't want to tell him what had happened with Emily until we were alone. It was almost impossible to keep secrets in Wildwood Cove, but I didn't want to be the one responsible for broadcasting Emily's mistakes.

We went in search of Hope and Lonny so we could say thank you and let them know we were leaving. Then we said goodbye to everyone else we knew before pulling on our coats and heading home.

* * * *

"I feel bad for both of them," I said to Brett later that evening.

I'd told him about Emily and Johanna on the drive home, and now we were in the front living room of our house, getting ready to decorate the Christmas tree we'd just brought inside. It stood majestically in the corner, its fresh scent filling the room.

"Sounds like they've been through a lot in the past year." Brett opened one of the boxes we'd hauled down from the attic.

"They have." I pulled a string of lights out of the box he'd opened and plugged it into an electrical socket. All but one bulb lit up.

Brett dug around and came up with a box of replacement bulbs. He handed me a green one.

I switched the bulbs and Brett passed me a second string to test. Fortunately, all the lights on that one worked.

I carried the lights over to the tree. "I hope they're able to have a good Christmas."

Brett came up behind me and wrapped his arms around my waist. "Johanna sounds like a good woman," he said. "I'm sure the two of them will be okay."

"You're right." I gazed up at the tree, deciding to focus on the moment. "We really picked out a beautiful Christmas tree."

Brett gave me an affectionate squeeze. "Three beautiful trees."

He turned me toward him and I set the strings of lights on a nearby chair so I could put my arms around him.

He kissed me. "Beautiful trees, beautiful house, beautiful life, beautiful wife."

"And a very charming, very handsome husband," I added.

We kissed again, only breaking apart when Bentley trotted in from the other room and nosed his way between us.

We laughed and patted him while his tail wagged happily.

Once Bentley was satisfied that we'd given him enough attention, he sniffed at the tree and pushed his way through the lower branches to get into the corner behind it.

"Easy there," Brett said, putting out a hand to steady the tree as it rocked in its stand.

Bentley lay down beneath the tree and rested his head on his front paws.

I grabbed my phone and snapped a picture of him. When Flapjack joined him under the tree a moment later, I took a few more photos and uploaded the best of them to my social media accounts. They were too cute not to share.

With the animals snoozing peacefully, Brett and I got back to work, trimming the tree while Christmas music played in the background.

"I talked to Ray this morning," Brett said as he hung a snowflake ornament on a high branch. "I meant to tell you earlier, but I forgot."

"Does he know something about Kevin's murder?" I asked, hopeful.

As the sheriff of Clallam County, maybe Brett's uncle Ray knew more than Kyle did.

"He knows Dwight Zalecki was a suspect. Sheriff Walczyk has been in touch with Ray, since Dwight lives in his jurisdiction."

"*Was* a suspect?" I asked, not failing to notice his use of the past tense.

Brett grinned and hung a shiny blue bauble on a branch. "I knew you'd catch that."

I poked him in the side before adding a cute owl ornament to the tree. "Dish the details, please."

"Was a suspect," he confirmed. "Apparently he's got an alibi."

"Really?"

"You don't sound convinced."

"It's not so much that…" I said.

Brett grinned again. "It's painful for you not to know all the details, isn't it?"

I glared at him. "Are you holding back?"

"Would I do that?" he asked with mock innocence.

"Drive me crazy, you mean?" I poked him in the ribs again. "Yes!"

He took my hand and pulled me closer to him. "I drive you crazy?"

I put a hand on his chest and tried not to smile in response to the humor in his blue eyes. "Usually in the best possible way. But in this case…"

"Okay. I won't keep you in suspense any longer." He gave me a quick kiss. "Remember how Lonny mentioned that Dwight's truck had more problems than the cracked windshield?"

"Yes." I got back to hanging ornaments on the tree.

"Apparently he was staying at Rustling Pines, another lodge up in the mountains, doing some ice fishing. His truck broke down and he was stuck there for a couple of days, until someone was able to come and help him get it running again."

"And he was stuck there at the time Kevin was killed?" I guessed.

"Exactly. And," he added just as I was about to ask another question, "Rustling Pines is at least ten miles away from Holly Lodge, and its owner attested to the fact that Dwight never left while his truck was out of commission."

He'd answered my question before I'd even asked it. "You read my mind," I told him.

"What can I say? I know you well."

I sent him a sidelong glance. "Are you implying that I'm predictable?"

"Only where your curiosity is concerned."

I had to smile at that. "Fair enough."

Thanks to Brett's information, I could cross one name off my suspect list. Dwight's supposed motive had never been all that strong, anyway. If he'd wanted to kill Kevin because of their neighborly disputes in the past, he likely would have done so a long time ago.

Striking Dwight off my list still left me with several potential culprits. Hopefully I'd get a chance to talk with Harvey in a couple of days. In the meantime, maybe I could find out more about the threatening note Lily had received.

That would have to wait until tomorrow, at the earliest. Right now, I wanted to enjoy my time with Brett.

When we finished decorating the tree, Brett put an arm across my shoulders and we admired our work.

"It looks fantastic," I said.

"It does, but there's one more thing we need." He dropped his arm from my shoulders and disappeared out of the room.

"I'm not sure there's room for more decorations on the tree," I called after him.

"It's not for the tree." Brett was grinning when he reappeared, and I soon realized why.

"You think of everything," I said with approval as he pinned a sprig of mistletoe to the top of the doorway that led to the foyer.

He took my hand and drew me in close so we were both standing beneath the mistletoe. "The most important things, anyway."

I put my arms around his neck. "This will be our first Christmas as a married couple."

"The first of many," he said, looking into my eyes. "I love you, Marley."

"I love you too."

When he kissed me, I forgot about everything except the two of us.

Chapter Twenty

The next morning Brett drove to Port Townsend to help a buddy install some shelving units in his garage. That same friend, a plumber, had promised to help Brett with the plumbing for our new bathroom. Since I had nothing planned for the day, I texted Patricia, asking if she wanted to go for a walk. I wanted some company, and I also wanted to talk to her about the note Lily had received.

It didn't take long for Patricia to reply with an affirmative response. I told her I'd be by her place soon, and got bundled up. The sun shone brightly down from the blue sky, but I could see frost out on the porch and the trees were swaying in the wind. A quick glance at the weather app on my phone confirmed that it was another chilly day outside.

Bentley didn't seem to mind. He charged out the door as soon as I opened it. I tucked his leash into my coat pocket and gave Flapjack a quick pat on the head. He was quite content to stay at home, curled up on an armchair.

A few brave birds explored the shoreline, and I spotted two people out walking their dogs closer to town. Otherwise, we had the beach to ourselves. I wasn't surprised that more people weren't out and about. As fresh as the air was, it had an icy nip to it that was already biting at my cheeks.

I zipped my jacket up higher as Bentley and I headed along the beach to Patricia's yellow and white Victorian. Sienna was at school and Patricia had told me via text that she'd already served her B&B guests breakfast. I assumed that Lily would be off doing something around town, perhaps spending time with Ambrose, but when I climbed the steps to Patricia's back porch, I spotted the author at the dining table.

Patricia greeted me at the french doors. "Come on in, Marley. I just need to grab my coat."

I told Bentley to lie down and wait, and he did so with only a tiny whimper.

"I won't be long," I promised him before stepping into the warm kitchen.

Lily had a laptop open on the table in front of her.

"Getting some writing done?" I guessed as Patricia headed off toward the front of the house.

"I'm hoping to," Lily said. "Patricia was kind enough to allow me to work here."

Patricia reappeared, pulling on a coat. "It's really no problem. And help yourself to tea or coffee, if you like."

Lily thanked her.

I rested my hand on the doorknob, but made no move to turn it. "I heard about the note you received. That must have been frightening."

"Oh." Lily seemed taken aback. She probably didn't realize how fast news traveled in Wildwood Cove. Rob's article wouldn't be published for another couple of days. "Yes. It certainly was upsetting."

"Any idea who's behind it?" I asked.

"None at all." Lily kept her gaze on the screen of her laptop.

Patricia zipped up her jacket, but she didn't seem impatient to get going. She probably knew I wanted to ask Lily more questions.

"Do you still have it?" I asked. "Would it be okay if I took a look at it?"

Lily frowned, and I wondered if I was being too pushy.

"I guess so," she said after a moment.

She reached down to a tote bag on the floor by her chair. She rummaged through it for a few seconds before pulling out a piece of white paper that was folded in half.

When she handed it over, I took it without thinking. It was a good thing I was wearing gloves, I realized as I unfolded the paper. I didn't want to add more fingerprints than Lily already had.

As Rob from the *Wildwood Cove Weekly* had told me, the note contained only two words—"you're next." The letters had been typed on a computer, and they looked tiny on the page. Their message, however, had a big impact. Even though the words weren't directed at me, reading them left me feeling uneasy.

"Why would anyone have something against both you and Kevin Manning?" I asked as I handed the paper back to Lily.

She stuffed it into her bag, making me wince. I hoped she wasn't damaging evidence.

"I can't even imagine," she said.

There was an edge of impatience to her voice, probably because I was keeping her from her writing. Or maybe she just didn't like my nosiness. Still, I couldn't bring myself to stop questioning her.

"Wasn't Ambrose the only one who knew both you and Kevin before you stayed at Holly Lodge?"

"Yes." She raised her gaze to meet mine. "But I can assure you that Ambrose had nothing to do with this or Kevin's murder. Ambrose would never hurt me. Or anyone."

That echoed what she'd told Rob.

Outside the french doors, Bentley sat up and let out a whine of impatience. I didn't want to leave him alone out there much longer, but I still had another question for Lily.

"Have you shown the note to Sheriff Walczyk?"

"The sheriff?" Lily seemed surprised by the question.

"That would probably be a good idea," Patricia said. "In case it's related to the murder."

A hint of pink showed on Lily's cheeks. "I'm sure it's not related. Honestly, it's probably just one of my readers trying to get my attention. Most of my fans are wonderful, but there's always one or two slightly unhinged people in every group."

That was probably true, but I wasn't convinced that the threat had come from a fan.

"I heard you found the note in your bag. Is that right? Could it have been there since before you left the lodge?" I asked.

"It was in my bag," Lily confirmed. "It definitely wasn't there before I came to Wildwood Cove. Someone must have put it in my bag while I was shopping the other day. A couple of the stores were quite crowded with holiday shoppers. I'm sure that's when it must have happened."

"That's scary. That means whoever wrote the note was in close proximity to you at some point." I didn't understand why she wasn't more frightened.

"It's unnerving," Lily admitted. "But if someone really wanted to harm me, they could have done so when they put the note in my bag. I really don't think I have anything to worry about."

I wasn't sure I agreed with her. Maybe the writer of the note wanted her to suffer psychologically before he or she struck out in a physical way. And I still wasn't buying the crazed fan theory, especially considering the wording of the note.

"I really do think you should show it to Sheriff Walczyk," I said.

Lily forced a thin smile. "You're probably right. I'll get in touch with her." She had her gaze fixed on her laptop again. She clearly wanted our conversation to be over.

Patricia exchanged a glance with me before saying, "We'll leave you to your writing."

She and I stepped outside, much to Bentley's delight. As we headed down toward the beach, he raced off ahead of us, bounding over a sun-bleached log and startling a seagull. The gull flapped into the air and flew away.

"Why would an unhinged fan say 'you're next'?" Patricia asked as we set off along the shoreline. "That sounds like something already happened to someone else."

"Exactly," I said. "I suppose it could be someone who's been targeting other authors as well, but I don't like the timing of it."

Patricia frowned. "Someone put that note in her bag while she was here in our town."

I glanced her way. "You're worried that Kevin's killer could be in Wildwood Cove," I guessed.

"It's a frightening thought."

I couldn't disagree with that.

"It also complicates things," I said.

"Because you don't know of anyone who would want to harm both Kevin and Lily?"

I nodded. "It doesn't make any sense."

"Maybe it only makes sense to the killer," Patricia said. "I really hope he or she will be arrested soon. I'm sure it must be tough for Rita, not knowing who killed Kevin."

"An arrest would definitely be a good thing," I agreed. "Are you going to Kevin's memorial service?"

"I was hoping to, but we have guests at the B&B on the weekend and John will be out of town for work. Are you going?"

I tossed a stick for Bentley and he raced after it. "We're planning on it. Chloe, too. She knows Rita's daughter, Zahra."

We continued along the beach, the frothy waves breaking rhythmically against the shore.

"Speaking of mysteries," Patricia said after a moment, "I understand you solved the ornament thefts."

"You heard about that?" I said with surprise.

"Johanna phoned me this morning," she explained. "She told me about what happened at the Wildwood Inn. I never checked if the basement windows at the seniors' center were locked. I saw that the glass wasn't broken and left it at that." She stepped over a clump of seaweed that had washed up on the shore. "Johanna's terribly embarrassed about the whole thing. She's bringing Emily by the festival after school today. I'll be meeting them there. She wants Emily to apologize in person."

I stopped to pick up a pretty shell. "I feel sorry for Emily. Not that I think she was right to steal, because I don't, but it sounds like her parents' divorce wasn't exactly amicable."

"Poor kid," Patricia said. "She's never been any trouble before, as far as I know. Hopefully she's learned her lesson."

"I think she has."

For the rest of the walk, we talked about more cheerful topics, like the Festival of Trees and our plans for the holidays. Even so, I didn't stop thinking about the note Lily had received. Not that it did me any good. By the time I'd said goodbye to Patricia and had returned home with Bentley, I was no closer to understanding how the note fit into the puzzle of Kevin's murder.

Chapter Twenty-One

I had high hopes the next day, even though I knew they probably weren't warranted. If I managed to meet up with Harvey in Port Angeles—and that wasn't a sure thing—there was no guarantee that he'd tell me anything useful. Nevertheless, I stayed positive during the drive from Wildwood Cove to The Codfather. As promised, Brett had come with me, and his presence helped to calm the fluttering of nerves in my stomach. No matter how much I wanted to talk to Harvey, and hopefully gather some clues from our conversation, I couldn't forget that he was one of my suspects.

We arrived in Port Angeles with more than an hour to spare, so we wandered around town, doing some Christmas shopping for family and friends. When we stopped at a jewelry store, I picked out a cute cat charm for Lisa's favorite bracelet. With green eyes and black fur, the charm looked exactly like Lisa's cat, Orion. We continued on to other stores, and I found gifts for Chloe, my mom, and my mother-in-law.

When we came to a bookstore, we didn't even have to ask each other if we should go in; that was a given. We browsed the shelves for over half an hour. I would have stayed longer if I wasn't worried about missing my chance to talk to Harvey.

I ended up buying a book for myself as well as one to give to my mom's husband, Grant, for Christmas. Brett managed to pick out some gifts as well, and by the time we left the shop we'd both worked up an appetite from shopping.

The Codfather was quite busy when we arrived, which wasn't a surprise. It was a popular place, thanks to its delicious food. As we headed for a free booth near the back of the restaurant, I carefully studied the other customers. Harvey wasn't among them.

"What if he doesn't show up?" I said to Brett after we'd ordered lunch and the waiter had brought us our drinks.

"Then you can talk to him on the weekend." Brett reached across the table and gave my hand a squeeze. "At least this trip wasn't a waste—we got lots of Christmas shopping done."

"True." I took a long drink of my root beer, my gaze fixed on the restaurant door.

When our waiter brought our fish, fries, and coleslaw, Harvey still hadn't appeared. I decided to do my best to enjoy my meal anyway. That wasn't difficult. The food was just as amazing as I remembered, and I savored every bite, even as I kept a close eye on the door.

We were halfway through our meals when Harvey finally made an appearance.

The owner of the restaurant called out a greeting to Harvey, clearly well acquainted with him. Several booths had freed up since Brett and I had arrived, and Harvey sat in one not far from ours. As eager as I was to talk to him, I decided not to ambush him right away. If I waited until he got his food, maybe he'd be less likely to storm out of the restaurant if he didn't like my questions.

I managed to finish my fish, coleslaw, and half of my fries before I nudged my plate away.

"Are you full or just anxious to grill Harvey?" Brett asked.

"Both." I pushed my plate closer to him.

He'd already polished off his food, but had no trouble finishing mine as well.

I drank the last of my root beer and then sat back, watching Harvey. Since he was facing away from me, I could keep an eye on him without being obvious about it.

"You don't want dessert, do you?" I asked Brett when he'd eaten the last french fry.

Brett grinned, clearly knowing why I was asking. "I won't delay you any longer."

He paid the bill and we gathered up our coats and purchases. I headed in the direction of the door, with Brett following behind me, but of course I had no intention of going that far. Instead, I stopped next to Harvey's booth.

"Hi, Harvey," I greeted. "Do you remember me and Brett? We met you at Holly Lodge."

Harvey was surprised to see us, but he recovered quickly. "Of course. How are you guys doing?"

"Not bad," Brett said. "How about you?"

"Getting along all right, considering the way things have been of late."

"Since the murder, you mean?" I slid onto the bench across from him, making room for Brett to join me.

If Harvey thought we were intruding, he didn't let it show. "That's right." He scooped coleslaw onto his fork. "We're not really in a festive mood at Holly Lodge."

"Understandable," Brett said. "Any news on the murder investigation?"

I could have kissed him for asking that question.

"Nope." Harvey cut into his battered cod. "The cops are keeping their cards close to their chests."

"I guess that's not surprising," I said. "But you knew Kevin well. Do you have any idea who killed him?"

He took a drink of coffee and set his mug down with a thud. "My money's on the real estate guy."

"Wilson Gerrard?" I asked.

He nodded as he munched on some coleslaw. "Didn't you guys hear him arguing with Kevin?"

"We did," Brett confirmed.

"But it seems like he doesn't really benefit from Kevin's death," I said.

Harvey shrugged. "Maybe he didn't think things through. Hotheaded types tend not to."

"And Gerrard is hotheaded?" Brett asked.

"I don't really know," Harvey admitted, "but there's something not quite right about him."

I recalled how Wilson had taken pleasure in people pointing fingers at each other. "I know what you mean." I hesitated, not knowing how he'd respond to my next words, but I forged ahead anyway. "You were outside around two in the morning the night Kevin died."

Harvey's gaze jerked up to meet mine. "What makes you think that?"

"I looked out the window and saw you," I said. "You were on snowshoes."

There was a hard glint to his eyes now. "Are you accusing me of something?"

"Not at all," I said quickly.

"Really? Because it sounds like you are."

"Hold on." Although Brett was maintaining an appearance of calm, I could tell he'd grown tense. "Don't put words in her mouth."

"I was just wondering if you'd seen anything unusual while you were out and about," I said. That was mostly the truth. Although in my book he wasn't free of suspicion. Not even close.

Harvey stared at me as he chewed hard on a french fry. "I didn't see anyone or anything, except for a light on in the lounge."

"Probably Lily, when she was reading," I said with a nod.

"So she says," Harvey grumbled. He grabbed the salt shaker and sprinkled some over his remaining fries.

"You think she's lying?" I asked with interest.

"*Someone's* been lying."

"I guess that's true." I considered how I could get more information from Harvey. "How long were you out that night?"

"You ask a lot of questions." The hard glint had returned to his eyes.

"Marley's solved mysteries in the past," Brett jumped in. "She's good at figuring these things out. You want Kevin's killer caught, don't you?"

Harvey studied us both as he continued to eat his lunch. "Sure, I do," he said eventually. The suspicion hadn't disappeared from his voice, but his eyes weren't quite as unfriendly as a moment ago. "But I don't see what it matters how long I was out."

"It could narrow down the window of time when Kevin was killed," I told him.

"If you don't have anything to hide, answering Marley's question shouldn't be a problem," Brett said.

I rested a hand on his knee, grateful for his support.

"Just because I have something I don't want spread around, doesn't mean I'm guilty of doing anything wrong," Harvey said.

A thought struck me. "Were you meeting someone that night? A woman, maybe?"

When Harvey locked his gaze on mine, I knew I was right.

Thoughts whirled around in my mind. Had Rita been having an affair with Harvey? If she'd cheated on Kevin, maybe their relationship was more troubled than we'd thought.

"It's...complicated," Harvey said.

I nodded. "Because she was married to Kevin."

Harvey's eyes widened. "What? No!"

A couple of other diners glanced our way.

Harvey noticed and lowered his voice. "I wasn't meeting Rita. I was on my way back from Evie's place."

It took a split second for the name to register in my mind. "The woman who lives near Holly Lodge? The one who brought fresh eggs for Rita?"

Harvey nodded.

Okay, so I hadn't been completely right after all.

"Is Evie married?" Brett asked.

Harvey drained the last of his coffee. "No."

I was still trying to connect all the dots in my head. "Then why the secrecy?"

"I was respecting Evie's wishes." Harvey paused as a waiter came by and refilled his coffee mug. When we were alone again, he continued to explain. "Evie *was* married. Her husband passed away three months ago. It wasn't a happy marriage, but Evie stayed true to him right till the end. She was worried that people might judge her if they knew we'd started a relationship just a few weeks after her husband died. We weren't going to keep it a secret for long, maybe another few weeks. Evie doesn't have anything to be ashamed of in my mind, but she felt better about keeping things quiet for now, so that's what we did."

"But you told Sheriff Walczyk where you were that night?" I checked, hoping he'd been truthful with her.

"I did, and Evie confirmed my story."

"So you've been cleared as a suspect?" Brett asked.

"Not entirely." Harvey took a sip of coffee. "I wasn't with Evie the whole night, and I still could have killed Kevin when I got back from her place. I didn't," he emphasized, "but I'm not completely free of suspicion. I'm not the only one, though."

"No, there are several people who could have committed the crime," I agreed.

"What about you two?" Harvey asked. "Are you under suspicion?"

"No." Brett glanced my way. "At least, I don't think so."

"We were able to give each other alibis and we'd only just met Kevin when he died," I said. "I don't think the police suspect us."

I certainly hoped that was true, but the sheriff and her deputies hadn't given us any reason to believe otherwise.

"Whoever did it needs to be caught soon," Harvey said. "The whole thing's tough on Rita and it won't exactly be good for business if there's a cloud of suspicion hanging over the place."

I considered his words. "So Rita hasn't been cleared as a suspect either?" I asked.

"I don't think so." Harvey rubbed his jaw. "It's ridiculous to think she'd kill Kevin, but I guess the police have to do their job. And since she doesn't have an alibi and she inherited everything from Kevin…"

I nodded. "They have to consider her as a suspect."

Rita couldn't have planted the threatening note in Lily's bag, though, since Zahra said her mother hadn't been anywhere except to Sheriff Walczyk's office, which was a good hour away from Wildwood Cove.

Harvey finished the last of his coleslaw and signaled to the waiter. "I should get going."

Brett stood up and I shifted along the bench so I could get up too.

"We won't keep you any longer," I said to Harvey. "Thanks for talking to us. Will you be at the memorial?"

He pulled out his wallet. "I'm in charge of organizing the hockey game."

"We'll probably see you on Saturday then."

We said our goodbyes, and Brett and I headed out of the restaurant.

"What do you think?" Brett asked as we walked back to his truck.

"I can't be certain, of course, but I don't think he killed Kevin."

"I got that sense too," Brett said. "But sometimes the most unlikely person turns out to be a killer."

Unfortunately, I knew that to be true. Still, I decided to focus my attention on my other suspects, unless and until something more came to light about Harvey.

We'd almost reached the end of the street when I stopped outside a shop's display window. A decorated Christmas tree took up much of the window, surrounded by boxes of pretty decorations.

"Don't you think we have enough decorations now?" Brett asked.

"We do."

I turned away from the display and continued walking with Brett, my hand in his. By the time we reached the truck, a plan had formed in my mind. While Brett drove us back to Wildwood Cove, I sent text messages to several of my friends.

Chapter Twenty-Two

My plan came together better than I could have hoped. On Friday evening, the doorbell rang, announcing the arrival of our first guests. I opened the front door to Chloe and Lisa, who'd shown up at the same time. They hurried inside, all smiles, Chloe with a box of craft supplies in her arms. I hung up their coats as they headed for the family room and fussed over an excited Bentley. I was about to follow them when I heard another car approaching. I stepped out onto the front porch and waved as Leigh parked her car next to Lisa's. All three of her daughters hopped out of the backseat.

"Hi, Marley!" they chorused.

"Hi, girls," I greeted. "Head on inside. Brett's making hot chocolate."

That news elicited squeals of delight. As soon as they stepped into the foyer, they called out Bentley's name and giggled when he raced down the hall to greet them.

"This was such a great idea," Leigh said as she followed me into the house.

Her daughters, Amanda, Brianna, and Kayla, had already disappeared into the family room with Bentley.

"To be honest, I wasn't sure what Johanna would think about the idea," I said as I hung up Leigh's coat, "but I'm glad she agreed to come."

Minutes later, Johanna showed up with Emily.

"I still can't believe you're doing this for us," Johanna said once we'd reached the family room and everyone had been introduced. Leigh's middle daughter, Brianna, was in the same class as Emily at school, but Lisa and Chloe hadn't met the Jessens before.

Leigh gave Johanna a hug. "We look after each other in this town."

"Thank you." Johanna directed the words at all of us, her eyes misty.

"It's our pleasure," I assured her. "Now, who wants hot chocolate and who wants eggnog?"

Once we had all the drinks sorted out, we got down to business. The kids were seated on cushions around the coffee table in the family room while the adults sat at the kitchen table. We all had clean seashells, paint, googly eyes, glue, ribbon, and a variety of other craft supplies.

Since Johanna and Emily had been forced to leave all their Christmas decorations behind when they'd left their previous home in Idaho, I thought it would be a nice gesture if we helped them make some new ornaments. I could have bought them some at the store in Port Angeles, but this seemed like a better idea. Not only would they end up with a decorated tree, but hopefully they'd also feel more connected to the community.

We spent the next two hours making little snowmen, angels, and other ornaments. Chloe painted a cute Santa Claus with a scalloped shell beard, and Brett surprised and impressed us by making silver stars and snowflakes out of a pile of bolts he'd brought in from the workshop.

While we worked, we chatted, laughed, drank eggnog and hot chocolate, and snacked on gingerbread and sugar cookies that I'd made the day before. The kids split their time between crafting, eating, and playing with Bentley and Flapjack, and they were all in good spirits. I watched them now and again, and was glad to see that Emily and Brianna appeared to be fast friends.

By the end of the evening, we had a box full of ornaments for Johanna and Emily to take home. When I handed them over to Johanna, her eyes filled with tears again.

"This is seriously the nicest thing anyone's ever done for us," she said, struggling to maintain her composure.

I hugged her. "We're just glad to help."

"You've helped more than you know," she said with a tremulous smile.

"Merry Christmas!" Emily called out as she bounded down the front steps, a big smile on her face.

"Merry Christmas!" I called back.

I stayed on the front porch until all our guests had driven away.

"I think that was a successful evening," Brett said, pulling me into a hug after I shut the front door.

"Very successful," I said with a smile.

I tried to hold onto the happiness that was bubbling inside of me. I knew that it might not last, since the very next day we'd be attending Kevin's memorial service.

Chapter Twenty-Three

I wasn't entirely sure what to wear to a memorial service that included an outdoor hockey game. Even though I wouldn't be taking part in the match, I'd likely be sitting outside watching Brett and the other players. I texted back and forth with Chloe to see what she planned to wear. After consulting with her, I decided to wear a dark blue dress and take a change of clothing with me, along with plenty of winter gear to keep me warm while sitting by the frozen lake. Brett had a similar plan; he was wearing a suit and bringing along other clothes as well as his hockey equipment.

We stashed our bags in the back of the truck's cab. We didn't want to put anything in the uncovered bed of the truck, in case it snowed before we returned home. We picked up Chloe on our way out of town and I scooted over on the bench seat so she could sit beside me.

"I'm not exactly looking forward to the service, since there's a sad reason behind it, but I am looking forward to watching you two play hockey," I said as we headed up the mountain.

Although Brett and I had been ice skating together at the rink on the outskirts of Wildwood Cove, I'd never seen him take part in a hockey game of any sort.

"I'm sure I won't be much use," Chloe said. "And I'll only take part if they're short on players."

"I haven't played hockey in years, so I might not be much use either." Brett glanced my way. "Don't expect me to be scoring any goals. I'm sure all my skills are rusty."

"You'll be great, no matter how rusty," I said. "And goals or no goals, I'm your number one fan."

"You haven't even seen me play yet," he pointed out.

"Doesn't matter," I said with confidence. "I'm still your number one fan."

Chloe nudged my arm. "If you weren't saying that to my brother, I'd think it was super cute."

Brett reached over to squeeze my hand. "It *is* cute. And mutual."

"Okay, lovebirds," Chloe said, "let's not go overboard."

The smile that had appeared on my face faded as I craned my neck to look out the windshield and up at the sky. The dark gray clouds hung heavily above us and the truck's thermometer displayed the chilly outside temperature, which had dropped as we climbed up the mountain.

"I know the weather forecast said it wasn't supposed to snow until late this afternoon, but I'm not sure I believe it." I fished my phone out of my coat pocket so I could check the weather app again.

"Try not to worry," Brett said, picking up on my anxiety, even though I'd tried to keep it contained. "We'll still be able to drive home safely even if there's a bit of snow by then."

I knew he was right, but I always felt safer when the roads were clear. I consulted the weather app. The forecast was still for heavy snow and strong winds, but the estimated time of the snowfall's onset had moved ahead by two hours to the early afternoon. I told Brett and Chloe about the change.

"If you want to leave when it starts to snow, we'll do that. Nobody would hold it against us." Brett gave my hand another squeeze. "Okay?"

"Okay."

That made me feel marginally better. I didn't want to bow out early, but hopefully it wouldn't come to that. The memorial service was scheduled to start at eleven, followed by the hockey game. After that there would be refreshments served in the lodge. If worse came to worst, we could skip the food, but if the hockey game didn't go on too long the weather might hold off until we were well on our way home.

I still had my phone in my hand when it chimed. "Sienna," I said as I checked my text messages.

"Will she and Patricia be at the memorial?" Chloe asked.

"No," I replied. "Patricia knows Rita and would have liked to come, but she couldn't leave the B&B. They've got guests and John is out of town. Patricia gave me a sympathy card to deliver on her behalf."

I tapped the message Sienna had sent me.

Finally get to start Lily's book! she'd written.

I wrote out a quick response. *Let me know how it is!*

She assured me that she would, and I tucked my phone back in my pocket.

When we reached Holly Lodge shortly before eleven, the temperature had dropped even more and a stiff breeze rustled its way through the surrounding pine trees.

"It's freezing up here!" Chloe exclaimed as soon as we'd climbed out of the truck.

I rubbed my arms. "I'm glad I brought lots of layers for later." Even through my thick winter jacket, I could feel the cold.

We left all our extra clothes and gear in the truck for the moment and hurried up the steps to Holly Lodge's front door. Stepping inside brought immediate relief. The lodge was pleasantly warm and I was glad to shut the door on the icy breeze.

The lobby was empty, but I detected the sound of low voices in the lounge, and classical music played quietly in the background. We were removing our coats when Zahra entered the lobby, wearing a dark purple dress.

"Hi," she greeted. "Thank you for coming."

Chloe gave her a hug. "How are you and Rita doing today?"

"All right, in the circumstances," Zahra said, returning the hug. "Here, I'll take your coats."

We handed them over and she took them into the office behind the reception desk before rejoining us.

"Everyone's in the lounge," she said, leading the way there. "We'll get started shortly."

Extra chairs had been added to the lounge, likely from the dining room. They all faced the fireplace, where flames danced and popped, adding warmth and comfort to the somber atmosphere.

Several people had arrived ahead of us, including Lily and Ambrose. They stood near the large window, looking out at the frozen lake, Lily's arm tucked through his. I wasn't surprised to see Evie and Harvey there, talking quietly near the fireplace, but I hadn't expected Wilson Gerrard to show up. He stood on his own by the bookcases, staring at his cell phone.

I nodded at Wilson, but didn't bother to speak to him. Instead, I set two sympathy cards—one from me and Brett and the other from Patricia—on a table where others had already set theirs. Then I introduced Chloe to Harvey and Evie.

"It was good of you to come all the way up here," Evie said. "Hopefully the weather will hold for you to get home all right."

"It should," Brett said.

I sure hoped he was right. As if reading my thoughts, he took my hand and gave it a gentle squeeze.

Harvey glanced around at the other guests. "We're expecting a few more neighbors. Then the service will get started."

I was glad he hadn't given us the cold shoulder. I'd been undeniably nosy when I'd talked to him in Port Angeles, but it seemed he'd forgiven me.

Cindy entered the lounge, wearing a dark green dress rather than the chef's uniform I'd seen her in during our previous trip to the lodge. She had a man in a suit with her. They came over to join us and we all introduced ourselves. The man with Cindy was her husband, Tom.

About ten minutes later, another couple arrived. They appeared to be in their late forties or early fifties. Cindy waved to them and informed us that they lived a few miles farther up the highway. Almost on their heels, a man and a woman in their early sixties came into the lounge with a younger woman—their adult daughter, according to what Cindy told us.

"They're neighbors too," Evie said. "Maybe they wouldn't be called that elsewhere, since they live several miles away, but around here it's not uncommon to live a mile or two away from your closest neighbor."

We fell quiet as Zahra addressed the room.

"Please take a seat, everyone," she said. "I think we're ready to start."

I couldn't see Rita anywhere, but as Brett, Chloe, and I settled into chairs that had been set up behind the couch, she walked into the room. She was stunning in a burgundy dress, but her expression matched the solemnity of the occasion. Despite the makeup that she wore, she looked tired, as if she hadn't slept well since Kevin's death. That was probably the case.

Zahra leaned in close and whispered something in her mother's ear. Rita nodded and then took a seat in one of the armchairs. Zahra stood next to the fireplace, facing the room.

"Thank you all for coming to help us celebrate Kevin's life. I grew up without a father, and although Kevin didn't come into my life until I was a teenager, he filled in a hole I hadn't fully realized was there."

I glanced down at my hands, trying to keep my emotions under control. I understood exactly what Zahra meant. Like her I'd gained and then lost a stepfather who'd played an important role in my life.

Brett covered my hands with one of his, bringing me immediate comfort.

"He was a father figure," Zahra continued, "a husband, and a friend to many." Her eyes glistened and she drew in a shaky breath. "I thought I'd tell you a bit about Kevin's past, and then if anyone else wishes to say a few words, you're welcome to."

She went on to tell us how Kevin was born in Bellevue and had lived in the Pacific Northwest all his life. Ever since he was young, he'd loved the outdoors and had looked forward to one day living up in the mountains where he could enjoy hiking and fishing on a daily basis. When he and Rita met, they decided to make that dream a reality together, leading them to purchase Holly Lodge.

After giving us a brief history, Zahra told a couple of funny stories about Kevin that elicited laughter from everyone in attendance, even Rita. By the time she wrapped up, Zahra had tears in her eyes again, but also a slight smile on her face.

Harvey stood up next and spoke about his friendship with Kevin. He mentioned how Kevin had given him a job at a time when he was in great need, having lost his employment at a sawmill.

After Harvey, Evie spoke briefly, and then Ambrose stood up.

"If it's all right, I'd like to read one of my poems." He addressed his words to Rita.

She nodded, sending him a grateful smile.

Ambrose opened his notebook and flipped through the pages. He read a brief poem about night falling over the land, which I figured was meant to represent death. It ended with a line about the sun rising again to warm those left behind. Like the poem he'd read during our last visit, it was full of references to nature.

When he was done, Ambrose shut his notebook, his eyes shining with unshed tears.

As he retook his seat, Rita stood and turned to address us all, clasping her hands in front of her. "Kevin was a good man. Infuriating, at times," she said with a brief smile, "and funny at others, but always steadfast and loyal. I'm crushed to have to go on without him, but I will always cherish those years we had together."

Her hands trembled, and she quickly sat down again.

Zahra stood up and smoothly took over for her mother. "Thank you again for coming. We truly appreciate your presence here today. For those of you taking part in the hockey game in Kevin's memory, it will begin in twenty minutes or so. If you need a place to change, meet me out in the lobby and I'll give you a key to one of the guest rooms. After the game, refreshments will be served in the dining room."

Slowly, everyone got to their feet. A couple of the neighbors approached Rita, giving her their condolences and apologizing for the fact that they weren't able to stay for the game or reception. Brett, Chloe, and I passed them by, meeting up with Zahra in the lobby. She gave us a key to the same room Brett and I had stayed in before, and Brett made a quick trip out to the truck to grab our bags.

Upstairs, Brett changed into jeans and a long-sleeved shirt. Chloe switched her dress for two pairs of leggings and a pink sweatshirt. I'd brought leggings, jeans, a long-sleeved shirt, and a sweater to wear under my puffy winter coat. We left our bags in the room and headed back downstairs, Chloe and Brett carrying their skates, coats, and the two hockey sticks Brett had brought along.

As we descended the stairs to the lobby, I spotted Zahra and Wilson near the front door.

"It's totally inappropriate," Zahra said in an angry whisper. "I think you'd better leave. *Now.*"

Wilson pulled on his jacket, unfazed. "If you insist."

Zahra yanked open the front door and glared at Wilson as he left the lodge.

"Everything all right?" I asked as she slammed the door behind him.

"Yes." She drew in a deep breath and let it out slowly. "Sorry about that. He wanted to talk business with my mom. On today of all days! How insensitive is that?"

Chloe put an arm around her. "Some people have no consideration for others."

Zahra nodded and took in the sight of all three of us. The rest of her anger seemed to drain away. "Two of you are going to play?"

"I'm going to try," Chloe said. "If you need me to make up numbers."

"I think we do." Zahra glanced down at her dress. "I'd better go get changed. I'll be back in a few minutes. You can head down to the lake, if you'd like."

She disappeared through the door that led to the Mannings' private quarters.

The lounge was empty now, but we could see some people heading down the pathway to the lake. We followed them in that direction. Harvey, wearing jeans and a thick winter coat, already had his skates on and was out on the ice, which had been cleared of snow near the shore. Evie was sitting on a wooden bench, tying up her skates. She, too, had changed into jeans. Scout wandered along the edge of the lake, sniffing here and there, his tail wagging gently.

Cindy was nowhere in sight, but her husband was seated on another bench, skates already strapped to his feet and a hockey stick in his hand. Some of the neighbors I hadn't met were also present and getting ready to take part in the hockey game.

Brett and Chloe joined the others on the benches and switched their winter boots for skates. I stood off to the side, wondering if I'd be the only spectator. Footsteps crunched through the snow behind me, and I glanced back to see Ambrose and Lily heading our way. Ambrose was carrying a pair of hockey skates, but Lily was empty-handed.

"Not playing?" she asked me as they drew closer.

"I'm not much of a skater," I told her.

"Same," Lily said.

"I'm not the greatest skater, either." Ambrose pushed his glasses up higher on his nose. "It's been years since I played hockey, but I'm going to give it a try."

"You'll do great," Lily assured him.

He gave her a grateful smile before finding a free spot on one of the benches.

Zahra arrived a minute later in jeans and a hoodie. She had a pair of skates under her arm and carried several hockey sticks.

"If anyone needs a stick, I've got some here." She addressed Harvey. "Are we okay for pucks?"

Harvey produced three from his coat pocket and held them up.

"Will Rita be playing?" I asked, noting her absence.

"No, she can't skate," Zahra said. "She's helping Cindy set up for the reception."

I glanced back at the lodge. "Should I go help?"

"They've got it covered, but thank you. If you get too cold, though, feel free to head back inside."

I figured it was a good possibility that I'd have to do that at some point. The wind was even stronger than before. It stung my cheeks and made my eyes water. I tugged my knitted hat farther down over my ears and tucked my gloved hands into my coat pockets.

The cold wasn't my biggest worry, though. As the players made their way out onto the ice, the first snowflakes of the day drifted down from the gray sky.

Chapter Twenty-Four

Zahra divided the players into two teams and then handed out jerseys—black for one team and green for the other. Brett and Chloe were on the same team, and both donned black jerseys.

"The ice is safe, right?" I asked, trying not to sound too anxious.

Evie was the only person on the ice who heard me. "Don't worry," she said. "Harvey tested it earlier. Everywhere the snow has been cleared is safe. Besides, this part of the lake is really shallow. It's out farther that it gets really deep."

That was one of my worries put to rest, at least.

I tried to ignore the snowflakes falling from the sky and took a seat next to Lily on one of the benches. Scout came over and lay down by our feet. The game got underway and I did my best to focus on it. Although I didn't forget about the weather, I quickly got into the game. The teams played three on three, and the area between the two goalie nets was about half the size of an average ice rink, maybe a little less. Harvey was the referee, and from time to time his whistle rang out across the frozen lake.

Despite Brett's warning on the way up the mountain, he did score a goal, with an assist from Chloe. I jumped up from the bench and cheered, momentarily forgetting that I had any worries about the weather. Evie also scored a goal, and Zahra scored two. After the first fifteen minutes of play, the teams were tied two-two. The players took a five minute break to rest up before going into the second period.

"Nice goal," I said to Brett as he stood near the edge of the ice, drinking from a water bottle.

He grinned at me. "Not quite as rusty as I thought I'd be." His grin faded away. "But you look like you need to head inside."

I tried not to shiver as the wind cut through my multiple layers of clothing. "I'm having fun watching the game."

"Your lips are turning blue," Brett pointed out. "You can always watch from the window."

"True," I conceded, giving in to the need to shiver.

I glanced up at the sky. The snowflakes were falling more thickly now. Out on the rink, Harvey cleared the fresh snow by pushing a shovel across the ice. I had a layer of fluffy flakes on my shoulders and knees, and probably my hat too. I dusted them off.

As usual, Brett knew what I was thinking. "If you're worried about the weather, we can head home."

I got up and stepped closer. "How much longer will the game be?"

"Half an hour or so," he said. "Two more fifteen-minute periods."

I turned to check out the pathway leading up to the lodge. Not even half an inch of snow had accumulated so far. A fierce gust of wind picked up some of the fresh powder and sent it swirling.

"I think we'll be okay to wait until the end of the game," I said. "But maybe we can leave right after?"

"We will," Brett assured me.

He skated off to join the others, who were getting ready to start the next period.

"I'm heading inside," I told Lily as I returned to the bench where she was still seated.

She jumped up. "I'll come with you. My fingers and toes have all gone numb."

Scout got up but didn't follow as we turned away from the lake. Harvey's whistle blew and the game got underway again. Lily and I headed up to the lodge together, walking briskly. The wind whistled around us and the trees surrounding Holly Lodge creaked and groaned as they swayed and trembled.

I let out a sigh of relief as soon as I set foot in the lodge, even though it would still take time for me to warm up. Simply being sheltered from the increasingly strong wind was a vast improvement.

Lily and I took off our boots so we wouldn't track snow through the lodge, leaving them on a rubber mat set out for that purpose.

"I'll stash your coat in the office if you want," Lily offered as she took off her own jacket.

"Thanks." I tucked my hat and gloves into the coat's pockets and then handed it over to her.

While she took our coats away, I stood by the crackling fire, holding out my hands to soak in the warmth. I wiggled my toes and the numbness slowly eased. A few minutes later, I heard voices in the dining room, so I headed that way.

Several tables had been pushed together and covered with a white cloth. Food had been set out on top, and just looking at the spread made my mouth water. Even though I hadn't taken part in the hockey game, sitting out in the cold had given me an appetite.

There were finger sandwiches, veggies and dip, crackers and smoked salmon spread, a variety of hot hors d'oeuvres, mini cupcakes, and cookies. There were also pitchers of ice water, a bowl of punch, and another bowl filled with eggnog.

Cindy set a stack of small plates at one end of the table. Lily was there with her.

"I just love your books," Cindy gushed. "The romances and the mysteries. I've read several and I've got your latest in my bag. I meant to bring it the last time you were here, but I forgot. Would you be able to sign it for me?"

Lily beamed at her. "Of course."

"How exciting! I'll be right back!" Cindy darted off, disappearing into the kitchen.

"I'm really looking forward to reading your books," I said to Lily as I came farther into the room.

"Thank you," she said with a smile. "I appreciate your interest."

The windows rattled as a particularly fierce gust of wind blew around the lodge.

"I'm sure glad we came inside," Lily said. "I'm not all that outdoorsy at the best of times. This weather is too much for me!"

"It's definitely a good day to be inside by the fire," I said as I wandered over to the window.

The snow was falling so thickly now that I could barely see the hockey players out on the lake. The nugget of worry that had been sitting in my stomach grew heavier. Now I wished I'd taken Brett up on his offer to leave before the end of the game.

Cindy reappeared and smiled brightly as Lily signed her book.

"Thank you so much!" Cindy hugged the signed book to her chest. "I can't wait to show my husband. He's a fan of your mysteries too."

Lily's cheeks turned a light shade of pink. "It makes me so happy to hear that."

Cindy reigned in her excitement. "Can I get either of you something hot to drink? You must have nearly frozen out there."

We both requested tea, and Cindy returned to the kitchen to make it for us. When she reappeared minutes later and handed us each a teacup, I wasn't sure if I'd be able to drink it. I wanted the warmth and comfort of the hot drink, but my stomach was so tied up in knots that I wasn't sure if I could fit anything into it.

I took a few deep breaths, trying to relax. Nobody else seemed anxious about the road conditions. I knew I worried more than most because of the mountain road accident that had killed my stepfather and stepsiblings several years ago, but knowing that didn't allow me to relax.

Although I didn't manage to set my nerves at ease, I did take a sip or two of tea. Remaining by the window, I watched the snowflakes swirling and blowing in the wind.

A figure appeared through the snow, heading towards the lodge. Another figure took shape behind the first.

With immense relief, I realized that it was Brett, followed by Chloe. I set down my tea and hurried into the lounge to meet them. They stopped outside the door, brushing snow off themselves before coming inside.

"Wow," Chloe said as she pulled the door shut behind them. "It sure is wild out there."

Brett gave me a quick, chilly kiss before working his feet out of his boots. "You okay?" he asked me.

"I'm worried about the roads," I admitted.

"We'll head out as soon as we get all our stuff together," he said.

"What about the game?" I asked.

"We decided to call it quits halfway through the third period," Chloe replied. "Too much snow and wind now. It was getting to the point where we could barely see the puck. The other team won by two goals, but we all had a good time."

Rita entered the lounge as Chloe spoke. "I'm glad to hear that," she said. "That's exactly what Kevin would have wanted."

"I wish we could stay longer," I told her. "But with the weather like it is…"

"I understand completely," Rita assured me. "Especially since you have farther to go than the neighbors do. I'm so grateful you were able to come."

We exchanged a few more words with Rita, and then headed upstairs to fetch the rest of our belongings. By then, the other hockey players had reached the lodge and were in the process of shedding all their outerwear.

When we returned downstairs, I tapped on the office door, just in case there was someone inside. There was no response, and the door was ajar, so I pushed it open, immediately spotting my coat draped over the back of a chair.

I dug my gloves and hat out of the pockets, knowing I'd want them on before going outside. A beautiful painting of the lake, as seen from the back of the lodge, hung on one wall. Although I'd noticed the painting the last time I was in the office, I hadn't done anything more than glance at it, same as with the diplomas and certificates on the other wall. I took a closer look at the painting now, wondering if the artist was someone local.

Zahra Omondi was written in the bottom right-hand corner.

I was impressed by Zahra's talent. The painting was really beautiful.

Not wanting to linger any longer, I pulled on my coat and rejoined Brett and Chloe in the lobby. We said our goodbyes to the other hockey players, who were now heading into the dining room, and then we dashed through the wind and snow to the parking lot.

I couldn't relax in the truck. Out on the highway, visibility was poor, the snow swirling around us. The wind had grown stronger and it rocked the truck in an unnerving way.

"I'm sorry, Marley," Brett said, his face grim. "We should have left earlier."

"It's okay," I said, not wanting him to feel bad. "I worry more than I should."

"I don't know..." Chloe sounded as tense as I felt. "This is pretty bad. Maybe we should—"

Crack!

A dark shape hurtled toward the windshield.

Chapter Twenty-Five

Chloe screamed.

Brett slammed on the brakes.

We all lurched forward and then back against the seat. It took a second for me to realize we hadn't crashed.

"Are you both all right?" Brett asked, his words tense.

"I am," I said in a shaky voice. "Chloe?"

She nodded, but she was clearly rattled.

"What about you?" I asked Brett.

"I'm fine, but we've got a problem."

That much was obvious. A huge evergreen lay across the highway, mere feet from the front of the truck. Brett had stopped just in time to avoid a collision with the falling tree. If he'd hesitated for a split second, we might have been crushed.

"Stay here." Brett was already getting out of the truck as he spoke.

I leaned forward, trying to get a better look at the tree. The trunk was so thick that it would have taken two of us with joined hands to form a circle around it when it was standing.

"I thought we were going to die." Chloe still sounded shaken.

I was more than a little rattled myself. I put an arm around her and gave her a squeeze. "We're okay."

Brett spent a few seconds surveying the situation before climbing back into the truck. Even though he hadn't been outside for long, a layer of snow covered his coat and hat.

"It's a mess. There's no way we can clear a path." He started the engine. "We'll have to turn back."

I was half relieved and half disappointed. Even without the tree in our way, the trip down the mountain seemed too treacherous now, but turning back likely meant we'd have to stay the night at Holly Lodge.

"You don't think…" Chloe started to say as Brett turned the truck around.

I figured I knew what she was about to ask. "That Kevin's killer is at the lodge right now?"

"We'll be fine," Brett said firmly. He sounded so sure, but I could tell he wasn't free of concern. That showed in his eyes.

I was worried too. Wilson had left earlier, but several people from my list of suspects were still at the lodge. I tried not to let my fear get the best of me.

"Even if Kevin's killer is at Holly Lodge, no one was harmed during the service," I said. "And if the killer achieved whatever he or she wanted by killing Kevin, there's no reason why any of the rest of us would be a target." I knew there was a gaping hole in what I'd just said.

Chloe didn't miss it either. "But we don't know what the killer was trying to achieve by murdering Kevin. So how do we know they don't have more people on their hitlist?"

"Speculating will only make you more nervous," Brett said. "We don't have much choice but to go back."

I thought about that for a second. "There are other lodges in the area, right? Maybe we can stay at one of those places instead."

"That's a good idea," Chloe said quickly, relief evident in her voice.

Brett kept his gaze firmly on the road. What he could see of it, anyway. "Let's start by getting back to Holly Lodge."

Fortunately, the trip back was short and uneventful. I let out a heavy sigh of relief when Brett pulled into the parking lot and stopped the truck. Since the murder, I never would have thought I could be so happy to return to Holly Lodge. Still, I hoped it would be a brief visit and we'd soon move on to another lodge.

Leaving all our belongings in the truck, we braved the wind and snow to make a dash for the front door. We shook the snow off our coats and boots as best we could before going inside, but we still had plenty of flakes on us that melted as soon as the warmth of the lobby hit us.

Zahra must have heard us arrive. She came into the lobby from the dining room, relief showing in her expression as soon as she saw us.

"Oh, thank goodness. I'm glad you came back. The driving conditions are terrible now."

"That's not the only problem," I said.

"A tree came down across the highway," Brett explained. "A big one. No one will be getting down the mountain until a crew can take care of it."

"And in this weather, that's not likely to happen anytime soon." Zahra took in the sight of our long faces. "Don't worry. You can stay here tonight, free of charge."

"We don't want to put you and your mom to any trouble," Chloe protested. "Maybe we could stay at another lodge close by?"

Zahra shook her head. "The only other place you could possibly make it to in this weather is fully booked. Some of the guests we had to cancel on moved over there."

Brett, Chloe, and I glanced at each other.

"Really, it's no trouble," Zahra assured us. "You can't go out there again. It's not safe."

We knew she was right. There was no getting around it.

"Thank you," I said. "We're so sorry for the inconvenience, especially when you and your mom are going through so much."

Zahra waved off my apology. "Really, it's no bother. This kind of thing happens up here in the mountains from time to time. You three won't be the only ones needing a place to stay. Ambrose and Lily can't get down the mountain either. Most of the neighbors already headed home, either in their trucks or on snowmobiles, including Cindy, but Evie's still here. She'll stay with Harvey tonight."

From the smooth way she said that, I figured she knew about Harvey and Evie's relationship. Had she known all along, or were they no longer keeping it a secret? I gave those questions a firm shove, sending them to the back of my mind.

Zahra handed me the key to the same room we'd used earlier. "Chloe, do you want a room of your own? Or you could bunk with me. I've got twin beds in my room."

Chloe hesitated, and I knew she was worrying about the possibility of Kevin's killer being somewhere in the lodge.

"Can I stay with you guys?" she asked me and Brett.

I gave her arm a reassuring squeeze. "Of course."

"I can bring a cot up if you'd like," Zahra offered. "Just let me know. In the meantime, be sure to come get some food in the dining room. There's still plenty and you must be hungry."

We thanked her and braved the elements again so we could retrieve our bags from the truck. Once back inside, we shook the snow off our coats and removed our boots before heading upstairs.

In the guest room, we dropped our bags on the floor and stared around us for a moment.

"It's a nice room," Chloe commented eventually. "If I weren't worried about a murderer lurking among us, I'd be able to appreciate it more."

I was tempted to switch on the gas fireplace, but decided to wait until we'd had some food downstairs.

I clutched my phone as my thoughts swerved in another direction. "What'll we do about Flapjack and Bentley?"

Brett gave my shoulder a reassuring squeeze and brought out his own phone. "I'll text my mom. She'll look after them until we're home."

He sent the message and received a reply almost right away. We'd left a house key with my in-laws so they could take Bentley for a walk while we were gone for the day, and Brett's mom told us she was happy to pet-sit for longer than originally planned. That was one weight off my shoulders.

Chloe plopped down on the loveseat. "You two really don't mind if I sleep here tonight?"

"Actually, I'd feel better with all of us together," I admitted.

"Me too," Brett said. "Not that I think we really have anything to worry about."

Chloe lay down on her side. "I don't need a cot. I can sleep right here on the loveseat."

"Are you sure?" I checked. "It's not very long."

"That's okay. I always sleep curled up anyhow."

With that decided, we made our way downstairs to the dining room. Despite the shock of our near accident and my trepidation about staying at the lodge, my stomach rumbled with hunger.

Zahra had already explained to the others why we'd returned, so they weren't surprised to see us. They did, however, pepper us with questions about the tree and the driving conditions. We didn't have to say much for everyone to agree that no one would be getting down the mountain that night.

"We're more than happy to have you all here with us tonight," Rita assured us. She sat at a table with Evie, nursing a cup of coffee. "And please, help yourselves to the food."

We didn't need another offer.

I took a plate and started adding food to it, Brett and Chloe doing the same.

"Are you sure you're okay?" Brett whispered to me once everyone else had gone back to chatting with each other.

I set two cucumber sandwiches on my plate. "I'm still feeling shaky," I admitted quietly, "but I'm okay."

He kissed me on the cheek before going back to filling his plate.

I knew he was worried that our near-accident had brought back bad memories and added to my anxieties. And it had, but I was managing better than I might have expected. Maybe it was because I had so much else on my mind, not knowing if we were about to spend the night a few doors away from a murderer.

As I moved away from the food table, already munching on a cucumber sandwich, Harvey came into the dining room. He approached the table where Rita and Evie sat, and rested a hand on Evie's shoulder. She looked up at him and smiled. There was no mistaking the love and affection in her eyes.

"I'm so glad they're together," Zahra whispered, joining me in a quiet corner of the room.

"I thought they were trying to keep their relationship a secret," I said as Brett came over and stood by my side.

"You knew about that?" Zahra sounded surprised.

"We talked to him in Port Angeles earlier in the week," Brett said.

Zahra's eyes lit up with understanding. "Right. As planned. Did he give you any clues?" Before I had a chance to respond, she added, "And he told you about Evie? He's usually so private about those things."

"It came out because she's his alibi for part of the night," I explained. "I looked out the window on the night of Kevin's death and saw Harvey out on snowshoes. It turns out he was on his way back from Evie's place. I don't think he would have told us if I hadn't brought that up. He said Evie didn't want people to know about them, at least not yet."

Zahra nodded. "He told me that too. About Evie wanting to keep it quiet, not the alibi. I know I didn't sound so certain at the Wildwood Inn, and I get that you'd suspect Harvey, but I've thought it over and there's just no way he ever would have killed Kevin. Or anyone. Even without an alibi, I'd be sure of that. Harvey's the type of guy who rescues injured animals and cares for them until they can be released again. He and Kevin were close. He wouldn't have hurt him."

"I think you're probably right about that," I said.

Zahra seemed relieved that I'd come to that conclusion. "As for Evie," she said, "I figured out they were together a while ago. It was so obvious from the way they looked at each other. I came across them kissing yesterday and told them they didn't need to keep it a secret from us. Mom and I love them like family."

"They look happy together," I remarked, watching as Harvey took a seat next to Evie and covered one of her hands with his.

Zahra smiled. "They do."

She headed for the food table and filled a glass with eggnog before wandering off to talk with Ambrose. They stood by the window, watching the blizzard, or what little of it was still visible. The daylight was already fading fast.

My phone buzzed in my pocket. I pulled it out and glanced at the screen. Sienna had sent me a text message, but I decided to read it later. I didn't want to seem rude by focusing on my phone, even if the official part of the memorial was over.

Chloe had been chatting with Lily over by the punch bowl, but now she came over to join me and Brett, a plate of food and a glass of punch in hand.

"I don't know if it's the weather or the stress, or both," she said, sitting down at a nearby table, "but I'm suddenly starving."

"So are we," I said, noting that Brett had nearly polished off everything he'd put on his plate.

"The food is delicious." Brett ate his last cracker, loaded with salmon spread. "I'm going back for seconds."

I still had a sandwich and crackers on my plate, so I pulled out a chair, intending to join Chloe at the table.

Before I had a chance to sit down, the lights flickered and then went out, plunging the room into darkness.

Chapter Twenty-Six

"Don't worry," Rita called out. "Stay put and I'll have a flashlight out in a moment."

I stood frozen by the table, my heart pounding. The sudden darkness had frazzled my already raw nerves. The first thought that had popped into my head was that Kevin's killer had arranged the blackout, intending to strike again. Now that my eyes had adjusted to the dim light, I could see that everyone but Rita was still where they'd been when the lights went out.

Thanks to the little bit of daylight left, the room wasn't in complete darkness. It had only seemed like that in the first moments because of the sudden change.

I sat down across from Chloe, and Brett took the chair next to me. He'd managed to snag a couple of sandwiches before the lights went out.

Across the room, Harvey got to his feet. "I'll go out and start the generator."

Rita returned from the kitchen, the bright beam of a flashlight bouncing around ahead of her. She had another flashlight in hand, which she gave to Harvey.

He switched it on, aiming the beam toward the floor. "I'll be as quick as I can."

As he headed out of the dining room, Rita addressed the rest of us.

"I have lots of battery-powered lanterns. The generator will allow us to keep the most essential things running, but we don't know how long this storm will last, so we don't want to run through the fuel too quickly. I'll make sure every room has a lantern so we don't need to use the overhead lights unless absolutely necessary."

"I'll get the lanterns, Mom," Zahra offered. "I know where they are."

"Thank you, honey," Rita said.

She handed the remaining flashlight over, and Zahra used it to light her way out of the dining room.

"I'm so sorry about all of this," Rita said to everyone.

"Please don't apologize," Lily said. "None of this is your fault."

"We're so grateful that you've given us a place to stay while we wait out the storm," Chloe added.

Rita gave us a brief smile. "I appreciate that you're so understanding."

Everyone went back to eating and chatting quietly.

"I nearly passed out from fright," Chloe whispered to me and Brett. "When the lights went out, I thought the murderer was about to kill again."

"Me too," I admitted.

"It's just the storm," Brett assured us. "We're going to be fine."

I hoped he was right, but I couldn't entirely banish the sense of unease that plagued me.

* * * *

Once Harvey had the generator up and running and we'd all had our fill of food, we helped Rita pack up the leftovers and put them away in the commercial refrigerator in the kitchen. Thanks to the generator, the fridge would keep running as long as the fuel lasted. Zahra had handed out the battery-powered lanterns, and Chloe, Brett, and I had two to share between us.

Rita stoked up the fire in the lounge, and all of us gathered in that room to chat and stay warm. We talked about Lily's books, Ambrose's poetry, the pancake house, and what it was like to live year-round up in the mountains. Although the conversation was friendly, I couldn't relax completely, but I tried not to let it show.

Brett had his arm around me, and Chloe sat on my other side, all of us on the couch. With the three of us all together, and with everyone else in sight, I knew we were safe for the moment. I just hoped that would stay true through the night.

Chloe picked up one of the Holly Lodge brochures that was lying on the coffee table and read it by firelight.

"Did you guys know that this place is haunted?" she whispered to me and Brett when she set down the brochure a minute later. She sounded more worried than before.

"It's Holly Lake that's haunted—supposedly—not the lodge," I said.

"And it's just a story," Brett added in a low voice.

I knew he was trying to allay some of Chloe's fears, so I didn't mention the woman Brett and I had seen while out snowshoeing. Chloe said nothing more about the ghost, but she remained tense, and I knew the story about Henrietta Franklin hadn't helped her already worried state.

Eventually, yawns punctuated the conversations going on around the room. Rita and Zahra disappeared for a few minutes and returned with a platter of leftover sandwiches for a makeshift dinner. We all dug in, and it didn't take long for us to empty the platter.

There didn't seem to be much reason to stick around after eating. Everyone was too sleepy to keep chatting and I was struggling to keep my eyes open. I was reluctant to leave the warmth of the fire, but Rita assured us that we could use the gas fireplaces in the guest rooms. Even without the generator, the fireplaces would still work, thanks to their battery backups.

I hesitated when Brett first suggested heading upstairs. As much as I was ready to get some sleep, I took comfort from being able to see everyone present at the lodge. If the killer was among us, at least I knew what they were up to. That wasn't going to last, though. Lily soon headed upstairs to bed, and Ambrose followed a few minutes later.

Harvey and Evie got bundled up, ready to make the short trek out to Harvey's cabin. They'd left Scout there and didn't want him to be on his own any longer.

Even with just the firelight to see by, I could tell that Rita was exhausted. Brett, Chloe, and I said good night, and headed upstairs by the light of our lanterns. Chloe curled up on the loveseat with extra pillows and blankets we'd found in the closet, and I burrowed under the covers on the bed, Brett beside me.

Chloe jumped up from the loveseat a moment later, startling me.

"What's wrong?" I asked.

The gas fireplace provided enough light for me to see her crossing the room.

"I want to be absolutely sure no one can get in," she said, grabbing the chair from beneath the small desk.

"I locked the door," Brett reminded her.

"I know." She tipped the chair, lodging the top rail beneath the doorknob.

"Does that really work?" I asked. "I thought it only did in the movies."

Chloe returned to the loveseat and snuggled under the blankets again. "I don't know, but I'm going to pretend it does."

I grabbed my phone from the bedside table, planning to check the weather app for some indication of when the storm might end. I really hoped we wouldn't be stuck at Holly Lodge for another day and night.

When I woke up the device, I remembered the text message I'd received from Sienna. I leaned back against the pillows and tapped on the message.

Reading Lily's book and guess what, the text read. *The murderer buried the victim in a snowbank to hide the body. Coincidence??? Unlikely, right?*

I sat up straight. "Holy buckets!"

Chloe peeked over the back of the loveseat. "What is it?" Her gaze darted to the door, and then to the window.

I waved away her obvious concern about someone coming into our room. "This text message from Sienna…I think she cracked the case!"

"What do you mean?" Brett asked.

I handed my phone over so he could read the message himself, but I explained anyway, for Chloe's sake. "Sienna bought one of Lily's books, one set on Mount Baker, and she started reading it this weekend. Apparently, the murderer in the story buries the victim in a snowbank to delay the discovery of the body."

Chloe's eyes widened. "You think Lily's the murderer? And she copied one of her books? Oh my gosh! I was chatting with a killer earlier!"

Brett handed my phone back to me, his expression serious. "But didn't you say Lily received a threatening note from the killer?"

I drummed my fingers against my phone. "Maybe that was a lie. Come to think of it, she was a bit cagey when I talked to her about the note, and she seemed a bit hesitant about showing it to Sheriff Walczyk."

"So the note was a fake?" Chloe wrapped herself in a blanket and hurried over to the bed, perching on the mattress by my feet. "Did she make it all up?"

"Probably," I said. "I bet she was hoping it would deflect suspicion away from her."

"But why would she kill Kevin?" Brett asked.

"I know she was annoyed that he didn't want her to set her next book at Holly Lodge," I said. "That seems like a flimsy motive, but maybe she was angry about something else too? Or maybe she just lost her temper while arguing with him about the book's setting again."

"Could be," Brett agreed, although he didn't sound overly convinced by the theory. "I guess it's not impossible. It's not like Lily's too short to have hit Kevin in the head with the ski."

That was true. She was a couple of inches taller than me, which put her at about five foot seven. She was a thin woman, but that didn't mean she wasn't strong enough to kill a man.

"Do you know what this means?" Chloe said in an urgent whisper. "Kevin's murderer is sleeping across the hall from us. We really are under the same roof as his killer. And we can't get away!"

"We'll be fine." Brett's voice was calm, but his face remained serious. "She has no reason to want to hurt any of us."

"Except..." I trailed off, not sure if I should finish my thought.

"Except what?" Chloe pressed.

I glanced at Brett, wishing I'd kept my mouth shut. I didn't want to scare Chloe any further, but I knew she wouldn't let me get away with not finishing my sentence. "I've been asking questions, and I talked to Lily about the note."

"Do you think she knows you've been trying to figure out who killed Kevin?" Brett asked.

I shrugged. "It's possible."

A chill that rivaled the howling winds outside settled into my bones.

Brett took my hand and gave it a squeeze. "We're still fine. Even if Lily thinks you could be onto her, there's no way she'd try to harm all three of us. As long as we stick together, we'll be okay."

"You're right." Knowing that didn't entirely erase my fear, but it helped to ease it. "Sheriff Walczyk needs to know about this, though."

I tapped out a message to Sienna, expressing my surprise and thanking her for telling me. She wrote back right away, letting me know that she'd told her mom, who in turn had looked up the number for the sheriff of the mountain community and had contacted Walczyk.

I breathed a little easier. "It turns out we don't need to worry about that. Patricia contacted the sheriff earlier today."

Chloe pulled the blanket more closely around her. "So maybe she's just waiting for a chance to arrest Lily."

"Or at least question her again," Brett said.

"So now all we have to do is wait out the storm." I set my phone on the bedside table and shifted closer to Brett.

Chloe got up and returned to the loveseat. "I don't know if I can sleep a single wink tonight, but I guess I should try."

"We're going to be fine," Brett said as I snuggled up against him.

Despite his words, I could tell that he wasn't entirely relaxed.

I didn't expect any of us to fall asleep, but I must have drifted off eventually, because I woke abruptly to the sound of a shrill scream.

Chapter Twenty-Seven

Chloe shot upright on the loveseat. "What was that? What's happening?"

Brett was already out of bed and heading for the door.

"Wait!" I scrambled to get out from beneath the covers. "We have to stick together, remember?"

Brett slowed down, although not by much. I thought I heard a noise out in the hall, but maybe it was just the sound of Brett shoving the chair away from the door. Chloe and I jumped up to join him. We were all fully dressed, not having brought any pajamas, so Brett wasted no more time. He yanked open the door and stepped out into the hallway. I peeked out from behind him. The hall was pitch black.

A terrible, keening moan came from somewhere not too far off. The sound sent a shiver of fear down my spine.

"We need the lanterns," Brett said.

I grabbed one, switching it on as I handed it to Brett. Chloe fetched the other, and we all cautiously made our way out into the hall.

A door farther down the corridor opened. Ambrose poked his head out, holding a lantern of his own in one hand and putting on his glasses with the other.

"What's going on?" he asked when he saw us.

"That's what we're trying to find out." Brett headed toward the stairway.

I grabbed Chloe's hand and we followed after him.

"What happened?" Zahra's voice came from below us.

When we were halfway down the stairs, Brett swore and then picked up his pace.

Chloe and I hurried after him as my heart thumped hard in my chest.

I didn't see what had caused Brett to swear until I reached the bottom of the stairs, where he'd crouched down.

Lily lay on her back at the base of the stairway. She let out a moan of pain that turned into a sob.

Zahra and Rita rushed toward us from across the lobby. They were both wearing dressing gowns over pajamas. Brett was on his knees next to Lily, his lantern on the floor beside him.

"Lily!" Ambrose had come down the stairs behind us.

"Give her some space," Brett cautioned as Ambrose made a grab for her hand.

Ambrose halted and took a step back, his eyes wide behind his glasses.

"What happened?" Brett asked Lily.

"Someone pushed me down the stairs," she choked out between sobs.

I exchanged a wide-eyed glance with Chloe.

Brett remained completely calm. "What hurts?"

Lily's face contorted with pain. "My ankle. The left one."

Rita hurried around the reception desk. "I'll turn the lights on."

A second later we all blinked as light flooded the lobby.

I moved a few feet away from Lily, taking Chloe with me. Rita and Zahra came over our way while Brett talked to Lily and assessed her condition, Ambrose hovering over them.

"Brett has first-aid training," I told the others. "Hopefully she's not hurt too badly."

Rita clutched at her dressing gown. "The blizzard's still going strong, and I doubt the tree's been cleared from the highway. There's no way an ambulance can get here if she needs one."

"Let's hope it's not that bad," Zahra said. She lowered her voice to a whisper. "Did she say someone pushed her?"

"She definitely said that." Chloe's voice shook.

I tucked my arm around hers. "Maybe she was mistaken?"

What I was really thinking was maybe Lily had concocted another lie to deflect suspicion away from herself. If she wasn't truly injured, that theory would have more credence in my mind.

"Lie still for a minute," Brett said to Lily before getting up and coming over to talk to the rest of us.

Ambrose stayed by Lily's side, crouching down and taking her hand in his.

"There's a good chance her ankle is broken," Brett told us. "Fortunately, that seems to be the worst of her injuries, but she needs to go to the hospital."

"There's no way that's happening until the storm is over," Rita said.

Brett's mouth formed a grim line. "That's what I figured." He glanced at Lily. "Let's at least get her somewhere more comfortable."

Rita moved behind the reception desk. "I'll call 911. An ambulance might not be able to get here now, but if they know we need one, they can send one as soon as possible."

As Rita pick up the phone, Brett returned to Lily's side. He spoke quietly with her for a moment, and then helped her to sit up before gently scooping her up into his arms.

"Where to?" I asked him.

"Probably the couch in the lounge."

All of us except Rita headed that way. Zahra flicked on the overhead lights and then returned to the lobby, where Rita was on the phone.

Brett set Lily on the couch and tucked a couple of cushions beneath her left foot. Ambrose pulled up a chair and sat next to Lily, holding her hand. She'd stopped crying, but her face was creased with pain.

I took Brett's arm and led him across the room, Chloe coming with us.

"Is she really hurt?" I asked in a whisper. "Could she be faking it?"

"I don't think she's faking it," Brett said. "I'm pretty sure her ankle's broken."

Chloe spoke so softly that I could barely hear her. "But if she's not faking it, who pushed her down the stairs? And *why*?"

I kept my voice equally low. "Maybe she threw herself down the stairs and didn't mean to get hurt so badly?"

Brett ran a hand down his face. "I have no idea what's going on. All I know is that she needs to see a doctor."

Rita came into the lounge and everyone except Lily turned her way.

"As we thought, an ambulance can't get here," Rita said.

"I'll be okay," Lily said, closing her eyes.

Rita held up a small bottle. "I brought some ibuprofen. Hopefully that will help with the pain."

Zahra appeared behind her. "And I've got a glass of water for you, Lily."

Lily opened her eyes as Zahra set the water on the coffee table. "Thank you."

Movement outside the back door startled me half a second before someone rapped on the glass.

"It's Harvey and Evie!" Zahra rushed over and unlocked the door.

The new arrivals hurried inside with a blast of cold air and a swirl of snowflakes. Zahra quickly shut and locked the door behind them.

"We saw the lights on," Evie said, pulling a knitted hat from her head. "We wanted to make sure everything was all right."

Zahra explained what had happened.

"Pushed?" Harvey said with a frown once Zahra had finished. "Are you sure?"

Lily nodded, opening her eyes halfway as she did so.

The rest of us looked at one another. I knew we were all wondering which one of us had given Lily the shove that sent her down the stairs. I doubted that anyone other than me, Brett, and Chloe knew there was a chance that Lily had thrown herself down the stairs, not intending to break any bones.

"Who was upstairs when it happened?" Harvey asked.

"Chloe, Marley, and I," Brett said. "And Ambrose."

We all looked to the poet.

"It wasn't me!" Ambrose said, on the defensive. "How can we know for sure that someone else wasn't up there too?"

"There is a back stairway," Zahra said.

Silence fell around us as we all eyed each other uneasily. I was glad when Brett broke the tense silence by speaking to Lily.

"Would you be more comfortable upstairs?" he asked her.

Her eyes shot open. "No!" She struggled to compose herself. "I mean, no, thank you. I...I don't want to be alone."

Rita fingered the collar of her dressing gown. "Maybe we should all stay here together."

From the way she darted glances at each of us, I suspected she'd finally come to terms with the fact that Kevin's killer could very well be among us.

"Good idea," Brett said. "Or at least in large groups."

I slipped my hand into his and he gave it a gentle squeeze.

Lily reached for a blanket that was lying over the back of the couch. Ambrose helped her unfold it and tucked it around her.

Zahra added more wood to the fire. "Is anyone else cold?"

"A little," Chloe said.

"Me too," I added.

"Hot drinks and blankets," Rita said. "That's what we need if we're all going to stay here in the lounge."

We all looked at each other for a moment.

"There's nine of us here," I noted. "Let's not split up into groups of less than three people."

Everyone nodded in agreement to that suggestion.

"Zahra and I will get blankets." Rita hesitated, glancing around as if wondering who should be the third person in their group.

"I'll go with you," Chloe volunteered.

"Are you sure?" I whispered to her.

She nodded and whispered back, "I trust Zahra."

Brett's hand tightened slightly around mine. I knew he wasn't keen on letting Chloe out of his sight. I wasn't either, but I did think she'd be okay in the company of both Rita and Zahra. Hopefully they wouldn't be gone for more than a minute or two.

Evie spoke up. "I'll make some hot drinks. Harvey and Ambrose, will you help me?"

Harvey didn't hesitate to agree. Ambrose was clearly reluctant to leave Lily's side, but after giving her hand a squeeze he got up and followed Evie and Harvey out of the lounge.

That left me and Brett alone with Lily.

This was my chance to get some answers out of her.

Chapter Twenty-Eight

I sat in the chair that Ambrose had vacated, facing Lily.

"How are you doing?" I asked as I tried to figure out how to pose my next questions.

She toyed with the edge of the blanket that was covering her. "All right. My ankle hurts, but I'm glad that's my only injury."

"So am I," I said.

Whether she was pushed or had thrown herself down the stairs, her injuries could have been far worse.

"Do you remember anything about the person who pushed you?" I asked. "Did you see anything? Hear anything?"

She shrugged. "Not much. When I reached the stairs, I heard the floor creak behind me. I started to turn around, but the push happened so fast. I remember seeing a shadowy figure at the top of the stairs as I was falling, but nothing more than that."

"Do you think it was a man? A woman?" Brett asked.

Lily shook her head. "I really don't know. It could have been anyone." She shivered and pulled the blanket up to her chin.

I asked my next question. "Why were you up at that hour?"

"I couldn't sleep. I wanted to sit down here by the fire. The wood fire is cozier than the gas one in my room."

I wasn't sure if I believed that explanation or not, but I knew I couldn't waste any more time. If I wanted to get to the heart of the matter, I needed to do it now.

"A friend of mine is reading one of your books," I said. "The one set on Mount Baker."

"Oh?" Lily wouldn't meet my eyes and shifted under the blanket.

Sarah Fox

She was nervous. I had no doubt about that.

"She told me a bit about the book," I continued. "Like how the body of the victim was buried in a snowbank."

Lily's nervousness morphed into fear. I could see it in her eyes when she finally met my gaze.

"So?" The single word came out as little more than a squeak.

"It seems like an awfully big coincidence that the same thing happened to Kevin," I said.

Lily sat up and clutched the edge of the blanket. "I didn't kill Kevin!"

"Then how do you explain the similarities with your book?" Brett asked.

I was grateful that he was supporting my quest for answers.

"I don't know!" Lily sounded close to tears. "I might not be super famous, but a lot of people have read my books."

"But you must have noticed the similarity right away," I said.

"I did," she admitted. "And I told Sheriff Walczyk about it. I didn't mention it to anyone else because I didn't want you guys to suspect me. I know how it looks, but it really wasn't me. What about the note?" she added desperately. "Remember that?"

"The note you made yourself?"

I didn't know for sure that I was right about that, but I was hoping to flush out the truth.

It worked.

Lily's eyes widened. "How did you..." She seemed to realize what she was admitting. "No...I..." She squeezed her eyes shut.

"Why would you do that if not to deflect suspicion away from yourself?" I asked.

Lily opened her eyes and wiped away an escaped tear. She winced with pain as she shifted on the couch. "I shouldn't have done that." She sounded weary now. "I regretted it as soon as I talked to the reporter in Wildwood Cove."

"Why did you do it?" Brett pressed.

She sighed heavily and wiped away another tear. "Publicity."

I stared at her for a moment. "You made it look like a murderer was targeting you so you could sell more books?"

"It's not easy to make it as an author!" she said in her defense. "I thought it might stir up some interest in my books." She sagged against the cushion behind her. "I know I shouldn't have done it. It was stupid. But I swear that's all there was to it. I didn't kill Kevin and someone really did push me down the stairs."

She seemed sincere, but I didn't know if I should believe her.

"If what you told us is true, why would anyone push you down the stairs?" I asked.

"Because I've been asking questions," she said. "I love mysteries, obviously. I've written several now and I thought maybe I could figure this one out."

Her admission gave rise to several more questions that I wanted to ask her. Unfortunately, our time for a private chat had run out.

I stood up as Rita, Zahra, and Chloe returned to the lounge, each of them with an armful of blankets. Evie, Harvey, and Ambrose appeared a moment later with an electric kettle full of hot water, a pot of coffee, mugs, spoons, hot chocolate powder, sugar, and cream, all set out on trays carried by the two men.

Once everyone had a blanket and a hot drink in hand, we found ourselves places to sit. Chloe nudged an armchair closer to the cozy loveseat where Brett and I settled. He put his arm around me, and together with the hot drink and blanket, that helped to ward off the worst of the chill. It didn't entirely banish my unease, though.

If Lily was telling the truth—and maybe she was—then someone had tried to harm her, likely because she'd been trying to solve Kevin's murder. If that someone knew that I'd been asking questions too, I could be a target as well. As much as I would have preferred being up in our room, I wanted to keep an eye on the others. As long as I knew where everyone was, I'd likely be safe, and Brett and Chloe would be too.

Rita lit some candles around the room and shut off the electric lights. We chatted quietly in small groups while Lily rested on the couch. She had her eyes closed, but I didn't think she'd fallen asleep. I didn't know if it was the pain from her ankle or her worries about her assailant keeping her awake. Maybe it was both.

Time seemed to pass at an excruciatingly slow pace. At first I watched everyone by the light of the fire and candles, searching their faces for any sign of guilt, even as I pretended not to be studying them. After a while, it became more and more difficult to keep my eyes open, despite my worries about a killer being among us.

I rested my head on Brett's shoulder, and the sounds of the crackling fire and hushed voices faded farther away.

I jolted awake sometime later. Everyone was where they'd been sitting earlier, except Evie, who now stood by the window. The fire was still burning brightly, but I didn't know if that was because someone had added more wood to it or because I'd slept for only a few minutes.

"The storm's dying down," Evie said.

I wondered how she could see anything out the window, but then I realized there was the tiniest bit of bluish light outside.

"The moon's even poking through the clouds," Evie added.

It was still snowing, but I couldn't hear any howling wind, and the snowflakes were falling straight to the ground rather than swirling in gusts and drifts.

"How long was I asleep?" I asked Brett.

He kissed the side of my head. "Almost two hours."

I rubbed my neck. Two hours of resting my head on his shoulder came at a price.

"Did I miss anything?" I whispered.

"No. It's been quiet."

I glanced over at Chloe. She was curled up in the armchair, sleeping.

Brett shifted forward on the loveseat. "I need to stretch my legs."

I got up at the same time as he did. "And I need to use the washroom."

Chloe stirred and opened her eyes. They widened as soon as she saw me and Brett on our feet.

She sat up straight. "What's going on?"

"I'm heading for the washroom," I replied.

She got up quickly, all vestiges of sleepiness gone. "I'll come with you."

I didn't even have to ask Brett to accompany us. He was already falling into step with us.

We took two lanterns with us so we wouldn't have to turn on the overhead lights and drain the generator's fuel.

"I can't believe I actually fell asleep," Chloe said with a yawn as we headed upstairs. "Talk about the creepiest night ever."

I unlocked the door to our room. "I'm surprised I fell asleep too. I wouldn't have been able to without you and Brett there beside me."

We didn't linger long upstairs, only staying long enough for each of us to make use of the washroom. On our way back down to the lobby, I told Chloe about the conversation that Brett and I had had with Lily earlier.

"So, do you think she's telling the truth?" Chloe asked after I'd finished sharing everything Lily had said.

"Maybe?" I looked to Brett for his opinion.

"She seemed like she was telling the truth, but it's hard to know for sure," he said.

We'd reached the lobby, but we came to a stop instead of returning to the lounge, so we could continue our conversation in private.

"If she's being honest," Chloe said, "who could have pushed her? We know it wasn't the three of us, and Evie and Harvey were at Harvey's cabin."

"So they said." Brett voiced the thought before I had a chance.

"Zahra and Rita came running from their private quarters," I added. "But there's a back stairway. If they were fast, one of them could have pushed Lily from upstairs and then run down the back stairs. For that matter, Evie or Harvey could have done that, slipping out the back door afterwards."

"I know it wasn't Zahra." There was no doubt in Chloe's voice. "She wasn't even here when Kevin was killed, right?"

I wasn't so sure that let Zahra off the hook completely. "But if Rita killed Kevin, and Zahra knows that, she might have wanted to stop Lily from asking questions."

"I don't think Rita's guilty either." This time Chloe didn't sound quite as sure.

"*Somebody* is," Brett pointed out. "Somebody who's in this lodge with us right now."

Chloe shuddered at that reminder.

I thought back to what had happened after we'd heard Lily's scream. "Ambrose came out of his room after we opened our door."

"Could he have pushed Lily and then run back to his room without us hearing him?" Chloe asked.

"That's exactly what I was wondering," I said. "I thought I heard a sound out in the hall after Lily's scream, but I don't know for sure if I did."

"But isn't Ambrose in love with Lily?" Brett asked. "He seems pretty concerned about her."

I rubbed my face. "I can't figure it out."

Brett rested a hand on my shoulder. "Hopefully we won't have to. With the storm dying down, maybe a crew will be able to clear the road. Then we can get an ambulance and the sheriff up here."

That would be a relief.

I nearly jumped out of my skin when a phone rang. The ringing wasn't from any of our cell phones, and the phone sitting on the reception desk remained silent. The sound was coming from the office, I realized. The door stood ajar, so I moved around the reception desk and pushed it open.

"Someone must have left their phone in here."

I spotted the glow of the cell phone as soon as I had the door open. The device sat on the desk. The ringing stopped and the screen went dark a moment later.

I held up the lantern I had in my hand. "Do you think I should take it to Rita?" I asked Brett and Chloe. "It's probably her phone."

I didn't hear their replies. I was too distracted by what I was staring at. By the light of the lantern, I studied the diplomas and certificates on the wall. I'd seen them before, but I hadn't paid enough attention on either occasion.

"What is it, Marley?" Brett asked from the office doorway.

I drew in a sharp breath. "I think I know who killed Kevin."

Chapter Twenty-Nine

The revelation had unsettled me so much that I forgot the reason why I'd come into the office in the first place. Whispering, I shared my new theory with Brett and Chloe. I didn't have any proof—yet—but I knew I had it right this time.

We left the office, intending to head back to the lounge so we could keep an eye on everyone. As we made our way around the reception desk, Ambrose emerged from the dining room, carrying a mug of steaming liquid.

I stopped short. "You're alone? What happened to staying in groups?"

He shrugged while holding the mug steady. "I was just going around the corner. I figured if I yelled for help, everyone would hear me. Besides, some of the others are sleeping."

He continued on into the lounge, and we followed him, my nerves taut. How much longer would we have to sit and wait in the dark with a murderer?

Rita had nodded off in her chair in our absence, as had Evie. Zahra sat staring at the flames in the fireplace, and Lily hadn't moved from the couch. She had her eyes closed, but when we entered the room, they fluttered open.

I sat on the edge of the loveseat, unable to relax. I tried to breathe normally, but despite my efforts my breaths remained shallow. I didn't know how much more of this I could take.

Brett sat next to me and put a hand to my back. The gesture brought me some comfort, but I still couldn't relax.

Chloe seemed equally ill at ease. She sat down in an armchair, but like me, she perched on the edge, as if ready to jump up at any moment.

Ambrose reclaimed his chair beside the couch. He held out the mug to Lily. "Here's your tea."

I jolted up out of my seat. "That's for Lily?"

My voice rang out like a shot in the quiet room. Evie and Rita stirred, and Lily's eyes widened. She nearly spilled the hot liquid on herself as she accepted the mug from Ambrose.

"I really wanted some peppermint tea," she said, sending a puzzled glance my way.

I felt everyone's gazes on me. I wasn't sure what to do next, until Lily raised the mug to her lips.

"Don't drink it!" I lunged across the room and grabbed the mug from her. A few drops slopped over the edge and spilled onto the floor.

Lily gasped, even though I'd managed not to spill the hot liquid on her. "What are you doing?" she demanded, looking at me like I was crazy.

Ambrose was on his feet now too. "Have you gone mad?"

I backed away, still holding the mug. I bumped into someone, and knew right away that it was Brett. He put an arm around my waist to steady me.

"What did you put in this?" I asked Ambrose.

"What do you mean? It's *tea*," he said. "Peppermint tea."

"And what else?" I set the mug on the mantel.

Everyone was alert now, focused on me and Ambrose.

"What's going on?" Rita asked me as she stood up. "Do you know something we don't?"

"I know Ambrose killed Kevin," I said, never taking my gaze off of him.

He stared at me from behind his glasses, the reflection of the firelight flickering in the lenses. I thought he was trying to remain impassive, but a shadow of something passed quickly across his face. *Fear? Anger?*

I suppressed a shiver, thinking it might be both. Maybe that made him more dangerous than ever.

"No way!" Lily exclaimed. "Ambrose wouldn't hurt anyone." She looked up at him. "Right, Ambrose?"

"Of course I wouldn't," Ambrose said. "Marley's lost her mind. Either that or she's trying to cover up for herself."

Brett tensed beside me. I knew he was about to speak out in my defense, but I took his hand and gave it a squeeze, letting him know he didn't need to.

"I thought you had something to lose by Kevin's death," I said, still addressing Ambrose. "That story about wanting to hold writing retreats here wasn't exactly true, was it?" I didn't give him a chance to deny it. "Maybe you do want to hold retreats here, but not big ones. You hate crowds. You like peace and quiet and prefer small groups of people. That's why you come to Holly Lodge. At least, that's why you came in the beginning. But now you have another reason, don't you?"

"What are you talking about?" Lily's voice practically dripped with scorn. "I know Ambrose. He's not a killer."

"I know you *think* you know him," I said, "and you probably think that your love for him is reciprocated. But he's in love with someone else."

"That's not true!" Lily sounded frustrated now.

I turned to Rita. She stood watching the scene unfold with shock in her eyes.

"Rita is short for Marguerite," I said. "I never gave your name a second thought until I saw your diplomas in the office." I shifted my gaze from Rita to Ambrose. "Marguerite is the name of a flower. The flower of your heart," I said, referencing the poem he'd read two weeks earlier. "You're in love with Rita and you wanted her for yourself. Lily was asking questions, trying to solve Kevin's murder, so you pushed her down the stairs. What did you put in her tea, Ambrose? Was this your second attempt at silencing her?"

"This is nuts!" Lily fumed.

"*She's* nuts." Ambrose stared at me, hatred simmering in his eyes.

Uncertainty flickered across Lily's face. "Except…"

"Except what?" Brett asked.

Lily hesitated before speaking, her wide-eyed gaze fixed on Ambrose. "There's that poem you wrote. Another one. Called *Marguerite*."

Ambrose's head snapped in her direction. "How do you know about that? I've never shared that poem with anyone!"

Lily shrank back in the face of his wrath. "I peeked at your notebook one day. I was curious if you'd written anything about me. About us. I thought maybe Marguerite was an ex-girlfriend from before we met."

Ambrose's mouth twisted, as if he was about to snarl.

Shock registered on Lily's face. "You really did do it, didn't you? You killed Kevin. And you copied my book. That made me look suspicious!"

He glowered at Lily. "I was hoping the body wouldn't be found so soon."

Rita let out a sob. "How could you?"

Ambrose only had eyes for Rita now. He took a step toward her. "I've cared for you for so long. Kevin made you unhappy. He always has. I couldn't stand to watch you suffering any longer. When I had a chance to set you free, I had to take it."

Rita shook her head, tears trickling down her face. "We argued, but we loved each other. He's the only man I wanted to be with."

Ambrose took another step closer to her. "No. I could make you so much happier." He reached a hand out to her. "I love you."

Rita recoiled from his touch.

That flicked a switch in Ambrose. He looked around at all of us, and seemed to realize the peril of his situation.

"I did it for you!" he yelled.

Then he shoved Rita aside and made a dash for the door.

Chapter Thirty

Shock kept the rest of us frozen in place for a second, but no longer.

Harvey was first to the door. He jammed his feet into his boots and then dashed out into the snow. I made a mad dash for the lobby and grabbed my own boots, pulling them on and running out the back door. Almost too late, I realized that the porch steps were slippery, covered in snow and ice.

I grabbed the railing to keep myself from falling and managed to make it down the steps safely. I knew Brett was right behind me, and others too, but I didn't look back.

Ambrose had made a beeline for the lake. I charged down the unshoveled pathway, my progress hampered by the deep snow.

The faintest hint of daylight lightened the sky, and only a few snowflakes drifted down from the clouds.

At the bottom of the pathway, Ambrose left the shore for the frozen surface, slipping and sliding on the snow-covered ice.

Harvey slowed his pace before leaving the shore, moving carefully.

I slipped on the path and nearly went down. Brett grabbed my arm, keeping me on my feet.

We slowed down as we reached the lake.

Harvey was shuffling his way across the ice. Ambrose was still well ahead of him, struggling along.

"Ambrose, no!" Harvey yelled.

Ambrose showed no sign that he heard him.

Brett and I stopped at the edge of the lake. I gasped for breath, the cold air hurting my lungs.

Zahra and Evie came running up behind us. For the first time, I glanced back. Everyone else had stayed at the lodge.

"Where does he think he's going?" Zahra asked. "He doesn't even have a coat or boots."

"That might be the least of his problems," Brett said grimly.

I realized why a moment later.

Harvey halted on the ice and cupped his hands around his mouth. "Ambrose, come back! The ice isn't safe out there!"

If Ambrose heard Harvey's warning, he ignored it.

Harvey took two steps forward.

"Harvey, stay back!" Evie called out.

He stopped again.

We all watched as Ambrose continued to flee across the lake.

Maybe he'd make it safely to the opposite shore and the police would track him down unharmed later on. I figured he'd probably decided to take the shortest route across the lake in the hope of finding a getaway car or snowmobile at one of the houses over there. Or maybe he'd reacted with no thought at all.

Those theories had barely run through my head when I heard a crack and Ambrose dropped out of sight.

Evie let out a strangled cry.

Harvey bellowed Ambrose's name and then turned around and hurried back to shore, shuffling and sliding across the snowy ice.

"We need a rope!" he called as he moved toward us.

He hit the shore running, heading back toward the lodge. Brett took off after him.

"What do we do?" Zahra sounded distraught.

"Nothing," Evie said, her voice bleak. "If we go out there without a rope, we'll end up in the water just like Ambrose."

I stood up on tiptoes, trying to get a better view of the spot where Ambrose had fallen through the ice. The snow on the lake made it hard to see clearly, but I thought I spotted his head bobbing in the water.

"How long can he survive in there?" I asked.

"Ten minutes, maybe," Evie said.

Harvey and Brett came running back down the pathway. Brett slid down the steepest part, but stayed on his feet. Harvey had a coil of rope over his shoulder and Brett was carrying a flotation device.

Harvey was already uncoiling the rope when he reached the edge of the lake. He quickly tied one end of it around himself and tossed the other end to Brett, who handed him the flotation device. Harvey tucked it under his arm and started out across the ice.

"Be careful," Evie called to him.

Brett stayed on shore with the rest of us, keeping a good grip on the end of the rope.

Each second seemed to pass slowly as we watched Harvey's progress. When he'd moved beyond the safe ice, he got down on his hands and knees. Then he slid forward on his belly, his progress hampered by all the snow covering the ice.

I could barely breathe from the tension. I couldn't see if Ambrose's head was still above the surface of the water.

Harvey had come to a stop on his stomach, near the edge of the broken ice.

He stayed there for at least two full minutes, barely moving, before he slowly turned around and slithered back toward us on his stomach. Brett reeled in the rope, helping him with his progress. When he was back on firm ice, Harvey got to his feet and shuffled to shore.

Apprehension settled heavily over my shoulders. There was no way he had good news to deliver.

"He went under when I was about halfway there," Harvey said, his face somber. "He didn't resurface."

I tried to process everything that had happened over the past few minutes, but my mind was too numb to make sense of any of it.

Brett put an arm around my shoulders and I realized that I was shivering. I hadn't noticed the cold until then, but now I felt chilled to the bone.

"Let's get inside where it's warm," Brett said, already nudging me in the direction of the lodge. "We need to call the sheriff."

We all trudged up the path to Holly Lodge, where the others were waiting to hear the grim news.

Chapter Thirty-One

We waited more than an hour for Sheriff Walczyk to arrive at Holly Lodge. By then the snow had stopped falling and the downed tree had been cleared from the highway. I even spotted a couple of patches of blue sky when I peered out the window, watching as the sheriff and two of her deputies headed down to the lake, Harvey walking beside them.

An ambulance had also arrived and had just pulled out of the parking lot, with Lily safely on board. Physically she was fine, aside from her ankle injury, but I figured it would take her a long time to recover from the shock of learning that Ambrose had been a murderer.

Another two hours passed before Sheriff Walczyk was content to let us head home. I was long past ready to get out of there. We'd all answered questions and given statements, and I wanted nothing more than to return to the comforting familiarity of home.

Chloe wanted to talk to Zahra one last time before we left, so she set off for the dining room, where we'd last seen Rita's daughter. I returned to the window, looking out toward the frozen lake. It would be Ambrose's final resting place, like it probably was for Henrietta Franklin, unless his body was recovered in the future. There wasn't much chance of that happening before spring.

I was horrified by what Ambrose had done, but his death had also left me shaken. I knew there was nothing more we could have done without ending up in the icy water along with him, but the memory of standing there helplessly on the shore as he drowned haunted me.

I was about to turn away from the window when something caught my eye. I peered out toward the forest, wondering if my eyes had played a trick on me.

No. I saw it again. A flicker through the trees.

Was that red hair and a green dress?

My coat and boots were by the back door. I pulled them on as quickly as I could.

"Marley?" Brett called from across the room.

"I'll be back soon," I said over my shoulder as I dashed out the door.

At the bottom of the porch steps, I stopped and scanned the forest. At first I saw nothing. Then I spotted another flicker of red between the trees.

"Everything okay?" Harvey came up beside me.

"I think I just saw Henrietta. Or, something…" I pointed at the woods on the eastern side of the lake. "What's the fastest way to get over there?"

Harvey didn't hesitate. "Snowmobile. Come on. I want to see the ghost again."

He jogged over to one of the smaller outbuildings and hauled open the double doors. Two snowmobiles were parked inside. He handed me a helmet and grabbed another for himself before getting onto the closest snowmobile.

"Jump on," he said before starting up the machine.

My helmet secure, I climbed onto the seat behind him. He drove slowly out of the shed and past the lodge. Then we picked up speed, zooming along the lakeshore.

Sheriff Walczyk and her deputies looked our way, but then they were out of sight.

I shouted general directions to Harvey. When the shoreline became too steep, he veered off into the woods, following the same trail Brett and I had taken on our snowshoeing trek.

We'd almost reached the far side of the lake without any further ghost sightings. I figured we were out of luck, but then I spotted the red hair again. Or, what I thought was red hair.

I tapped Harvey on the shoulder. "Stop here."

He brought the machine to a halt between the shore and one of the houses that was almost directly across the lake from Holly Lodge.

Someone had just disappeared inside the A-frame house.

I climbed off the snowmobile and ran through the snow. I jogged up the steps to the large porch and then rapped on the french doors.

Inside a brightly lit kitchen, a woman spun around, her eyes widening when she saw me. She shoved something onto a chair and out of sight before opening the door.

"Marley?" she said, clearly surprised by my appearance. "What are you doing here?"

"Hi, Cindy. I guess you could say I'm ghost hunting."

Her face paled, but she didn't say anything.

"Except," I continued, "I think the ghost I was chasing is very much alive."

Cindy's shoulders sagged and she let out a resigned sigh. She stepped back. "You'd better come inside."

I gestured to Harvey and he joined us in Cindy's warm kitchen. She retrieved the wig and the dark green dress she'd stashed on the chair. Both items were soaking wet and bedraggled, the fake red hair tangled.

"Please don't bother Rita about this," Cindy requested. "She has far too much to deal with already."

"Rita was in on this?" I asked.

Harvey stayed quiet, listening.

"It was her idea," Cindy explained. "She thought if there were some sightings of Henrietta, it might help to draw more people to Holly Lodge. We thought it would be especially good if Lily Spitz saw the ghost while she was here. She has lots of followers on social media. If she talked about her ghost sighting online, it could stir up a lot of interest."

"But today of all days?" I said.

"No. I didn't mean for there to be a sighting today." Cindy dropped the wet dress and wig onto the kitchen table. "I wore these yesterday morning, in the hope that Lily—or anyone—might spot me flitting in and out of the woods. I had to take them off before I returned to Holly Lodge, so I hid them in a hollowed tree. Then the blizzard hit. Thanks to the wind, they got covered in snow, even in their hiding place. I almost didn't find them today. I was just bringing them home. I wasn't even wearing them. I didn't realize someone would see me carrying them."

"So the ghost isn't real," I said, not particularly surprised.

"Oh, she's real all right," Cindy said. "I was serious when I said I've seen her myself."

Harvey nodded in agreement. "I've seen her too. Twice."

"But she doesn't appear on command," Cindy said. "There haven't been many sightings recently, so that's why Rita came up with this scheme. But the ghost...she's no hoax."

I wasn't sure what to make of that, but I did know one thing for sure—I really wanted to go home.

Chapter Thirty-Two

I added soap to the dishwasher, shut the door, and turned it on.

That was the last of the cleanup done.

Our Christmas Eve dinner had been a great success. Ivan, Lisa, and Chloe had come over for the evening, and they'd all brought some food to contribute to the meal. Brett and I had taken care of the rest of the cooking. After eating, we'd all enjoyed glasses of eggnog while listening to Christmas music and exchanging presents. Our guests had left happy, and I still had a smile on my face.

My mom wouldn't be here for Christmas this year. She and Grant had gone to Boston to visit Grant's family, but she'd be coming for a visit soon. On Christmas Day, Brett and I would spend a quiet morning together before heading over to his parents' place in the early afternoon. Until then, it would be just the two of us. Plus Flapjack and Bentley.

I wandered into the front living room, where we'd gathered with our guests after dinner. Bentley trotted ahead of me, proudly wearing the red and green plaid bowtie Lisa had brought for him. Flapjack was already in the living room, curled up beneath the Christmas tree, sleeping in the glow of the multi-colored lights.

Brett was there too, collecting scraps of wrapping paper destined for the recycling bin. He stopped what he was doing when I came into the room. He put an arm around my shoulders as I stopped to admire the Christmas tree for the umpteenth time. Bentley sniffed at the remaining wrapped presents before turning in a circle and lying down on the edge of the tree skirt.

The Flip Side's festival tree hadn't won the competition—Marielle's cupcake tree was voted the favorite—but, as biased as I might have been, I thought the tree in front of me was the most beautiful one I'd seen all season.

"I think everyone had a good time," Brett said.

I turned to face him and put my arms around his waist. "I think so too. Ready to head up to bed?"

"Almost." He kissed my forehead. "There's still one more present you have to open first."

"I thought we were leaving the rest until tomorrow."

"Except for this one." Brett reached into his back pocket and pulled out a plain white envelope.

I accepted the envelope and glanced from it to Brett. "Is it a time-sensitive present?"

"Not exactly. I just can't wait any longer to give it to you."

Intrigued, I opened the unsealed envelope and pulled out a piece of paper. I unfolded it and studied it. It appeared to be a print-out of e-tickets of some kind. I read the print on the page and then raised my gaze to see Brett grinning at me.

"We're going to Hawaii?" Excitement bubbled out of me, almost making my voice squeak.

"You want to go, right?"

I threw my arms around Brett's neck and kissed him. "You know I do!"

We'd talked about going to Hawaii, but we hadn't yet managed to make any real plans in that regard. At least, I hadn't. Brett obviously had.

He wrapped his arms around me. "I know we said we'd stick to staycations, but I couldn't resist the thought of ten nights on Maui in early January."

"It'll be perfect," I said, still giddy with excitement. Something occurred to me. "Except…"

"All taken care of," Brett said before I could finish my sentence. "I've already talked to your mom. She'll look after the animals and help out at The Flip Side while we're gone."

I beamed at him. "You really do think of everything."

Brett kept his arms around me as he walked me slowly backwards. He stopped once we were beneath the mistletoe.

"You're happy?" he asked.

"Very."

I kissed him, and several minutes passed before we spoke again.

"Now are you ready to go upstairs?" I asked.

Brett squeezed my hands. "As soon as I let Bentley out one last time. I'll meet you up there."

He called to Bentley, and the goldendoodle scrambled to chase after him. I heard the front door open as I switched off the Christmas lights and blew a good night kiss to Flapjack. He made no move to come out from under the tree.

I was about to head up the stairs when Brett poked his head in through the front door.

"Marley, come see."

He disappeared from sight without saying anything more.

Curious, I joined him out on the front porch. I barely noticed the cold air cutting through my clothes. I was too enchanted by the fluffy white snowflakes falling from the sky.

"Snow for Christmas," Brett said. "That doesn't happen all that often in Wildwood Cove."

I gazed up at the sky. "It's beautiful."

Bentley trotted past us into the house, but we didn't move. There was something almost magical about the large flakes drifting lazily down from the dark sky.

Brett put his arm around me and held me close. "Merry Christmas, Marley."

I snuggled up to his side, still watching the snow fall, thoroughly content. "Merry Christmas, Brett."

Acknowledgments

I'd like to extend my sincere thanks to several people whose hard work and input made this book what it is today. I'm forever grateful to my agent, Jessica Faust, for helping me bring this series to life, and to my editor at Kensington Books, Elizabeth May, for helping me shape this manuscript into a better book. The art department has created gorgeous covers for the series, and I appreciate all the work the entire Kensington team has put into this book. Thank you to Marguerite Gavin for doing such a great job of narrating the audiobooks, and to Jody Holford for cheering me on and helping me with Ambrose's poem. Thanks also to all the readers who have returned for another of Marley's adventures in Wildwood Cove.

Recipes

Pumpkin Scones with Maple Glaze

Scones

1 cup pumpkin purée
2 cups all-purpose flour
1/3 cup brown sugar, packed
1 tablespoon baking powder
1 teaspoon cinnamon
1/2 teaspoon ground ginger
1/4 teaspoon nutmeg
1/8 teaspoon cloves
6 tablespoons unsalted butter
1 egg
1/3 cup heavy cream
1/4 cup milk
1 tablespoon molasses
1 teaspoon vanilla

Preheat oven to 400°F.

Spread the pumpkin purée on a baking sheet lined with parchment paper. Roast the purée in the oven for about 8 to 10 minutes (this will enhance the pumpkin flavor). Watch carefully as you don't want it to burn. Remove from the oven and set aside to cool.

In a large bowl, mix together the flour, brown sugar, baking powder, cinnamon, ginger, nutmeg, and cloves. Cut the butter into small pieces and cut it into the dry ingredients with a pastry cutter or fork until it resembles coarse oatmeal.

In a separate bowl, whisk together the egg, cream, milk, pumpkin purée, molasses, and vanilla. Stir into dry ingredients.

Line a baking sheet with parchment paper. Place the dough on a lightly floured surface. Knead lightly, about 8 to 10 times. Form dough into a ball and place on the baking sheet. Flatten the ball into a disc approximately 1 inch thick. Cut into 8 pieces but do not separate the pieces.

Bake at 400°F for approximately 18 to 20 minutes, until golden brown.

Maple Glaze

    2 tablespoons pure maple syrup
    1/2 cup icing sugar
    2 teaspoons cream

In a small bowl, mix together glaze ingredients until smooth. Once the scones have cooled, drizzle with glaze and serve.

Cinnamon Pancakes

2 tablespoons melted butter
1.5 cups milk
2 teaspoons lemon juice
1.5 cups flour
1/4 cup brown sugar
3 teaspoons baking powder
1/4 teaspoon baking soda
1.5 teaspoons cinnamon
1 large egg
1 teaspoon vanilla
1/4 cup chopped pecans

Melt the butter and set aside to cool. Combine the milk and lemon juice and set aside.

Mix together flour, sugar, baking powder, baking soda, and cinnamon. In separate bowl, beat together egg, milk/lemon juice, vanilla, and butter. Make a well in the dry ingredients and add the liquid ingredients. Combine. Mix in chopped pecans. Ladle batter into greased skillet and cook on medium heat until bubbles form on the top and don't disappear. Flip and cook second side until golden brown.

Gingerbread Muffins

1 cup unsweetened applesauce
1/2 cup brown sugar
1/2 cup molasses
1/3 cup vegetable oil
1/2 teaspoon vanilla
2 eggs
1 1/2 cups flour
1/2 teaspoon salt
1 1/2 teaspoons baking soda
2 1/2 teaspoons baking powder
1 1/2 teaspoons cinnamon
1 teaspoon ginger
1/4 teaspoon nutmeg

Preheat oven to 420°F.

Mix together the applesauce, sugar, molasses, oil, and vanilla. Add the eggs, one at a time, mixing after each addition. Sift together the dry ingredients and add them to the egg mixture. Mix well. Fill the muffin tins to the top.

When you place the muffin tins in the oven, reduce the heat to 375°F and bake for approximately 15-16 minutes. Remove from the oven and let sit for five minutes. Take the muffins out of the tins and allow to cool before serving. Makes 12 muffins.

Keep reading for a special preview of the new
Literary Pub Mystery by Sarah Fox!

THE MALT IN OUR STARS
A Literary Pub Mystery

There's some shady business in Shady Creek, Vermont, this spring—in the third mystery by USA Today bestselling author Sarah Fox featuring pub owner and amateur sleuth Sadie Coleman . . .

Sadie is delighted to have booked famous romantic suspense novelist Linnea Bliss for an event at The Inkwell, her literary-themed pub, housed in a renovated grist mill. The author and her personal assistant Marcie are staying at Shady Creek Manor, a grand historical hotel that was once a private mansion and is rumored to still hold hidden treasure somewhere within its walls.

But the hotel's storied past is nothing compared to its tragic present when Marcie plummets to her death from an open window on the third floor. After Sadie discovers signs of a struggle in the room, it's clear that someone assisted the assistant out the window. But Marcie is new in town—who would have a motive to kill her?

In between pulling pints and naming literary-themed cocktails, Sadie takes it on herself to solve the case, wondering if the crime is connected to the vandalized vehicles of a film crew in town to do a feature on local brewer Grayson Blake, with whom Sadie shares a strong flirtation. Or could the poor woman's defenestration have anything to do with the legendary treasure? As Shady Creek Manor prepares for a May Day masquerade ball, Sadie is determined to unmask the killer—but when she uncorks a whole lot of trouble, will she meet a bitter end?

Look for *THE MALT IN OUR STARS*, on sale now.

The Malt in Our Stars
Chapter One

Shady Creek Manor was an impressive sight to behold. The three-story stone building sat in the middle of several acres of neatly trimmed lawn, immaculately kept gardens, and serene woodland. The clear blue sky made the scene even more spectacular. I cracked my car window open as I followed the long driveway, breathing in the heavenly scent of the spring air. The smell of flowers and freshly cut grass buoyed my already good mood, and I soaked in the warmth from the sun shining through the driver's-side window.

Instead of following the branch of the driveway that looped around a fountain to the front door of the manor, I drove along another arm, past the hotel to a parking lot beyond a row of trees that prevented the parked cars and cement from spoiling the view from the front of the property. The lot was only half full, and as I pulled into a free spot my nerves danced a little jig. I was about to meet one of my favorite authors, Linnea Bliss.

When I climbed out of my car, I smoothed down the skirt of my green dress and tucked an errant strand of red hair behind my ear. I wanted to be as professional as possible and I was determined not to fangirl when I met the author. Not too much, anyway. Still, as I headed across the parking lot, I had to take a deep breath to settle my still-dancing nerves. I reached the edge of the parking lot and was about to walk along a pathway that led around to the front of the manor when the sound of hushed but angry voices reached my ears.

I paused, seeking out the owners of the voices. A second later I spotted Brad Honeywell, one of the manor's owners, outside a rear door of the hotel. He was in the midst of an argument with a twenty-something woman with dark brown hair cut in a sleek, short bob with blunt bangs. Although I'd never formally met Brad, I knew him by sight since he came to my pub, The Inkwell, on occasion. The young woman with him was a complete stranger to me, however. I couldn't hear what the two of them were arguing about, but just as I was going to continue on my way, the young woman took a step back from Brad.

"Stay away from me!" she fumed.

Before Brad had a chance to say anything in response, she spun on her heel and disappeared into the manor, almost slamming the door behind her. Still agitated, Brad ran a hand through his thinning dark hair.

I didn't want him to catch me gawking, so I quickly set off along the pathway. I couldn't help but wonder what was going on between Brad and the young woman. It wasn't any of my business, but I was curious by nature and couldn't stop a list of possibilities from scrolling through my mind. I brought those thoughts to an abrupt halt when I reached the front of the manor.

Although I'd glimpsed the hotel while driving past on a few occasions, I'd never been inside, or even this close. Built in the first half of the twentieth century by a wealthy man named Edwin Vallencourt, the manor was originally a private mansion. According to local stories, Vallencourt had entertained other wealthy and sometimes famous figures and had thrown legendary parties at his extravagant home. After his death, his heirs had been unable to afford to keep the massive property and it had changed hands several times over the years.

Almost a decade ago, Brad Honeywell and his wife, Gemma, had purchased the property and restored the manor to its former glory before opening it as a hotel. It was the fanciest and most expensive place to stay in the small town of Shady Creek, Vermont, and I was almost as eager to get a look inside as I was to meet Linnea Bliss.

A short flight of wide stone steps led up to the elegant double doors. When I stepped into the spacious lobby, I had to pause on the threshold to take in the beautiful sight before me. A crystal chandelier hung from the high ceiling, but it was almost unnecessary at the moment, with all the daylight streaming in through the large windows. I couldn't spot a speck of dirt on the white marble floors, and the tasteful antique furnishings allowed me to feel as though I'd momentarily stepped back in time, until I noticed the computer on the reception desk.

On my left and next to a leafy potted plant was a settee so gorgeous that I wished I could have it for my own, even though it probably would have looked out of place in the cozy little apartment I called home. It had a beautifully carved crest and legs, and was upholstered with cream fabric. It likely cost more than all my furniture put together.

When I first entered the lobby, the reception desk to my right was unmanned, but as the door drifted shut, Brad Honeywell strode toward me. I experienced a brief moment of apprehension until he directed a welcoming smile my way. Most likely he was unaware that I'd witnessed him arguing with someone minutes earlier.

"Good morning and welcome to Shady Creek Manor," Brad said. "It's Sadie, isn't it?"

"That's right," I replied. "I'm here to meet with Linnea Bliss and her assistant."

"Yes, of course," a woman's voice chimed in. Gemma Honeywell entered the lobby through an arched doorway that appeared to lead to a sitting room. She wore a light gray pantsuit with a silk blouse, and her curly fair hair was tied back in a fancy twist. "We're all very excited to have such a famous author staying here at the manor."

"And I'm excited to meet her," I said.

Gemma introduced herself, since we'd never officially met, and told me she'd call Marcie Kent, Linnea's assistant, and let her know that I'd arrived.

I took the opportunity to try out the beautiful settee. I half expected it to be uncomfortable because of its formal appearance, but that wasn't the case. Perhaps it wasn't quite as comfy as my couch, but it was still a nice place to sit.

While I waited, Gemma had a hushed conversation on the phone behind the reception desk. I twisted one of the rings on my right hand, butterflies circling around each other in my stomach. Gemma was still on the phone when a woman in jeans and a flannel shirt with rolled up sleeves appeared in the lobby. She had cropped brown hair and carried a toolbox. I'd seen her at my pub and around town a few times. If I remembered correctly, her name was Jan and she had her own plumbing business.

As soon as Brad spotted her, he hurried out from behind the reception desk.

"Problem all fixed?" he asked.

"As good as new," Jan replied.

"Excellent. I'll write you a check." Brad ushered her down a hallway that led toward the back of the manor.

Gemma hung up the phone and smiled at me. "Ms. Kent asked that you meet her and Ms. Bliss in the parlor for tea. I'll show you the way."

Thanking her, I followed her through the archway into the sitting room. Although, *parlor* seemed like a much more suitable term. The room was bigger than my whole apartment and it reminded me of sitting rooms I'd seen in British movies featuring grand estates from days gone by. The rugs alone probably cost a fortune, never mind the ornate furnishings. The artwork on the walls might not have been created by the grand masters, but each piece was still gorgeous.

A marble fireplace was the focal point along one wall, while the opposite wall featured a row of arched windows, currently shaded with sheer curtains to filter out some of the bright sunlight. At the far end of the room, four chairs sat tucked beneath a round table covered in a white cloth.

Gemma nodded at the table. "If you'd like to take a seat, I'll be serving tea shortly."

"Thank you," I managed to say, even though most of my attention was taken up by my beautiful surroundings.

As distracted as I was, I tried to collect myself. I didn't want to seem scatterbrained when Linnea arrived. That didn't take long. I hadn't yet had a chance to pull out a chair from the table when footsteps drew my gaze to the doorway.

I recognized Linnea Bliss right away. I'd seen her picture many times online and on the dust jackets of her best-selling romantic suspense novels. She was in her late fifties, slightly plump, with gray streaks in her brown hair. Her warm smile put me immediately at ease.

"You must be Sadie Coleman." She offered me her hand. "Such a pleasure to meet you."

"You as well." I smiled as I shook her hand.

The woman who'd come into the room behind Linnea stepped forward.

"And this is my assistant, Marcie Kent," Linnea said. "I know the two of you have spoken on the phone."

I'd talked to Marcie a few times as we'd arranged for Linnea to come to Shady Creek to give a talk and sign books at my literary-themed pub. I'd never seen her picture before, though, and I had to catch myself quickly to mask my surprise at the fact that she was the woman I'd seen arguing with Brad behind the hotel.

We exchanged pleasantries and the three of us settled at the table, Gemma appearing a moment later with a tea cart. She set a teapot and cups on the table along with cream and sugar and a tiered plate that held scones and little cakes.

"I'm so happy you decided to come to Shady Creek," I said to Linnea once Gemma had left.

"It was Marcie's idea," Linnea said. "And since the book I'm currently writing is set in Vermont, I thought it would be a great way to soak in the local atmosphere and add authenticity to my writing."

"I can't wait to read it." I tried to keep my excitement at least somewhat under control, but there was still a good deal of enthusiasm behind my words. "I've read and loved everything you've written."

"Thank you, dear. That's a lovely thing to say."

"It's the absolute truth," I assured her before turning to Marcie. "Have you been to Shady Creek before?"

Since it was Marcie's idea to add the town to the end of Linnea's latest book tour, I was curious if she had a connection to the area. Although Shady Creek was a small town, it was popular with tourists, especially during leaf-peeping season, and I wondered if she'd vacationed here in the past.

Her reply quickly dispelled that idea. "I haven't, but I read about the town and Edwin Vallencourt while doing some research for Linnea. It sounded like such a nice place and I knew Linnea was hoping to make a trip to Vermont before she finished writing her book."

"I'm so glad you chose Shady Creek for your visit, and The Inkwell," I said to both of them.

Linnea added strawberry jam to a scone. "I can't wait to get a look at your pub. It sounds so charming and the pictures I saw online are delightful."

"Thank you," I said, my smile probably outshining the sun.

As we drank our tea and snacked on the delicious cakes and scones, we chatted about the upcoming event at The Inkwell, going over some final details. We'd nearly covered everything when approaching footsteps drew our attention to the doorway. My surprise probably showed on my face when I realized that Eleanor Grimes was hurrying toward us, her expression determined and her eyes fixed on Linnea.

Eleanor ran the Shady Creek Museum and didn't exactly have the sweetest disposition. When I'd moved to town ten months ago, she'd had her eye on the beautiful old gristmill that housed the local pub, hoping the town would buy it so she could move her beloved museum into the space. She hadn't been happy when I'd purchased the building and business. I'd never actually spoken with her, but she'd sent an icy glare my way on more than one occasion.

"Ms. Bliss," Eleanor said as she approached, "I wonder if I could trouble you for a moment of your time. I'd like to speak to you about a cause very dear to my heart."

"This is Eleanor Grimes," I said by way of introduction. "She's in charge of the local museum."

Eleanor didn't so much as glance my way. Her bony hands clutched a book to her chest. I couldn't see much of the cover, but it didn't appear to be one of Linnea's novels.

She continued on as if I hadn't spoken. "One writer to another, I'm sure you'll understand—"

"Eleanor!" Gemma rushed into the room. When she reached our table, she lowered her voice, although we could all still hear her clearly. "I asked you to please *not* interrupt Ms. Bliss."

"Donations are vital to the continued operation of the Shady Creek Museum. Our history is the backbone of our community and—"

"Yes, yes." Gemma forced a smile that wasn't far off from a grimace. "But Ms. Bliss doesn't want to hear about that right now."

She put an arm around Eleanor's thin shoulders and attempted to turn her away from the table.

Eleanor resisted and addressed Linnea again. "I brought you a copy of my book." She placed the volume on the table next to Linnea's plate.

I glanced at the cover. It was titled *Shady Creek: A History* and Eleanor's name was printed near the bottom in fancy script. I'd heard that she'd recently self-published a book about the town, but I hadn't seen a copy of it before today.

Marcie spoke up. "I've read that."

I'd never seen Eleanor smile before, but she did now.

"Have you?" She sounded ridiculously pleased. "Then I'm sure you appreciate—"

"In chapter nine you state that Edwin Vallencourt amassed his fortune through wholly legitimate business dealings and that the rumors about him earning money from shadier ventures are completely baseless."

Eleanor stood up straighter. "That's right."

"But in actual fact, there's plenty of documentation to back up those rumors," Marcie said, sounding a bit like a know-it-all. "Vallencourt had his fingers in several less-than-honorable pies and was heavily involved in bootlegging during prohibition."

The remains of Eleanor's smile slipped away. She pursed her thin lips and her eyes hardened. "Those are all lies!"

"Historical facts, actually," Marcie countered, her cool demeanor a sharp contrast to Eleanor's growing fury.

"How dare you come to our town and spout such filth about one of Shady Creek's most revered citizens from the past! I'll have you know that—"

"Eleanor!" Gemma cut her off sharply, her forced smile long gone. "I apologize for the interruption," she said to us before turning Eleanor around and herding her from the room.

"Sorry," Marcie said to me and Linnea, although she didn't sound all that contrite. "It drives me crazy when people spread factual errors."

Linnea poured more tea into Marcie's cup. "There's no real harm done, dear."

I realized that my fingers had a painfully tight grip on the napkin lying across my lap. I hadn't expected such tension when I'd arrived for tea. Marcie and Linnea appeared to have already put the encounter behind them, so I tried to do the same. That wasn't easy when Eleanor's indignant protests could still be heard off in the distance. Eventually, however, her voice died away and we were left in peace.

Chapter Two

Fortunately, we met with no further interruptions and drew our meeting to a close shortly after we'd finished off the pot of tea. Aside from the one brief disturbance, our conversation had gone smoothly and pleasantly. I'd enjoyed spending time with Linnea, and Marcie as well, and I was now looking forward to the author's visit to The Inkwell more than ever. Plenty of townsfolk had expressed interest in hearing the author speak, and I knew many people planned to show up at the event the next day. The members of The Inkwell's romance book club would be in the audience and had told me they intended to show up as early as possible so they could claim the best seats.

Now that I'd met Linnea, I didn't have a single doubt that she'd be a hit with her fans. She was charming, engaging, and full of colorful stories. There wouldn't be one bored person in the audience. I was still a tiny bit nervous, simply because I desperately wanted the event to go off without a hitch, but mostly I was excited.

After saying goodbye in the lobby, Linnea and Marcie had gone up to their rooms, taking the broad, curving staircase to the next floor. Instead of heading for my car, I stopped in the lobby and glanced at the reception desk. There was no one behind it at the moment. I could hear voices in the distance but there was no one around to stop me from venturing deeper into the manor.

I wasn't planning to explore the entire hotel, even though I desperately wanted to. Getting a look at the lobby and parlor had only made me all the more eager to check out the rest of the place. I didn't want to annoy anyone, however, so I exercised restraint and bypassed the staircase. I wasn't going to leave without a little exploration, though.

Following a wide hallway that led toward the back of the hotel, I walked as quietly as possible in my high heels. An arched doorway to my right led to a dining room, where about a dozen hotel guests were sitting down to an early lunch. A few feet farther along, arched double doors stood open on my left. I was hoping I'd found the ballroom and I soon discovered that I had. The room I peeked into was large enough to host dozens of dancing couples with plenty of space to spare. The polished parquet floors gleamed in the sunlight that poured into the room through the numerous tall windows that lined the wall across from me. Two sets of French doors also let in streams of daylight and one set stood open, leading out onto a large patio.

The ballroom was empty at the moment, so I crept inside for a better look. An enormous crystal chandelier hung from the ornate plaster ceiling high above me. It was turned off at the moment, but I could imagine what it would look like lit up at night, each one of the dangling crystals sparkling and glittering. The rest of the light fixtures were wall sconces designed to look like old-fashioned gas lamps. At one end of the room, a balcony overlooked the dance floor and beneath it was a small stage, likely where live music would be played on the night of the May Day masquerade.

I hadn't yet lived in Vermont for a full year—I'd moved to town during the summer—so I hadn't experienced Shady Creek's annual masquerade before. I'd heard it was not to be missed and I'd already purchased my ticket. I didn't have a mask yet, or a dress for that matter, and I made a mental note to address those issues soon.

Movement outside the windows caught my eye and I realized that someone was out on the patio. When he turned so his profile was lit up by the sun, I crossed the ballroom to the open French doors.

"Hi, Judson," I greeted.

"Hey, Sadie," he said with a smile. "What brings you here?"

Judson was a regular patron at The Inkwell and was employed as the manor's gardener. He was in his mid-thirties and single, from what I'd heard. He wasn't, however, short on female attention. It was easy to see why so many women found him attractive. His eyes and his wavy hair were both the color of milk chocolate and he had a lean and well-toned physique from all his gardening work. I'd spoken to him several times at the pub and I found him to be a pleasant, easygoing guy.

"I had a meeting with Linnea Bliss and her assistant," I said in answer to his question.

"The famous author? She'll be at the pub tomorrow, right?"

"That's right. I'm hoping she'll be a hit."

"She probably will be. She seems nice."

"You've met her?"

"She stopped to talk to me this morning," he said. "She was out for a walk and I was weeding the flower beds out front. Some guests pretend I'm invisible and others look down their noses at me, but not her."

"She does seem nice," I agreed.

I watched as he grabbed a hose with a nozzle attachment and watered the colorful flowers growing in large stone pots on the patio.

"The gardens look amazing," I said. "You've done great work."

"Thanks. The Honeywells want everything to look even more immaculate than usual with the masquerade coming up. Hopefully they'll be as impressed as you are."

"I'm sure they will be."

Hearing a noise behind me, I glanced over my shoulder. A fair-haired woman in a gray dress and white apron rolled a housekeeping cart into the ballroom from the hallway. When she spotted me and Judson, she left her cart in the middle of the room and came out onto the patio. I recognized her as she stepped into the light.

I'd met Connie Archer two weeks earlier when she came by the Inkwell for lunch. Apparently, she was new to town. She was about forty years old and maybe a bit jaded, but she seemed nice enough.

"Hey, Connie," Judson said as she joined us.

I added my own greeting and she cracked a brief smile.

"Gorgeous day," she observed, her gaze going to the clear blue sky. "I'd much rather be out here than stuck inside."

"You're working here as a housekeeper?" I figured that was a safe guess, judging by her uniform and the cart she'd left inside.

"Yep. I'm supposed to get the walls washed in the ballroom before the interior decorator comes with her team to get the place ready for the masquerade."

"That seems like a big task," I said, not envying her.

She shrugged. "It's not really so bad. I don't need to clean every inch, just any smudges or dirt I find. How come you're here?"

I repeated what I'd told Judson about meeting with Linnea. "This is my first time at the manor, so I thought I'd take a peek at the ballroom."

Judson tugged on the hose and moved along the patio to water another set of flowerpots. "It's something, isn't it?"

"It really is."

"You should see the rest of the place," Connie said. "Fit for a queen, if you ask me. Must be nice."

I wasn't sure what she meant by that. "Staying here, you mean?"

"That too, but I meant the Honeywells. It took a lot of dosh to get this place turned into a hotel. Word is they inherited millions and that's how they were able to buy the place. The only thing I ever inherited was my glaucoma." She said it with a wry grin, softening the complaint.

Judson shut off the water. "If the Honeywells find the hidden treasure, they'll be even richer." He pulled off his work gloves and ran the back of one hand across his forehead.

"Hidden treasure?" I echoed, my curiosity piqued.

Connie rolled her eyes. "Not that story again."

"It's a good one," Judson said. "That's why everyone likes to repeat it."

"What treasure?" I asked, eager for more information.

"You know this place was originally owned by Edwin Vallencourt, right?" Connie said.

When I nodded, Judson picked up the thread. "Rumor has it that he loved his secrets and stashed away some of his valuables before he died."

"But no one's ever found them?" I guessed.

"That's because there's nothing to find." Connie turned for the door. "I have to get back to work."

"Don't worry, Con," Judson called after her with a grin. "When I find the treasure, I'll give you a trinket or two."

She muttered something under her breath, but I didn't catch the words. Judson laughed and pulled his gloves back on.

"Do you really think there's hidden treasure?" I asked him.

"Probably not," he admitted, "but it's fun to speculate." He grabbed the hose. "I'd better get back to work too. I'll see you at the pub sometime soon, Sadie."

"See you."

As he headed off around the corner of the manor, pulling the hose with him, I returned to the ballroom. The housekeeping cart still sat in the middle of the room, but Connie was nowhere to be seen. Since it was time for me to get back to The Inkwell, I resisted the temptation to explore more of the manor and instead set off for my car.

* * * *

When I made my way onto the village green the next morning, my original plan was to cut across the northeast corner and make a direct line for the Village Bean, the local coffee shop. I'd had a cup of coffee with my bowl of oatmeal an hour earlier, but now I had a hankering for a mocha latte and the Village Bean had the best lattes around.

As eager as I was to get my first taste of mocha deliciousness, my steps slowed when I reached the grassy village green. Signs of spring were all around me and, not for the first time, I was almost taken aback by the incredible beauty of the town I now called home. The white bandstand in the middle of the green had recently received a fresh coat of paint, and hanging baskets bursting with colorful flowers hung from each of the old-fashioned lampposts lining the streets around the green. Many of the storefronts around the square also had hanging baskets or flowerpots flanking their doors, and all around me birds chirped and sang.

Pulling my phone from my purse, I turned my back on the green and snapped a photo of my beloved pub, which also doubled as my home. Housed in a renovated grist mill, the pub and the apartment above it practically oozed charm and character. The stone building had red-trimmed windows and a bright red water wheel. With the lush green forest and the bold blue sky as a backdrop, the pub made for an eye-catching sight. I planned to post the photo on The Inkwell's Instagram account, but that would have to wait for the moment.

I resumed my progress over to the corner of Sycamore Street, where the Village Bean was located. I lingered for a minute or two as I chatted with the coffee shop's owner, Nettie Jo, but then I took a seat by one of the windows and pulled out my phone again. Once I had the picture of The Inkwell posted on social media, I checked my email and text messages. Marcie hadn't contacted me to cancel the event last-minute, much to my relief. Not that I'd expected her to, but I'd had an unsettling dream that Linnea had suddenly decided to leave Shady Creek and set sail for Tahiti.

When I set down my phone, I sat back and tried to relax. For the first time since my arrival, I studied the other customers in the coffee shop. I smiled at a woman who walked past me with a coffee and muffin in hand, heading for a free table at the back of the shop. I recognized a couple of faces, but the other customers were strangers. Some of them might have been tourists, but the man and woman sitting three tables away from me didn't look like they were on a relaxing vacation.

The woman appeared to be a little older than my age of thirty and had her straight black hair cut in an asymmetrical bob. Her high-heeled boots, skinny jeans, and leather jacket probably cost more than my entire wardrobe. Her companion was probably a few years younger than her and his curly hair was a shade lighter.

"You don't get it, Alex," the woman said to him, her face intense. "This is a test. Everything has to go perfectly or they'll think I'm not cut out for the job."

"Everything will be fine, Liv." He sounded unconcerned, but the tension in his jaw suggested that he wasn't as relaxed as he was trying to appear.

"Fine?" She practically spat the word out. "Our windshield got smashed!"

"And it's getting fixed," Alex said, his voice even. "Besides, this town is so small we can probably walk everywhere we need to go."

"In these heels?" With a frustrated sigh, the woman whipped out her phone and started tapping away at it, her thumbs little more than two blurs.

I finished off my latte and got up to leave. Listening to those two made it impossible for me to relax. It was time to get back to The Inkwell, anyway.

When I got to the pub, I swept my gaze around the main room, making sure everything looked perfect. I hoped Linnea would appreciate the rustic charm of the place, with its exposed wide plank floors and stone walls lined with my sizable book collection. Earlier that morning I'd set up an easel to hold a large sign advertising the event. I nudged the sign half an inch to the left before standing back to make sure it was perfectly centered.

"Please tell me you aren't going to start dusting again." Mel Costas, one of my employees, watched me from behind the bar, where she was setting out clean mugs and glasses. She wore her blue and blond hair in tousled spikes. The short style showed off her latest tattoo: a line of small birds in flight, curving around from the back of her neck to up behind her right ear.

"Of course not," I said, although I'd been thinking about grabbing my feather duster. I'd already dusted and cleaned everything three times over since we'd closed the Inkwell the night before, but my restless energy was making it hard to stay still. "But I'll have one last look at the Christie room."

"Everything's perfect," Mel called after me as I headed for one of the pub's two overflow rooms. "Just like it was an hour ago."

I could hear the smile in her voice and knew she was teasing. She was right, though. The room I'd named for Agatha Christie was spotless and all set up for the event, with rows of chairs facing one end of the room. I'd decided to have Linnea's talk in the Christie room to give it a cozier, more intimate feel. Plus, any customers who weren't taking part in the event wouldn't disrupt the talk or feel like they were intruding.

When I returned to the main part of the pub, I glanced at the clock. Linnea and Marcie would be arriving at any moment. A knock on the front door made me jump and my heart skipped a beat. I recovered quickly and hurried to greet my guests.

It was finally time for the Inkwell's first author visit.

Printed in the United States
by Baker & Taylor Publisher Services